The Country Village Summer Fête

CATHY LAKE

ZAFFRE

First published in the UK in 2021 by
ZAFFRE
An imprint of Bonnier Books UK
80–81 Wimpole St, London W1G 9RE
Owned by Bonnier Books
Sveavägen 56, Stockholm, Sweden

A CIP catalogue record for this book is
available from the British Library.

ISBN: 978–1–83877–282–6

Also available as an ebook and in audio

1 3 5 7 9 10 8 6 4 2

Typeset by IDSUK (Data Connection) Ltd
Printed and bound in Great Britain by Clays Ltd, Elcograf S.p.A.

Zaffre is an imprint of Bonnier Books UK
www.bonnierbooks.co.uk

For my husband and children, with love always

The Country Village Summer Fête

Cathy Lake is a women's fiction writer who lives with her family and three dogs in beautiful South Wales. She writes uplifting stories about strong women, family, friendship, love, community and overcoming obstacles.

Also by Cathy Lake

The Country Village Christmas Show

Chapter 1

Emma Patrick shivered as she shuffled around the small Tesco Extra. It was eerily quiet, reminding her of a scene in a TV show about London during a zombie apocalypse. There had been no other living people on screen as the main character limped around the shop, looting what she could while the lights flickered on and off and zombies lurked around every corner. Emma had been terrified watching it alone in her flat, but had been desperate to see if the suspense of the book had been captured on film.

When Emma got to the self-service checkouts the area was cordoned off with orange cones surrounding a large red and white puddle on the floor, complete with lumps. Either someone had dropped a trifle or they'd blown up a zombie so she turned and went to the one open checkout, hoping that the cashier wouldn't be in a chatty mood.

'Forget to change, did you, love?'

The cashier, a man with a bright pink Mohican and pierced eyebrows, gave her the once-over.

'Pardon?'

'Looks to me like someone left the house in a hurry.' He winked and Emma's confusion deepened. 'Still got your PJs on.'

Emma placed the ice cream, vodka and dental floss on the conveyer belt and looked down at herself.

'Oh!' She grimaced, thinking fast. 'Actually, it's lounge-wear.' Heat filled her cheeks and she hung her head, wishing she had a curtain of hair to hide her face but, of course, it had been a while since she'd had long hair and the stylish brown pixie cut did nothing to spare her blushes.

'Of course it is. But between us, you're not the first and you won't be the last.' He flashed her a smile before scanning her shopping. 'I once found myself in Macdonald's at 5 a.m. in just a pair of tighty-whities, Doc Martens and a beanie. I was only nineteen and I'd been out clubbing all night, but even so, to this day I don't remember choosing to wear my sensible undies. I mean, imagine if I'd pulled?' He shook his head and sighed.

Emma pulled her smartphone from her pocket and paid with contactless then picked up the paper bag containing her shopping and headed for the doors, keen to escape Chatty Man before he shared any more anecdotes.

Out on the street, she looked at her phone. It was 2.23 a.m.

She'd had no idea it was that late. Or should that be early? She'd been working all hours recently, trying to make a dent in a flurry of editing jobs and had lost all sense of time. The days had blended together, the nights too, but shopping at 2 a.m.?

What was going on?

And as for her shopping . . .

The dental floss she needed, she realised, as she poked her tongue against the molar where she had a bit of sweetcorn trapped, but the other things? Well, something had made her do it. All she could think was that she'd been on autopilot, going through a familiar routine like a well-trained dog. Shame she hadn't thought to get dressed first, though; she'd just left the flat in her flannel two-piece, unaware of anything other than her desire to feed, exactly as she imagined a zombie would.

She tucked her phone into the pocket of her pyjama trousers, the handle of the bag over her arm, and set off in the direction of her flat, hoping she wouldn't bump into anyone she knew.

Faces swam around Emma, perfect faces with white teeth, full lips and long lashes, surrounded by glossy hair. They held up babies with cute smiles and headbands, dressed in sweet little baby grows and fashionable trainers, or tiny dogs that peered out from behind floppy fringes and designer handbags.

Couples hugged each other tightly and headlines flashed above their coiffured hair: *MADLY IN LOVE! PERFECT*

COUPLE! RESCUED ME FROM MYSELF! THIRD TIME LUCKY FOR LIAM AND LILA!

Wedding bells pealed loudly, paparazzi shouted, cameras flashed and, somewhere beyond it all, crickets chirped.

'No more! No . . . please, no more!' Emma pushed her hands to her ears and shook her head. 'Enough!'

She sat up in bed, heart racing, chest rising and falling rapidly, sheets twisted around her legs. Between her breasts sweat trickled and she was aware of moisture around her hairline.

'It was a dream,' she reassured herself. 'Just a stupid dream.'

But the crickets were still chirping so she grabbed her phone and turned off the alarm then flopped back against the pillows. Her head felt tight and her mouth dry – and no wonder. After she'd got home from Tesco Extra, she'd been unable to sleep so had cracked open the vodka and ice cream and spent her time flicking through her phone, hopping from one social media platform to another. When she'd felt sated enough to sleep, she'd gone to bed with her phone and wrapped herself up in the quilt, tucking a pillow next to her so she'd feel as if someone else was there with her. Usually, she didn't give in to her craving for hugs, but last night she'd longed for someone to hold her and tell her everything was going to be all right. She was clearly working too hard. And there was something else that she couldn't deny to herself; she hadn't felt right for months. Something had been making her feel disjointed and unhappy, niggling at her like toothache. She'd been trying to ignore it and perhaps that had led her to wander out of her flat at silly o'clock.

Unfortunately, booze, sugar and night sweats had combined to give her nightmares and she was as tired now as she'd felt before she'd gone to bed. Recovery from indulgence did not happen as quickly at forty-nine as it had when she was younger and she knew she'd pay for it all day. Recently, she often felt as if she could never get quite enough sleep, however many early nights she had. It left her feeling as though she was sleepwalking through the days, slightly numb and outside herself, and only coffee and sugar seemed to help.

However, with a deadline looming, she needed to be firing on all cylinders. Sloppy work would lead to fewer jobs coming her way and, as a freelance editor, she couldn't afford to have a black mark against her name; in this business, reputation was everything.

It was time for paracetamol, strong coffee and an almond croissant.

The café was Emma's sanctuary, a place she could retreat to when the walls of her small flat started to close in on her and she longed to be near other people. She loved her flat and was usually perfectly comfortable on her own, but every so often she needed company and it was nice, then, to head to the café to work, surrounded by other human beings without being bothered by them.

With one tall skinny latte inside her and another on the way, and an almond croissant that she was taking her time over, savouring the rich flaky pastry and sweet marzipan filling, she felt much better than when she'd woken that morning at just after seven. She set the alarm for the same time every weekday, aware that she needed to have a routine even though she was self-employed. Some people struggled with the self-discipline necessary to work from home, but Emma had done it for nine years. Prior to that she'd worked as an editor in several big publishing houses, although even then she'd been able to work from home when she had lots to get through.

Of course, there were some days when she struggled to get going, but on those she'd start a bit later then make up the time by working through the evenings. The wonderful thing about being single and childless was that she had that flexibility; there was no one relying on her to make their dinner, wash their uniform or listen to them talk about their day. Emma had always patted herself on the back for not settling down and having a family, for not moving out of London and buying a pretty little cottage somewhere rural, for not allowing tradition to claim her. Not that it hadn't been difficult at times, especially when she'd noticed the yearning in her parents' eyes to see their daughter married or the fond smiles playing across their lips as they spoke about a friend's newly arrived grandchild. But Emma had also known that her mum and dad accepted her choices and would never deliberately put pressure on her to become a wife and mother. In spite of that awareness, she'd always felt that she'd let her parents down in some way.

And now it was too late. In more ways than one . . .

When her name was called, Emma got her coffee from the counter then settled back into her seat. Her laptop was open in front of her and she allowed her eyes to run over her list of emails. There were so many unopened ones that she'd let mount up, some of them flagged as important – and that was completely unlike her. A lot were from retailers and mailing lists she'd subscribed to, but even so, in amongst them were messages from publishers and authors, some offering her work and some following up jobs in her queue.

She closed the inbox and stared at her desktop photo. It was of her and Lucie Baxter-Cheng, her best friend and one-time colleague, grinning at the camera as they held up espresso martinis during a weekend away. Their smiles were tipsy, their eyes shining and they looked happy and relaxed. At forty-six, Lucie was three years younger than Emma and they'd shared a lot of nights out over the course of their friendship. That had been before, six years earlier, Lucie met and married magazine editor, Phoebe Baxter-Cheng, and they'd begun their fertility journey. Until Lucie had met thirty-five-year-old Phoebe, she hadn't shown a flicker of interest in parenthood, but being with Phoebe had changed all that and they'd invested in private fertility treatment using a sperm donor as a way of trying to become parents. Emma was happy for her friend but at times she found it strange being around her because their conversations were so different these days.

Emma stuffed the last bit of croissant into her mouth and chewed it slowly, trying to make it last. If her jeans weren't currently digging into her waist, she might have ordered another one, but her self-indulgence over the past year and a lack of healthy meals at regular times had led to a lot of her clothes being a bit tight for her liking. At the times when it did play on her mind, she'd tell herself that she was nearly fifty and menopausal, so some weight gain was to be expected. It didn't worry her, but she knew that she needed to be careful if she didn't want to invest in a whole new wardrobe – and, of course, she knew the importance of staying fit and healthy. Elasticated waist joggers had their time and place, but Emma had always liked a nice pair of jeans and a pretty blouse and knew that the latter wouldn't look quite the same tucked into her baggy comfies.

'Time to get to work,' she told herself, 'or you'll never get this job finished on time.'

She opened the document and scrolled to the last page she'd read. It was a good book, one she believed could catapult the debut author to the top of the charts, so she would ensure that she gave it her full attention and expert polish.

Three hours, two more skinny lattes and a peppermint tea later, Emma looked up from the screen and stretched her back. The story had sucked her in, which was a good sign, and everything around her had faded away. But now she was back, her senses stirring, along with the awareness that she was hungry. She picked up her phone to check for messages and jumped as it started ringing.

Unknown caller . . .

It could easily be work as the numbers for the big publishing houses were often withheld. Alternatively, it could be a cold caller trying to sell her something or the bank wanting her to transfer the balance of her credit card to one that would seem like a good deal but would actually result in higher fees over a longer period of time.

Curiosity won and she swiped to answer. She could always tell them they'd got the wrong number.

As the person at the other end began to speak, Emma realised it was not a cold caller, the bank or a publishing house. Her heart sank and cold fear flooded through her veins.

Chapter 2

'Darling, I'm so sorry I couldn't get here sooner.'

Lucie Baxter-Cheng pulled out a stool and sat down opposite Emma at the high table in a swanky central London bar.

'It's fine. I'm just grateful you could make it at all.'

'Emma, you're my best friend.'

'I know how busy you and Phoebe are at the moment, though, and I promise I won't keep you long. I just needed to see a friendly face.'

'Of course you did, poor love.' Lucie pushed her sleek black bob behind her ears and set her clutch bag on the table. 'Shall we order?'

Emma nodded, glad that she had her friend's attention for an hour at least, grateful that she'd have the chance to share her concerns.

Drink in hand, Emma braced herself to repeat the phone call she'd received earlier that day at the café. It had only been three and half hours but felt like much longer. It's funny, she thought, how stress and worry can stretch out time, deplete energy levels and disperse common sense. She'd abandoned the manuscript she'd been working on, unable to focus on anything other than the churning in her gut, the ache behind her eyes and that awful word that kept flashing in front of her like a neon sign.

'Tell me, then.' Lucie sipped her gin and tonic and stared hard at Emma, her brown eyes looking almost black in the dim lighting.

'I had a phone call today from the GP back in Little Bramble. Dad isn't well.'

Lucie put down her drink. 'Oh no! I gathered that something was wrong from your message, but is it serious?'

Emma swallowed hard. Her dad was her only surviving parent. They'd lost her mum four years ago, so she knew how hard it was to grieve for someone she loved deeply, but the thought of losing her dad as well was too much. It made her want to run back to her flat and hide under the duvet. She'd had to force herself to come back out this evening to meet Lucie, but she'd known that if she didn't, she'd be likely to finish off the vodka and ice cream and didn't fancy another headache in the morning. The hangover anxiety she used to get after work nights out would not help her right now, so she'd ordered lime and soda.

'He – he was found waiting in the bus stop at six o'clock this morning in his dressing gown and slippers. He didn't know who he was.' The image of her dad being so vulnerable was something she couldn't get out of her head and it made her heart ache.

'Oh, how awful. Who found him?'

'The village postman, Marcellus David. He took Dad to see Dr Creek at her home because he was so worried, then they took him to the surgery and Dr Creek checked him over. They gave him a cup of tea and some toast and he seemed to come round and remember his name and address. He was incredibly embarrassed.'

'Poor Greg.' Lucie shook her head. She'd met Emma's dad on several occasions over the years and they'd got on well.

'I've been aware that Dad hasn't been himself lately. He hasn't really been the man I used to know since we lost Mum over four years ago. His memory hasn't been great and when I went back to Little Bramble at Christmas, he kept getting confused, but I tried to put it down to that Christmas show he was involved in and told myself that old age and stress are bound to affect his memory. I mean, he's eighty-four now and he doesn't look after himself as well as when Mum was around.'

'Poor Greg and poor you.'

Emma pressed her lips together and sucked in a deep breath. 'Dr Creek said that it's possible that Dad has – has dementia.'

A chill washed over her like a winter wind and she shivered violently. Saying the word out loud made it feel more real. Her dad had always been so strong and reliable, such a force of nature, constantly busy making and mending things, singing and playing his guitars, an eternal optimist who had supported her through many decisions and difficult times. A mechanical engineer by trade, he'd worked with transport companies all over the UK before retiring twenty years ago. He'd been a keen musician in his spare time, playing lead guitar with The Little Bramblers, collecting guitars to add to his extensive collection, playing at Christmas shows, wedding parties and summer fêtes. He was her dad, her rock, the man she could rely on to be there for her, but now, after today's phone call, she wasn't sure how long he would be around – at least, not as the dad she knew and loved.

Dementia. The word carried so much within it and the thought was terrifying.

'I'm so sorry, Em.' Lucie reached across the table and took Emma's hand. 'What can I do to help?'

'Nothing at the moment, thank you. But I'm going to have to go back.'

'To Little Bramble?'

Emma nodded. 'I need to see him for myself. Dr Creek said that she won't know for sure if it's dementia until she's run some tests, which could take a while, and she'll probably need to refer him, so a diagnosis could take time. Meantime, Dad needs someone to look after him and make sure he doesn't go wandering off alone at all times of day and night. Some of the neighbours have been keeping an eye on him since Mum died, Dilys in particular, but that can't go on indefinitely. It's not fair on him or them. And of course they are not there at night or in the early hours of the morning.'

'When will you go?'

'First thing tomorrow. I'm in the middle of a job I need to finish, but I'll take my laptop with me and do it there. I'm the only one left who can help Dad.'

'Will your brother be able to do anything?'

Emma thought back to her conversation with Ted earlier that afternoon. It had been gone midnight in Sydney but he'd still been up and, although he'd been concerned, he'd told her he was really busy and couldn't get to England at the moment. Emma had understood. If it had been the other way around and she'd been 17,000 kilometres away, she'd probably have expected Ted to be the one to rush to their dad's side.

'Not from Australia.' Emma sighed. She really was on her own in this.

'I guess he's got a lot on with his business?'

Emma nodded. 'He always has. The last time he visited was for Mum's funeral. He does video call Dad at least once a month, but with his business and his young family he's got a lot on his plate.'

'A seven-year-old son and five-year-old twins certainly are a lot. I'm sure it's too much for his wife to manage alone for any length of time – but could they all come over?'

'He said they will at some point.'

Lucie nodded.

'There's something else.'

'What is it?'

Should she tell Lucie this? She had her own worries, as Phoebe had been trying to get pregnant using donor sperm for the past two years and so far they'd had no luck. Emma knew it had been a stressful time for them both. But if she didn't share this with Lucie, who could she tell? Just getting the words out might help her to shake off the way she had been feeling.

'I-I haven't been feeling great myself.'

'Well, of course you haven't, darling. You're clearly worried sick about your dad.'

'It's not just that.'

'Is it cancer?' Lucie's eyebrows shot up her forehead and disappeared underneath her short fringe. 'Oh no, please tell me it's not cancer.'

'No! I don't have cancer. Or anything else that I know of, apart from some menopausal symptoms. But . . . I think I might be having some sort of meltdown.'

'Meltdown?'

'Yes. See, I haven't been sleeping very well lately and I've been worrying a lot more than usual about things. I feel anxious a lot of the time and – and I found myself in Tesco Extra at 2 a.m. yesterday with no idea how I got there. *And* I was wearing my pyjamas. That was before I even *knew* about Dad.'

'What on earth were you doing there at that time?'

'Buying dental floss, vodka and ice cream.'

'Essentials, then.'

'Ha! Yes.'

'Is it the first time you've done that?' Lucie steepled her hands on the table in front of her.

'The first time I've been there in my pyjamas.'

'You weren't!'

'I was.'

'Oh, Emma, you poor love. You really are burnt out, aren't you?'

'D'you think that's what it is?'

'It could well be and . . . I have to apologise, Emma. Since Phoebe and I got caught up in wanting to become parents I haven't been there for you as much as I should have been.'

'You don't need to apologise. You've had your own journey and been through so much. I really hope it works out for you both – more than I can say. As far as I'm concerned, I think I'm just spending too much time working and on social media. I jump from Twitter to Facebook to Instagram to Zoom and back again, and then it's emails, tax forms, LinkedIn and more. I'm afraid to turn down jobs in case the publishers don't come back to me and there's no one else to help if I can't pay the bills, and so I feel like I'm on a treadmill, running constantly and it's . . .' She blinked and cleared her throat.

What was happening to her face? It seemed to be contorting in all sorts of funny ways and she realised she must look like some grotesque gargoyle. Was she going to cry? She never cried!

'Emma?' Lucie leant towards her. 'Are you OK?'

'I . . . uh . . . I . . .' A solitary tear squeezed from the corner of her eye and trickled down her cheek. 'Oh dear.'

'Emma!' Lucie slid off her stool and wrapped Emma in a Chanel-scented hug. Emma sniffed hard, not wanting to deposit snot or mascara on Lucie's shoulder. 'It's OK, darling, it's all going to be OK.'

When Emma felt certain that the waterfall of tears had receded and that she was back in control again, she said, 'I'm not actually sure that it will be. Something needs to change and I think I know where to start.'

'By going home?'

'Yes. I need to see my dad.' Saying the words made her feel five years old again, like that time she'd fallen in the park and cut her knee and her dad had scooped her up in his strong arms and carried her home. He'd stuck a Barbie plaster on her knee and they'd eaten ice lollies in the garden while he told her the names of the garden birds. Then he'd played her an Eagles' medley on one of his guitars and all had seemed right with the world again.

Lucie leant back and met Emma's eyes. 'What do you need to sort out before you go?'

Emma shrugged. 'Not much at all. I've a few plants that will need watering but I can ask my neighbour, Jayden, to pop in and do that and–'

'You think the City boy can be trusted not to kill them with kindness?'

Emma smiled. 'Jayden's all right. I know he's a bit of a party animal, but his flat is like a greenhouse, full of plants.

17

I've watered them for him when he's been away so I'm sure he'll return the favour.'

'Well, that's it then.' Lucie reached across the table for her glass, drained it, then waved it at Emma. 'Want another?'

Emma picked up her lime and soda and frowned. 'Tell you what, I'll have a glass of red – but just the one.'

'Good idea to get some antioxidants inside you. One large vino coming right up. While I'm gone, have a think about whether or not you want me to come with you. I can juggle things around a bit and come for a few days to support you.'

'Thanks, Lucie.'

She watched as her friend sashayed to the bar, turning heads all the way. In her killer heels and fitted black dress, Emma wasn't surprised Lucie was attracting attention. Lucie had style and she knew it. She also had an incredibly kind heart and Emma was grateful for her friendship, but she knew that she had to do this alone. Lucie had her own life and worries, a wife to support and plans to make. Emma was independent, self-employed and on the cusp of turning fifty. There was no one to hold her hand and that was just fine; it was how it had been for almost thirty years.

She just wished all of this was happening another ten or twenty years down the line and not when she was already feeling slightly wobbly about her life. It seemed too soon after losing her mum for her dad to be unwell. Being an editor, she'd worked on novels featuring characters with dementia, and so she'd done some research into the condition. Dementia itself was a terrible condition for both the person affected and for their loved ones. Dad might still be physically present and yet no longer the man she knew.

Not yet.

And, of course, though she wished she could push them away, there were other reasons why she didn't want to spend much time in the village she'd grown up in. Reasons she'd buried deep a long time ago. Reasons that made her long to turn the clock back so she could deal with things better.

But until someone invented a time machine, she had no choice but to put her big girl pants on, don her stiff upper lip and head home to Little Bramble. She just hoped the inhabitants of the pretty country village were ready for her return.

Chapter 3

Emma pulled her suitcase behind her as she walked from the station in Little Bramble the following morning, cursing her decision to wear sandal wedges as the gravel path that led from the platform to the car park was not suited to her choice of footwear. The heavy rucksack on her back wasn't helping and she was already starting to sweat in the balmy June air.

When she reached the car park, the ground evened out and she exhaled a sigh of relief. A broken ankle would not help her to deal with the current situation. She was expecting things to be hard enough as it was.

As she passed people making their way to the station, she felt their eyes on her. Were they wondering who she was and why she had come to their village? Did any of them recognise her? She knew she was being paranoid and yet she scanned faces from behind her large sunglasses, searching for someone familiar, yet hoping she would remain anonymous. So much had changed since she'd lived in the village, but then she had left, what was it? Almost twenty-eight years ago. She'd been just twenty-two. She'd only returned for very brief spells since and encouraged her parents to visit her in London whenever possible, although that hadn't been as often as she would have liked. But then time flew past, promises to get together more often were forgotten and life – and mainly work in her case – got in the way. There was always one more job to complete, one more to accept, and one more to line up ready so that Emma's life had existed around her editing.

At the far side of the car park, she shuffled through a narrow gateway and paused. There was the village in all its early morning glory. Everything looked so green and open, so pretty and rural, so fresh and vibrant. There was even a smell that shouted *country village* at her, a combination of woodsmoke, flowers, freshly mown grass and the tang of manure from nearby fields. Even after all the years that had passed, all the time she'd lived in the city, this smell brought goosebumps to her skin and a lump to her throat because it would always be the familiar smell of home.

She trundled her suitcase past the village green, noting that the huge Norwegian Spruce still held its spot at the centre like some kind of sentry guarding the village. Growing up, she'd spent a lot of time at the green, playing with friends, gasping at fireworks, singing carols and watching the turning on of the Christmas lights. The green and the village hall had been the heart of Little Bramble. The old hall had burnt down and

Emma didn't know much about the new one, other than that her dad had been due to sing there as part of a Christmas talent show. Then, when she'd been visiting, a terrible snow-storm had prevented some performers from attending and she'd advised her dad to stay home in the warm because she'd sensed he was somewhat fragile, even then. She'd only stayed in the village for a few days after that. As soon as the trains had been running again, she'd hopped on one and headed back to London, trying to forget her concerns about her dad as the fields and buildings whizzed past behind the smeared glass of the train windows. She should have stayed to see in the New Year as her dad had asked, realised that it was a cry for help, but just like always, she felt compelled to flee the village as soon as possible.

Guilt washed over her and she stopped walking, took a few deep breaths, unsteady on her wedges as her heart pounded behind her ribs. She shouldn't have left him – there was no avoiding the truth; she had put herself first and now look what had happened! Her lifelong rock was crumbling and she hadn't even been around to support him.

Dementia . . . The word seemed to be whispered on the breeze that had suddenly picked up, whistling around the green, shaking the green leaves of the trees and the soft petals of the flowers in pots and beds. The rainbow of colours seemed to shimmer around her and she closed her eyes for a moment then yelped as something flicked against her cheek.

Emma opened her eyes and looked down, relieved as she realised that she had not been attacked by an insect or bird, but by a small sheet of colourful paper. She plucked it from the ground where it had landed and held it out, laughter juddering through her as she glanced around self-consciously.

She scanned the piece of paper, taking in the smiling cartoon faces and excellent sketch of the green where stalls had been erected and bunting hung from every available lamp post and tree.

'The Little Bramble Country Village Fête,' she read, 'Saturday 31st July.'

She folded the paper as the memories came rushing through her.

Across the green she saw people, stalls, animals, heard shouts and laughter, music and birdsong. The aromas of hot dogs and crepes filled the air and the warmth of the sun made her cheeks glow and her shoulders relax.

She stepped closer to the grass and searched the faces, knowing that she was looking for him, for the source of the music. And there he was, standing in a semi-circle with his small band, guitar hanging from a strap around his neck, his face a picture of happiness as he sang and played.

'Dad,' she whispered, love and nostalgia rushing through her.

As she watched, a woman approached the band, wearing a long denim skirt and flowery smock top, her shiny brown hair falling down over her shoulders. She was holding the hand of a girl who was around eight or nine with a tiny heart-shaped face and long dark hair like the woman's.

Mum. And the little girl was her.

Emma gasped then shut her eyes tightly, banishing the image from her past, unable to cope with the emotions it brought.

Not here. Not now.

She slipped the leaflet into her bag. No doubt her time here would bring a host of memories back to the surface. And with good memories came some bad ones, but what was the point of regretting what she couldn't change?

Emma took a deep breath and walked on until she reached a small row of cottages as pretty as those in a picture book. Little Bramble was one of the loveliest villages she had ever seen, and every time she returned, its beauty never failed to take her breath away.

She was here now, home at last, and she would try to help her dad in whatever ways she could.

Hopefully, she hadn't left it too late.

Connor Jones sipped his black coffee and winced. It was cold. He'd made it over fifteen minutes ago, before his mobile had rung and he had returned to the small office above the workshop at The Lumber Shed. He had a thousand things to get done today but he didn't mind because business was booming and, as a result, admin was building up.

He'd grabbed a coffee from the machine in the staff kitchen then headed up the staircase that led to his office in the converted barn, hoping to get his head down and clear some of the email orders from his inbox. His daughter, Grace, who still lived with him, even though she was twenty-five, was with her mother today and so he had the day to do with as he wished. Initially, Grace had lived with her mother, Sadie, after her parents had split up, but following a series of arguments when Grace was sixteen, she'd asked to live with her father. Connor had been hesitant to agree at first, not wanting to hurt Sadie or to make the rift between mother and daughter worse, but it had turned out to be a sensible move. With some space between them, Grace and Sadie had got on better and Connor had been happy to see it, knowing how important having a good relationship with both of her parents was for Grace.

For Connor, whenever he had free time on his hands, it was work that he chose to do. His whole world revolved around Grace and The Lumber Shed and, after his past experiences, that was quite all right with him. He hadn't seemed to be good at romantic relationships, had made a mess of the two he'd had, and so his daughter and his business were his priorities. He didn't want anything else in his life and was quite happy with the way things were.

He thought about the phone call he'd just had with Grace's mother, Sadie, and a familiar sadness gripped him. Sadie was a good mum and he could never fault how much she loved Grace, but she wanted more from Connor than

25

he could offer and it had been that way for years. This often led to phone calls where Sadie would become increasingly frustrated with Connor, berating him for being a failure as a man and as a father, and he tried so hard not to retaliate because it only made things worse. Their relationship had left Connor with a prevailing sense of inadequacy, a belief that he was incapable of making Sadie happy, and so he had finally summoned his courage and ended their relationship when Grace was fifteen. It had been one of the hardest things he'd ever had to do, but years of trying to be what Sadie wanted him to be had left him drained.

Sadie had never accepted the break-up. He wished she would find something to make herself happy, then she could move on and forget about him, but she just didn't seem to want to do that. It was as if she enjoyed being miserable. Connor wondered if any man could have made her happy and in the ten years since their split, Sadie's behaviour had been a growing concern. She was all over the place. He had asked her to seek help, but she'd turned on him and accused him of trying to make out that she was unstable.

The latest phone call had started innocuously enough as Sadie had told Connor she wanted him to get Grace a new suitcase to take with her to Paris because the one she intended taking was too old and small. Connor had already discussed the suitcase situation with Grace and she'd reassured him that the one she had was fine, so, as with many of Sadie's reasons for phoning him, he suspected that it had been an excuse to have a go at him yet again. Connor wondered how she would manage when Grace left. Her parents were ageing and she spent a lot of time at their home, had even bought the cottage next door so she could be close to them; apart from that she had her part-time job behind the bar at the Red Squirrel and not much else. Grace had been her whole world, even when she didn't live with her, and her absence was going to leave a big hole in Sadie's life. Connor was worried about the impact this would have on her and, in turn, on Grace, because he knew that Sadie's rants often spilled over to Grace.

He stood up and carried the mug of cold coffee out of his office, down the stairs and through the workshop to the kitchen, then tipped it down the sink. Back in the workshop, he surveyed the large open space with workbenches and tools, machinery and works in progress. He loved the space when it was busy, when the machines hummed, music blared from the radio and the scent of sawdust and varnish drifted through the air. There was such a sense of productivity, of moving forwards and getting things done. He also liked knowing that they were taking wood and old furniture and giving everything a new lease of life, creating new from old and helping the planet.

The business had come a long way from when his father had started it in his shed when Connor was just seven years old. They had moved premises several times over the years as the demand for reclaimed wood furniture had grown and then, six years ago, Connor had rented the converted barn from a local farmer and had been able to hire more workers. His father had seen the new premises and given it his approval, had even shed a tear as they'd sat in the office the day work had begun there and cracked open a 25-year-old single malt. Connor's father had told him how delighted he was to see the business he'd started doing so well and how proud he was of Connor, his only child, for working so hard. Just thinking about his dad made Connor's throat tighten. John Jones had died just six months after that day, a sudden heart attack tearing him away from his family. Of course, Connor and his mother, Zoe, had been shocked at John's sudden death, but the fact that he had always been a heavy smoker and refused to quit, despite warnings from his GP, had meant that they'd had to accept that he'd been gambling with his life every day.

But God, Connor missed his father so much. They'd been so alike, so close; John had been father and friend, advisor and mentor. There was no replacing a bond like that. Grace had been wonderful, grieving for her grandfather yet stoic in a way that Connor admired, and while he would never have cried on her shoulder, not wanting to burden her with that, he had been aware of her attempts to reassure and comfort him. She was a remarkable young woman and he was still in awe of the fact that she was his daughter.

His mobile started vibrating in his pocket so he pulled it out and peered at the screen.

Sadie again . . .

Emma parked her suitcase outside her dad's front door and stretched her neck from side to side to try to release the tension. She had a feeling that she was on a precipice, that life as she knew it was about to change and she could be about to lose the control she'd tried so hard to exert over her life.

When she opened the door and went into the cottage where she'd grown up, there would be no going back. It was a strange feeling, but one that she knew she had to embrace. Until now, she'd lived her adult life for herself, working as hard as she liked, eating and drinking what she fancied, getting up and going to bed at times she chose. However, if her dad needed her as much as she suspected he did, while she was here she would need to adapt to a way of life that suited them both, would have to compromise and consider his needs too; it was going to be a challenge.

She opened her handbag and rooted around for the door key. She had kept it, even though she didn't return here very often, because her parents had insisted that their home would always be *her* home and that she should come back whenever she felt the need. Strange, now, that when she was returning for a longer period of time it was because of her dad's needs and not her own. But then wasn't that how life went? You started off weak and vulnerable and ended up the same way if you were lucky enough to live that long.

Well, there was nothing else for it other than to go inside and find out exactly how her dad was doing. She located the key, pushed it into the lock and opened the door.

Chapter 4

The hallway to her dad's cottage was cool and dark. Emma parked her suitcase and rucksack in the corner out of the way of the door, steeling herself for what was to come. The cottage smelt like home, the combined scents of life greeting her as she slid off her wedges and pulled a pair of flip-flops from her handbag. There were layers to the familiar smell – years of baking in the kitchen at the end of the short hallway, the lavender polish that was used on the woodwork and the coal tar soap that her parents had used since before Emma was born. They had steadfastly refused to try other products, believing that the soap they had always used was far superior to fancy shower gels and the packaging of a simple paper wrapper better for the environment. How right they had been.

Emma considered calling out but worried that, if she did, she might startle her dad, so she went through first to the lounge off the right of the hallway, but it was empty.

The curtains weren't fully open, so the room, with its two wingback armchairs and three-seater sofa, was gloomy apart from the strip of light that shone through the gap in the curtains and fell across the threadbare rug in front of the hearth. Dust motes swam in the beam of sunlight, minute diamonds that floated around slowly, as if they too were afraid of disturbing the peace.

When Emma's mum had been alive, the house had always been filled with noise: the clattering of pots and pans, the vacuum being run around upstairs, her dad strumming on his guitars and the albums that her mum used to play on her old record player. Her mum had had an eclectic taste in music, enjoying the likes of Frank Sinatra, Queen, The Beatles, The Eagles, Whitney Houston and more, but her favourite had been The Carpenters. Emma found listening to 'Close to You' or 'We've Only Just Begun' incredibly emotional, as the songs always brought back vivid memories of happy times. She wanted to enter the lounge and look around, to allow herself to think about her mum, but she didn't have time right now. She had to find her dad and see how he was before she did anything else; she had to keep moving.

She went to the kitchen, peering around the door, and was rewarded by the sight of her dad's neighbour, Dilys Martin, standing at the sink, her back to the room. She was wearing faded jeans, crocs that looked too big and were probably her husband's, and a white shirt with a tiny bird pattern that looked too small. She'd filled out since Emma had last seen her at Christmas, but now that Emma thought about it, she hadn't really paid Dilys much attention then. Emma had known Dilys since childhood – she had been sixteen years older than Emma and often babysat her. Dilys had always lived next door, inheriting the house from her parents and raising her own two children there. She was a grandmother of five now, ranging from twelve to four, and Emma knew that had been something her own mum had envied. Dilys's house was always busy with children coming and going, large family gatherings and chaotic celebrations of special occasions. In contrast, after Emma and her brother had left the village, her parents had been left without either of their children and their only grandchildren were on the other side of the world.

'Knock knock!' Emma called softly and Dilys turned around.

'Emma! I did hear you come in but wanted to finish this quickly.' She dried her hands on a towel and opened her arms. 'It's so good to see you.'

They hugged briefly, then Emma set her shoulder bag down on the kitchen table.

'Cup of tea?' Dilys offered.

'Yes, please. How's Dad?'

'He's resting at the moment. I tucked him in upstairs because he was exhausted after a restless night.'

'Thank you so much for staying with him.' Emma cleared her throat. 'I'm so grateful for your help.'

'No problem, Emma. You know I care about your dad, as I did about your mum. They were great friends to me over the years and helped me out many a time when the children were small. Nothing was ever too much trouble for them. Not many people have such wonderful neighbours, especially these days.'

'I don't know how we'd have managed without you and Fred.'

Dilys handed her a mug of tea. 'Well, you don't need to, so don't worry.'

'Thank you.' Emma sipped the tea, milk no sugar, exactly how she liked it.

Life in Little Bramble was very different from life in London. Yes, she knew her neighbours there to talk to and to water their plants, but here in the village people like Dilys knew how you took your tea and remembered your birthday, even years down the line. It was very different, and although Emma had, for quite a while, liked the anonymity of London, enjoyed being able to lose herself within a crowd and walk the streets without bumping into a soul she knew, there was something comforting about coming home and knowing that people cared. However, she had to admit that there were some people she would be happier bumping into than others.

They sat at the table and Emma drank her tea while Dilys told her how her dad had been. It seemed that some days were worse than others for him and while he forgot things that had happened the day before, he could remember things that happened long in the past, in particular before Emma's mum had died, with startling clarity. Dilys also said that Greg seemed to struggle more when he was tired or stressed and that there were long periods of lucidity when he seemed to be his normal self.

'How long are you staying, Emma?' Dilys asked finally.

'I was thinking a month but I'll see how things go.' She swallowed hard, as if to suppress her fears that it might not be long enough, that there might be plans that had to be made and medical staff consulted on how to proceed.

'Try not to worry, Emma.' Dilys patted her hand. 'I'm sure that having you home for a bit will help your dad no end. He misses you terribly, and your mum, of course. Hopefully you being here will be the tonic he needs.'

Emma nodded and smiled but she knew that Dilys was well aware that her dad would probably need more than a few weeks with his daughter to get better. He might improve but he was unlikely to ever be the same man again.

Dilys got up and took the mugs to the sink and turned the tap on.

'It's all right, I'll do those,' Emma said.

'OK, Emma, thank you. But don't forget, Fred and I are here for you and your dad. Day or night, give us a knock and we'll come right round.'

'Thank you . . .'

Emma saw Dilys out of the back door and the older woman went through the gate that her dad had installed between their gardens, then she went back into the kitchen and closed the door. She leant against it, listening to the

34

creaks and groans of the old cottage, hugging herself as the mugginess thickened in her brain and she realised that she felt bone-weary. It was only when she was alone that she could let reality properly sink in. Her mum was gone, her dad was poorly, and life was forever altered.

The creaking of floorboards from above dragged her from the daze that had settled over her. She went to the sink and splashed some cold water over her face then patted it dry with a hand towel. The last thing she wanted was to upset her dad because she seemed distant or confused herself. Something about coming back to Little Bramble had affected her, had settled over her like a thick fog as if her mind was trying to suppress emotions she'd long ago buried, preventing them from floating to the surface like bubbles in champagne.

Champagne . . . She gasped.

Back then, almost thirty years ago, her parents had bought so many bottles of champagne that the kitchen had been an obstacle course for weeks. There had been bottles on every surface, boxes on the table and tucked underneath, along with numerous small jars of her mum's jam and marmalade adorned with white and silver ribbons and her dad's best suit hanging on the kitchen door, ready to be dry cleaned.

Her parents had been so excited.

Friends and neighbours had been so excited.

Emma had swayed between joy and despair.

Emotions ebbed and flowed like waves and Emma had suddenly felt as though she was drowning, being dragged under by forces beyond her control. She had been seized by a panic that told her that she was throwing everything away when she'd barely lived! And so she'd made a life-changing decision. In an instant, everything she'd thought she'd had and known had disappeared in one devastating explosion.

Footsteps on the stairs made her turn to the sink, run the cold tap and splash more water over her face. She drank some water as well, then filled the kettle and turned it on.

'Oh, hello.' Her dad shuffled into the kitchen in his dressing gown and slippers and she froze, unable to tear her eyes from him. He looked so old and so frail, as if a sneeze could knock him over. 'I didn't know you were here.' He frowned. 'Did I know you were coming?'

'I didn't speak to you, but Dilys said she'd let you know.'

His frown wavered and she saw that he was trying to remember if Dilys had told him.

'Is there a reason why you're home? Not that I'm not delighted to see you but . . .'

'It's OK, Dad. I know there's normally an occasion when I come back but this time I'm back for a different reason.'

His face contorted then and her heart squeezed.

'Is it because of me? Because I've been . . . forgetful?'

A thousand excuses fought in Emma's mind for precedence and she opened her mouth several times to reply but then realised that she could soften the blow without misleading him.

'Yes, Dad. I've come back to spend some time with you because you need to have some tests.'

'Tests?'

She nodded.

'To find out if I'm . . . going to get worse?'

She nodded again, feeling as though she might choke on the emotion.

'Oh, I'm glad you're home,' he said. 'I won't have to do this alone.'

He smiled though his eyes shone and Emma couldn't help herself; she rushed towards him and threw her arms around his waist, burying her face in his neck and holding him as tightly as she dared because she feared she might break him. He patted her back gently and she trembled with the shock of seeing him so fragile.

'How are you feeling, Dad?' She released him and leant back to look at him.

'I'm OK, Emma. At least, I think I am.' He had a few days' worth of grey stubble on his face, which wasn't at all like the man Emma knew and loved. Her dad had always shaved in the morning, so she knew he wasn't feeling his best. 'Carrying on with life as best I can.'

'Oh, Dad!' She hugged him again.

'Hey, hey!' He gave a small laugh. 'Why so sad?'

Had he already forgotten their conversation of moments ago?

'I'm just worried about you. You know . . . after yesterday.'

He frowned. 'Yesterday?'

'Yes, you know when you . . . uh . . .'

'Have you boiled the kettle?' His eyes lit up and Emma swallowed what she was going to say.

'Yes. Would you like tea?'

'Please. I'm sure there are some of Dilys's raisin and oat cookies here too.' He started opening drawers and cupboards and rooting around. Emma watched him for a moment, then scanned the kitchen, spotting a foil-covered plate on the Welsh dresser. She picked the plate up and peered under the foil; sure enough, there were cookies on it, so she removed the foil and set it on the table.

'There you are, Dad. You sit down while I make some tea then we can have a nice catch-up.'

'Lovely,' he said as he sat down then started nibbling at a cookie. 'Just lovely. Why are you here?'

Emma filled the kettle, biting hard on her bottom lip, determined to stay strong for both their sakes.

Connor raised his wine glass and smiled at the beautiful young woman sitting opposite him.

'To you and all that you've achieved.'

She smiled, the candlelight flickering over her pretty features, from her small nose to her pale eyelashes and eyebrows, making her blue eyes seem to glow as if lit from within and her blonde hair shine like spun gold.

They clinked glasses then drank and Connor felt the day easing away as the alcohol hit his empty stomach, warming him and making him realise how hungry he was.

'This place is lovely, Dad.'

Grace looked around and he followed her gaze. The Bistro had opened the previous month and was a welcome addition to the village. The owner, Lorna Osborne, had come to Little Bramble to stay with an old friend from university. She'd seen the small empty premises between the King's Arms and the veterinary surgery, that had briefly been a wool shop then a juice bar, and fallen in love with it and with the village. She'd bought the premises from its elderly owner, who wanted a quick sale, and after an impressively speedy renovation, mainly due to her boyfriend's carpentry skills and a team of friends and acquaintances with plumbing and electrical experience, they'd created a cosy, quaint bistro. Lorna's boyfriend, Serge, was also a chef and so with her out front, Serge in the kitchen, and a small staff of locals, they'd opened last month and had been busy ever since.

This was the first time Connor had booked a table and he had to admit that he was impressed too. Lorna had come to The Lumber Shed looking for tables and chairs and Connor had done her a good deal, pleased to see a new business coming to Little Bramble. She'd offered him a table whenever he wanted it in exchange for his help, but Connor had never been one to take advantage of a situation, and so he'd waited a while. He'd done Lorna a good deal because it was good for the village and not for his own gain, but he had been keen to find out if the food was as good as everyone claimed.

The bistro had ten tables to seat a maximum of four people each, although he imagined they'd move tables around for larger parties. They'd been seated at a table near the bay window that was framed with red curtains and had a deep mahogany windowsill. There was a red and white checked cloth on the table and a small red votive holder in which a candle flickered. The lighting was low, the music soft and mellow and the atmosphere relaxed and informal. It was Connor's kind of place.

He returned his attention to Grace and felt a tug at his heart. She was about to head off to Paris and he wasn't sure how he would manage without her. Of course, she'd been to university in London for four years, where she'd studied fashion and design, one of those years being an industry placement, and he'd found that difficult but knowing that she'd be back for holidays and probably after graduation had made it easier. Since then, she'd lived at home for three years, going between his house and her mum's.

Never one to take it easy, Grace had set up an Etsy shop selling fashion she made on her sewing machine in the small spare bedroom. She'd blogged, growing her voice as a respected member of the fashion and design community and creating a platform for her designs. He'd enjoyed those years, especially in the summer evenings when he'd sit in the garden with a book, soothed by the sounds coming from the open bedroom window of the snipping of her sharp scissors as she cut out patterns and the whirring of the sewing machine. Connor was extremely proud of her talent and creativity, her work ethic and zest for life. She was also brave, ambitious and determined, but never in a rush to get anywhere; she knew that it took time to get where you wanted to be and so she'd been happy to return home for a few years while she built a name for herself and honed her skills. At times he allowed himself to compare Grace with her mother, almost, he suspected, to reassure himself that he'd done a good job as a father, and the difference was startling. It was as if growing up under Sadie's shadow had made Grace determined to live her life for herself, to never feel the need to find a man to rely on, and he thanked the stars that Grace was so independent. She would make her own way in life, create her own happiness.

'I can hardly believe you'll be leaving so soon.' He swirled the wine in his glass then set it back down as heaviness filled his chest.

'I know.' Her eyes flashed as they met his. She was excited, and so she should be. 'I can't wait. It's like I've done all this work and finally it's paying off. It's a dream come true, Dad.'

'What you've always wanted ever since you were a little girl and you used to cut up my shirts to make new ones.'

She rolled her eyes. 'Don't remind me. It used to drive Mum mad.'

Connor nodded. Sadie used to freak out every time she found another item of clothing that Grace had chopped up, but he thought it amusing as well as fascinating, because even at ten years old she was thinking about how colours and materials went together, about how she could change the sleeves on a garment to make it look different, about how she could attach ribbons and buttons and glue on glitter and costume jewellery to completely change an outfit. Of course, sometimes his friends had laughed when

41

he met up with them wearing one of her creations, but as long as it had made Grace happy, Connor hadn't cared.

'Remember when I took that old yellow suede jacket Mum had and dyed it?'

'You meant to turn it red but it ended up salmon pink.' He cringed at the thought of how anxious Grace had been when she'd shown him the jacket and how worried he'd been when he'd thought about how Sadie would react.

'What were you then? Thirteen?'

'Twelve!'

He nodded. 'Good times.'

'You know, Dad, you two were never a good match.'

'Sorry?' Connor looked up but Grace was gazing into her glass. 'You and Mum. I always knew it, deep down, even if I didn't want to believe it. No one wants their parents to split up but some people just shouldn't be together. I mean, I'm glad you were, because you had me, but you never made each other happy so what was the point?'

Connor cleared his throat and wriggled in his chair. He'd spoken to Grace about this before, of course he had, but it was never a comfortable conversation and he always tried to discuss it gently. He could never say anything bad about Sadie to Grace because that would hurt his daughter, but he had tried to be as honest as he could, telling her that he respected her mum and cared about her but didn't love her in the way he should, in the way that Sadie deserved to be loved. The main problem was that Sadie wasn't always quite so calm and respectful when speaking about Connor, but he also knew that Grace let Sadie rant and tried not to let it get to her. She knew her dad, she knew how much he loved her, and however many times Sadie might insist that Connor loved only himself, he hoped Grace knew that wasn't true.

'The thing is, Dad, I've been fine about you being single for so long because I've been here to look after you, but now that I'm going away – properly – I'm worried about you.'

'What? Why?' She thought she'd been looking after him? Her brows met. 'In case you'll be lonely.'

'I won't be lonely, Grace. I've got my mum, the business, friends and I'm always busy.'

'I hope you won't but I do wish sometimes that you had someone.'

He shook his head. 'I don't need someone else in my life.'

'You're still young, though. You've only just turned fifty and you're a good-looking man. You have that grey-hair George Clooney thing going on that lots of women like and you're in quite good shape.'

Connor snorted. '*Quite* good shape? What, for my age?'

'No, Dad, for any age. All my friends say you're quite hot, a bit of a silver fox, and that they're surprised you're single.'

Heat filled Connor's cheeks. This was not a conversation he'd imagined having with his daughter. He was flattered but also acutely embarrassed. He was a father and an employer and he hadn't thought about himself in *that* way for a long time. Not since . . . Well, not for a long time. Sadie had helped with that, made him want to forget that he could be dating or in a relationship, because it was just so difficult with her around and he didn't want to hurt her more than he already had. It was a huge responsibility when someone else's emotions were reliant upon him and Little Bramble was a small village, so it wasn't like he could go on a date and not have Sadie find out about it.

'I'll never understand why you and mum got together. I know you were at school together, but you just don't seem to have anything in common at all.'

Connor sipped his wine then put the glass down. 'We have you in common, Grace, and for a while that was all we needed. But we are very different people and while that might work for some, it didn't for us.'

'I wish she could find someone else too.' Grace's expression changed and for a moment she looked like a little girl again and all of Connor's protective instincts surged. If he could have loved Sadie for Grace's sake, then he would have done.

'That would be nice.' He picked up a menu. 'I'd like to see your mum happy. However, I think we should order soon. My stomach's rumbling.'

'It would be nice to see you both happy . . . and settled.'

Grace picked up her menu and Connor glanced at her, his heart filled with love for his only child, a child he hadn't planned on having but one he wouldn't be without.

Chapter 5

The next morning Emma woke with a start. She had slept soundly, lulled to sleep by the surroundings of her old home, the comfort of her bed and the darkness of the room, by the hooting of owls and the barking of foxes. Living in London for so long she was used to the constant hubbub, the sirens at all times of the day and night, the lights she could see from her window that signposted familiar landmarks, the hum of the air conditioning, the ping and whir of the lift and the soft swish of the doors as someone got out on her floor.

In London, there had been people all around her all of the time: above and below, to each side, opposite and behind, and yet she had been alone. After she had decided to go freelance nine years previously, her life had changed. For a while, she'd still met old friends and colleagues for coffee and drinks, still attended publishing events and danced in clubs until the small hours. But as the years passed, things had begun to change. Some of the colleagues she had been close to had married or moved to better school catchment areas; some left to carve out careers in publishing houses in New York and Chicago, and some just got swept up in their busy lives. Soon, her world had shrunk, her phonebook far smaller than it had once been and she'd become isolated, often spending days and weeks without seeing another soul except for her neighbours as they passed in the hallway and the other late-night shoppers in Tesco Extra or Little Waitrose. Her way of communicating with the world had become through her laptop and smartphone, through the ever-growing range of social media platforms. She'd often lost hours as she'd hopped from one to another, chatting to people she felt she knew but had never met and offering support to those who seemed sad or lost, cheering for those experiencing success and stepping back from the trolls who struck out at anyone and everyone just for the sake of an argument. It could be a wonderful world and a scary one. But human contact had become very limited as even Lucie, who'd always been available, got caught up in her own personal challenges. It was just how things were and Emma didn't feel sorry for herself, just tired and a bit lonely.

Lying here in her childhood room with the lemon walls, the white ceiling with its thick beams and the window that overlooked the large back garden and trees beyond, she realised that she felt safer than she had done in a long time. She hadn't even realised how bad things had got, but comparing how she felt now with how she had been feeling recently made everything clearer. If she let her mind wander she could pretend that she was a child again, that the years had not passed as quickly as they had and that her mum would be downstairs right now, drinking coffee on the back doorstep, watching the birds making the most of the nuts in the feeders while her dad was restringing one of his acoustic guitars.

Outside, a chorus of birds sang in the trees of the garden and cool air scented with roses crept in through the gap in the window that she'd left open last night. She breathed in the fresh country air deeply, savouring the sensation and the scents.

Since her arrival yesterday, her laptop had remained in its bag, her phone had run out of battery, and she'd stepped away from the world she'd become accustomed to and into her old one. She'd been so immersed in making dinner, in watching TV with her dad as they ate, then making sure that he got to bed all right, that she'd not thought to plug in her phone or even turn her laptop on. At just gone 10 she'd closed the curtains that her mum had made many years ago, purple with a tiny silver moon print, crawled under the duck down duvet and passed out without even checking her notifications.

Panic seized her now and she swung her legs over the side of the bed, grabbed her bag, then rooted around for her phone. What if she'd missed something? What if someone had tried to contact her and been unable to? She could lose a job, lose a follower, lose . . .

Lose what, exactly? What difference would another hour make? It was hard to take a step back, to relinquish control over her carefully constructed life, but while she was here she'd have to make some changes – and not being a slave to social media was one of them. Surely her mini meltdown in Tesco Extra had served as a warning of something worse to come? She hadn't wanted to admit it fully to herself, hadn't said the actual words to Lucie when they talked about how Emma was feeling, but she suspected that she was suffering from burnout and she needed her strength if she was going to be able to help her dad, so it was time to practise some self-care.

She set her phone down on the bedside table, plugged in the charger, then sat back down and stretched her neck from one side to the other. This break from the norm was certainly a challenge; she usually scanned her phone on waking, then while she sat on the loo, and again as she sipped her first strong coffee. But she felt the need to do things differently today. She would check her phone and her emails after breakfast, but for now she needed to use the bathroom then drink a large mug of tea.

***

'Hello, Dad,' Emma looked up from her mug as he entered the kitchen.

'Good morning!'

He ambled across the kitchen and she got up and hugged him. He felt slight, as if he'd lost more weight since yesterday. She vowed to try and feed him up while she was home.

'Right, what do you fancy for breakfast?' she asked.

'I don't mind.' He looked around the kitchen. 'Can I smell toast?'

'You can. I just polished off a piece, but I can make some more.'

'You're a good daughter.'

'Thanks.' Her voice wavered as guilt pierced her chest. Was she?

'Sit down and I'll make some tea too. The paper's there for you.'

'Perfect.'

He patted his dressing gown pockets and frowned.

'What is it?'

'My glasses. I don't know where I put them.'

'When were you wearing them last?'

His mouth fell open and his frown deepened. 'Uh . . . not this morning.'

'Last night watching TV?'

He nodded. 'I should wear them all the time now, really, as I can't see far. Can't read without them either.'

'Hold on!' She dashed from the kitchen and found his glasses on the arm of his chair in the lounge then took them back to him.

'You're an angel, Emma, a true angel.'

She shrugged the compliment away; she felt far from angelic and his kindness was just making her guilt throb like a fresh burn.

'Right, breakfast.'

They sat and ate toast and drank two pots of tea, Greg reading his paper and Emma flicking through a supplementary magazine as the sunshine poured through the kitchen window, warming the floor tiles and showing up the haze on the glass. Emma made a mental note to try to clean the windows or phone a window cleaner while she was here. The curtains looked like they could use a wash too.

But that could wait. There was no hurry. She had time.

'Are you sure you're up to this?' Emma asked as she helped her dad into his jacket.

'Oh yes, I'm looking forward to it.'

When he'd buttoned up his jacket, she gave him his flat cap and he pulled it onto his head. He already looked better, more like himself, because he'd shaved and dressed and the leisurely breakfast had put some colour into his cheeks. Perhaps it was having some company too, she thought, as she slipped her feet into white plimsolls and her arms into a denim jacket.

'You look very pretty, love.'

She laughed.

'You do,' he insisted. 'Always such a pretty girl you were, just like your mum.'

'It must be the French ancestry.' She used the reply her mum had always used whenever she received a compliment. Dawn Patrick had been born Donatienne but when she'd come to England in the sixties, she'd unofficially changed her name to Dawn because that was how people tended to pronounce the start of her name anyway.

'The Marseille link runs strong in your mum's genes.'

Emma nodded. Her mum had often told her stories of her grandfather's time working on the railroad and his involvement in the liberation of southern France. Her grandparents had lived in Marseille after World War II and her grandfather had helped rebuild the city. Dawn had come to England aged twenty-four, to visit a pen pal from Little Bramble and met Greg at a village dance. They fell in love and Dawn stayed in England, seeing her parents once or twice a year until their deaths in the seventies. Emma had been a young child when they died so had few memories of them, other than the ones her mum had told her that made them seem so alive. The realisation that she had no children to tell about her own mum had hit her several times recently, but that had been *her* choice and for the most part she had enjoyed the life she'd led. Thinking about her grandparents again made Emma think about the plans she'd had to visit Marseille to see where her mum had grown up and to lay flowers on her grandparents' graves – it was another thing she had planned to do then not found the time for. Life was slipping through her fingers faster than she could believe. Would she find the time one day soon to make that trip and try to connect with her mum's past? Try to recall the French her mum had taught her when she was younger and use it in person? Or had she left it too late, left the language of her ancestors to wither inside her until it felt completely foreign to her tongue?

'But I'm hardly a girl any more, am I?'

Emma caught sight of herself in the hallway mirror and had to agree; she hadn't been a girl for a long time. With short hair, lines around her eyes and a softening to her chin, she thought she looked as though someone had drawn her when she was younger and then more recently smudged the picture around the edges, as if who she had been was slowly being deleted and replaced with a faded, hazy version.

'You'll always be a girl to me.' Her dad stood next to her and wrapped his arm around her shoulders, squeezing her tightly. Considering how slight he had become, there was a lot of strength in his embrace and she sent out a silent thank you that she still had a dad to hug her.

'Come on then, let's get some air.'

Outside, the morning was mild, the air sweet with the fragrance from the roses that ran around the front door and across the front of the cottage. Emma turned to look at them, admiring the beautiful baby pink and milky white of the flowers, their centres golden yellow. Then there was the ivy, dark green leaves that contrasted with the grey-brown stone of the cottage, winding around the faded white of the window frames and up towards the old tiles of the sloping roof. It was like a cottage from a chocolate box; not for the first time, Emma experienced a warmth that came from having grown up in such a beautiful home. The cottage still held a place in her heart – and right now it was tugging at something inside her, creating feelings that she didn't know how to deal with.

She tucked her arm through her dad's. 'Where shall we go, Dad?'

'Well, I don't think there's much point getting my hair done, is there?' He rubbed his forehead under his cap and they both laughed.

'Not really, no.' Emma pushed a hand through her own cropped brown hair. 'Nor me.'

'I like that style. It suits you. Very Audrey Hepburn.'

'I should come home more often if I'm going to get so many compliments.'

Her dad smiled but she winced at her own insensitivity. He had needed her after Christmas but she'd left him alone. She couldn't forgive herself for that.

She slid her free hand into her bag and pulled out her oversized sunglasses then put them on. Something about being home and spending time with her dad had stirred a whole range of emotions and she didn't fancy having anyone look into her eyes this morning and witness what was going on inside her.

A sudden urge to ring Lucie gripped her, to grasp at her London life and escape from this small corner of

England where her emotions had once run so high, a place she simultaneously adored and feared. In London, Emma was smart, successful, professional, independent, removed. In Little Bramble, she was Emma Patrick, daughter of Greg and Dawn. In one world she could exist without her days being clouded by emotions she'd rather not feel. In another, there was joy to be found in the company of her dad and in other villagers like Dilys, but there was also long-buried pain that she didn't want to face again. There was a deep, dark guilt that could overwhelm her and drag her down if she let it, and experiencing the full onslaught of those emotions was something she didn't want and would avoid for as long as possible.

'Let's go to the green and have a sit on a bench, shall we?' her dad asked as they walked.

'Good plan.'

At least there they could watch the world go by and she could hope that not many people would recognise her with her short hair and sunglasses, and that ghosts from the past would just glide on by.

Connor tucked the folder into the filing cabinet next to his desk then closed the drawer. Another job completed and paid for, another happy customer. Even after so many years, he still found completing a job and seeing the customer happy incredibly satisfying. There was a sense of achievement to it that he didn't find in any other area of his life. Perhaps it was because his personal life was so unfinished in many ways. Years ago, after leaving school at sixteen, he'd joined the family business as an apprentice. He had experience in carpentry already from weekends and holidays spent working with his dad, but becoming an apprentice meant that he could earn some money and know he was entering the world of work. He had money in his pocket and a spring in his step back then, as well as a beautiful girlfriend and a good group of friends. Life had seemed promising, with plenty to offer. It was only when he reached his twenties that he started to wonder if he'd been wrong and if, in fact, life wasn't going to be quite as kind to him as he'd originally believed.

He'd had plans, hopes and dreams, then one day had changed everything and life had seemed to freeze. He'd been on pause for a while, existing rather than living, and he'd lost his youthful optimism, drifted through the days without really caring what happened any more. A serious error of judgement had led him to Sadie's arms and Grace had been conceived soon after, but then he'd had a focus again, a reason to succeed and keep trying.

He gave himself a mental shake and pushed his shoulders back, trying to stretch out the knots that had formed there while he'd been at his desk sorting out paperwork. He'd much prefer to be behind a saw or brandishing a paintbrush, but someone had to do the admin and most of it fell to him now that his dad was no longer around to help. His mum did what she could, but he didn't like to put on her because she had her own life to lead and, at seventy-five, he believed she deserved to spend her time on far more enjoyable things. Like rescuing greyhounds.

'Knock-knock!'

The door opened and his mum entered, carrying a Tupperware container and a reusable coffee mug.

'Hi, Mum, I was just thinking about you.'

'All good, I hope?' She smiled, making the skin around her eyes concertina. Her white wavy hair was windswept and her cheeks and the tip of her nose were pink, so he knew she'd probably been out walking Digby and Toby, her greyhounds. She looked good, but losing his dad had aged her in the past five years and he knew that she still struggled without her husband. They'd been close and his death had rocked her. 'I've brought you some lunch. I knew you'd be catching up with paperwork today and was worried that you wouldn't make time to eat.'

'Thanks, Mum. What is it?'

She handed him the container and set the coffee down on the desk.

'Tuna niçoise salad with wholegrain penne in home-made pesto.'

'Sounds great.' Connor nodded but he was already imagining how his office would smell later on. The combination of tuna and eggs would not be pleasant in the confined space.

'You can always eat it outside on one of the picnic benches.' His mum cocked an eyebrow, clearly reading his reaction. She had always been able to guess what he was thinking or feeling just by looking at him. Even when he tried his best to hide his feelings, she just knew. Grace had a similar ability, so he guessed it was hereditary on his side of the family.

'I might do that later and enjoy the air.'

'Well, make sure you put it in the fridge so it stays fresh.'

'Yes, Mum.'

'How's Grace today?'

'Good. She was already at her sewing machine when I left this morning. Said something about whizzing up some more tote bags for your stall at the summer fête.'

'It's such a shame she won't be here for it. If only she could have delayed leaving for another few weeks.'

'It is a shame.' Connor knew his mum was going to miss Grace desperately. They were very alike with a creative flare for making things and, since his mum had got involved with the greyhound rescue charity two years ago, they'd done a lot to raise money for the dogs. His mum had gone to the greyhound kennels at a local farm and met Digby, a large black greyhound. She'd applied to adopt him but, on the day she'd gone to collect him, another greyhound had been running around in the paddock and he'd run right up to the fence and barked at her. She'd fallen in love with him too and ended up coming home with Digby *and* the fawn greyhound that she named Toby. Connor was glad she had the dogs because they'd definitely been a tonic, giving her a reason to get up and out of the house every day. They were such loving and devoted creatures that they had brought his mum happiness he'd worried she'd never feel again. Working with the charity had also restored her sense of purpose and Connor was relieved to see the improvements in her.

'Never mind, I'm sure the fête will be a great success. It's lovely to have it to look forward to. Have you got much ready for your stall yet, Connor?'

'Just a few bits and pieces.' He shrugged but his smile gave him away. He had plenty ready for the fête. It was the big event of the summer and a wonderful opportunity to find new customers and spread awareness of his business.

'Did you make the mini chairs?'

'I've made five so far, along with two small desks, and I'm working on a rocking horse.'

'Your dad would have loved to help out.' His mum's face contorted and he tensed, worried she was about to cry, but then she bit her bottom lip so hard it went white.

'He surely would.' Connor stepped forwards and hugged his mum. 'He'd be so proud of you.'

'And of you.'

His mum patted his back then stepped out of his embrace, visibly pulling herself together and forcing herself to adopt the stoicism that had got her this far. Inside, she was warm and kind, but she was able to appear cool and calm even when grief was tearing her apart. It was one of the things that helped her to be strong when a wounded greyhound was brought into the kennels, one that was too badly injured to save or that had to have extensive surgery

58

and rehabilitation. His mum often fostered those dogs too, taking them into her home and helping them on their journey as they healed then watched as they headed off to their forever homes. She was so strong, patient and compassionate and he admired her grit and tenacity.

'Connor . . .'

'Yes?'

'Will you be OK when Grace goes?'

'In what way?' He tucked his hands in his jeans pockets and felt his belt tighten around his waist, almost like a signal from his unconscious mind to stay strong.

'Well, I know you'll miss her but so will Sadie and I'm worried that she'll become even more . . . Sadie.'

Her green eyes clouded with concern.

'I'm sure it will be fine. Perhaps this will actually be a good thing for Sadie and she'll have the chance to make some changes.'

His mum inclined her head but he wondered if he'd convinced her, because try as he might, he didn't feel particularly convinced himself.

Emma's walk around the village with her dad had been a lot more enjoyable than she'd anticipated. They had perched on a bench by the village green, sipping coffees from the café and watching the world go by. With her new hairstyle and large sunglasses, she felt as if she was wearing a disguise and that gave her some comfort that she might not be recognised by anyone.

Little Bramble looked basically the same as it had done when Emma was growing up but there had been some changes, like the new village hall that had been built and the pretty little bistro that her dad told her had recently opened. As they'd sat side by side, her dad had seemed relaxed and he'd recalled details from the past without hesitation. Dilys had told Emma that his memory seemed better when he was happy and relaxed and she witnessed this first-hand now. He'd reminded her of the time he'd taken her out in his car after she got her provisional driver's licence and she'd oversteered and mounted the pavement by the old village hall. Emma had screamed but her dad had calmly taken the wheel and turned it the other way, correcting her error without batting an eyelid. She'd been in awe of his composure. It was only when they arrived safely home and her dad had hung up his hat and coat and placed the keys in the dresser in the kitchen that she saw any anxiety in him at all. He'd poured himself a large single malt and downed it in one then went to his music room and played ten songs in a row to calm himself down. Emma had wished that she could join him, sing or play along next to him, but she lacked his musical talent – it was something she felt sad about but that her dad seemed to accept. He'd been very accepting about most things when she was growing up and she knew she was lucky to have such a patient, accepting father and gentle, loving mother.

A few people had passed them and waved or stopped to say hello, but no one that Emma would have felt uncomfortable seeing. Her dad had asked about her life in London, something that he always liked to hear about, and she'd relayed a few stories about stressed editorial directors on tight deadlines who'd begged her to complete edits almost overnight and about an uppity thriller author who hadn't liked having his debut novel polished at all. In fact, he'd insisted on having a different editor look at the manuscript then raged on Twitter when the second one had made even more changes than Emma.

Surrounded by the sights and sounds of her childhood, her dad at her side, London had seemed like a million miles away. It was, if she allowed her mind to drift, almost as if that life had been a dream she'd had, as if the clock had been turned back and at any moment her dad would say they'd better get home because her mum would be wondering where they were.

As they'd walked home, her arm tucked through his, she'd found herself wishing that her mum would be waiting for them, her long grey hair twisted into a loose bun at her nape, her round glasses perched on her nose, her warm brown eyes filled with love. She would be wearing her multicoloured dungarees or a cotton smock top and the house would smell of baking and spices. Her mum had a small stone outbuilding in the garden that they referred to as her studio, where she made her jams and chutneys, but she still sometimes used the cottage kitchen. Emma could remember trying to avoid the splodges of jam on the floor tiles and being offered a wooden spoon with some new recipe her mum had concocted to taste, then wriggling as she hugged her if Emma had approved the new recipe. The memories were so vivid that the longing made her breathless.

Just before they reached home, they bumped into Marcellus David. He greeted Emma with his usual gusto, his accent warm and still laced with hints of the Caribbean even though he'd been the postman in Little Bramble for over thirty years. In his navy uniform, with his bright red bag across his body, he looked exactly as he always had done and Emma's heart filled with warmth. Some things didn't change, and that was surprisingly comforting. Marcellus had handed her the post as well as a colourful leaflet, then wished them both a good day and said he hoped to see her again soon.

Back in the cottage, her dad had a cup of tea then said he fancied a nap before lunch and Emma agreed that was a good idea. When she'd tidied the kitchen and pegged out a load of washing that she'd put on before they left, she sat at the table with another cup of tea, the warmth of the sunlight falling across her naked feet in the cosy kitchen.

Her eyes fell on the pile of letters Marcellus had handed her and she thumbed through them, but they seemed to be bills and circulars, nothing of interest. Then she came to the colourful leaflet. It was the same as the one that had blown into her face on her arrival in the village. Little Bramble was having a summer fête in just over five weeks' time.

In the past, the weeks leading up to the fête had been filled with preparations and had always increased her mum's productivity as she'd made more jams, marmalades and chutneys to sell on her stall. She'd no doubt have been the same right now, preparing for the highlight of the summer. The summer fête had always been a joyous affair, like a big village party, and it had been a wonderful time to celebrate the community spirit of Little Bramble and appreciate living in such a beautiful place.

Would this fête be the same as she remembered? Things from childhood are often disappointing to an adult. Childhood memories seen through rose-tinted lenses could never be recaptured. Emma had only imagined that she'd stay in the village a month, but the fête was a week later than that and she really wanted to be there for it. Should she plan to stay a bit longer? Who knew how long her dad's tests would take – and if dementia was confirmed, then she would need to rethink anyway. Attending the fête, having it to look forward to, would be good for her dad, and after spending the morning with him and seeing how frail he had become, but also how delighted he seemed to be to have her with him, she wanted to be there for him and to help create some lovely memories while they still could. He would pick up during her stay and she'd be able to leave again, secure in the knowledge that he was absolutely fine.

She suspected that the reality would not be half so simple or positive but, for now, she would enjoy being with him,

63

take things day by day and treasure living in the moment. It wasn't something she was good at doing, especially not without work to escape into, but she intended on giving it a bloody good try. Besides which, she could still work while she was here as long as she made an effort to fit it around her dad's naps and TV programmes, so she could maintain some sort of normalcy to her time in Little Bramble.

Chapter 6

Emma spent the next day going through paperwork that her dad had stuffed into the kitchen cupboards and drawers. According to the dates on the envelopes Emma found, he had been filing things in this way for quite some time. It was as though he'd been trying to forget they existed, as if it was too much to deal with. Or maybe he'd been trying to keep the place tidy in the way he used to. She had vivid memories of her dad being the one who did most of the tidying up around the house and the one who sorted the family finances. Her mum liked to vacuum, but her dad liked to put things away, and perhaps a part of him was still trying to do that, only not quite as effectively.

Since emailing the people she worked with to let them know that she was taking some time away from London to deal with a personal matter, while reassuring them that she was on top of deadlines, she was making a conscious effort to ignore her laptop. She'd tucked it inside her wardrobe upstairs and only checked her email on her phone once in the morning and once at night in case of emergencies. She didn't want to be distracted by her other world, not yet, when there was so much to do here. There were a few weeks left until the deadline for her current job, five at a push, as it had been sent to her well in advance, so she didn't have to rush to complete it.

First, she piled up everything she found on the kitchen table, then she started to sift through it, creating smaller piles of bills, personal letters and junk mail. Next, she tore up all the junk mail and put it in the paper recycling, checked all the bills to ensure that they had been paid – the last thing her dad needed was to have his electricity or water cut off – and the post that looked personal she put on the dresser for her dad to look through. There was a definite sense of achievement in sorting things out like this, but she knew it was only the tip of the iceberg and that there would be more to do during her time in the village.

Later that afternoon she donned her large sunglasses and popped to the small grocery shop in the village. She picked up some pasta, mixed baby leaf salad, fresh salmon and a bottle of white wine for their dinner. Thankfully, the village had a grocer, butcher and a few other small shops, so she didn't need to go further afield, but if she had she could borrow her dad's Toyota Yaris. She knew from Dilys that he hadn't driven far since buying the car the previous year, which she thought was a good thing as he was so frail. He'd bought the new car because he was finding his old Jaguar hard to drive and park. This new one was small and automatic, so he found it easier.

She put the shopping away and made her dad a cup of tea then took it through to the lounge. He was watching a Beatles documentary on TV, apparently engrossed in it, so she kissed his forehead then left him to it.

Back in the kitchen, she realised that she wanted some fresh air, so she opened the back door and peered outside. The garden had been her mum's pride and joy. She had spent many hours out there planting, weeding, nurturing and eventually relaxing. Emma had tried to keep this love of growing things alive in London, but with only a small balcony attached to her flat, she'd had to concentrate on indoor plants. They brought her a lot of pleasure, but she'd never had a whole garden at her disposal and wondered for a moment if that was something she'd missed out on.

She stepped outside then paused, remembering the wine in the fridge. A glass of cold white wine would be perfect to enjoy in the warm afternoon while she looked around the garden. Wine poured and glass in hand, she went back outside and gazed at the beauty before her.

On the patio area in front of the kitchen window was a wooden arbour that hadn't been there during her last visit. It consisted of an enclosed two-seater bench made of a light-coloured wood with a panelled back and sides and a felted weatherproof roof. The sides were carved with leaves and flowers and the craftsmanship was exquisite.

The bushes and trees that bordered each side of the garden were full and green. Birds sang in the branches and a warm breeze played with her floaty skirt, brushing it against her legs and ankles. Her feet were bare except for flip-flops and she kicked these off to walk on the grass. It was springy beneath her soles and too long, so she made a mental note to locate the lawnmower and cut it as soon as she had a chance.

As she made her way further along the garden, using the stepping stones that ran in bends through the grass, she breathed in the scent of sweet roses and honeysuckle and beneath that, the sharpness of lavender that grew in abundance in the flower beds in front of the trees and bushes. The garden narrowed at the end of the lawn to an archway created from bamboo that was adorned with deep purple, star-shaped clematis flowers.

To one side of the archway was a well-established crab apple. Bird feeders hung from its branches, empty and rusting, and next to it lay a bird table with a small arched roof and a ledge that her dad had added for pigeons to sit on. As well as being a musician, her dad was a skilled carpenter and liked to make things like the bird table for her mum. He hadn't built anything bigger than that, calling it a busman's holiday after the job he did, but small constructions gave him pleasure, especially when they made his wife happy. The table appeared to have been knocked over and left where it had fallen in the grass, abandoned and forgotten. Her mum would be devastated if she knew her garden had been left like this, that her beloved birds had been neglected, her bird table left to rot. Emma's throat tightened as if someone had squeezed it hard. She considered righting the bird table but the wood looked rotten and probably now provided shelter to woodlice and worms. The thought of touching anything that wriggled or crawled made her shiver and regret removing her flip-flops. She would attend to it another time as well as getting some new bird feeders and cutting the grass.

Through the archway was the second part of the garden, where there were raised beds for herbs and vegetables, an abundance of fruit trees, a large greenhouse, a picnic bench and her mum's stone studio. She sipped her wine then strolled past the apple trees; some had already dropped apples that lay on the ground in various stages of decomposition. A voice in her head told her this was June drop and nothing to worry about and she recognised it as her mum's; it was something she'd heard many times before. In one of the beds, rhubarb burst outwards in an explosion of red and green, and the memory of it in crumbles and jams with creamy vanilla custard made her mouth water. Some of the raised beds looked reasonably well tended, and had things growing in them. Perhaps her dad had worked on them or maybe it had been Dilys, a keen gardener herself. The garden had become a mixture of care and neglect, some things receiving attention, some not, and it made her think of herself for a moment, how she worked hard on her career but not on her mental or even her physical health. Why her dad would have dug the raised beds and planted things but not righted and repaired the bird table she couldn't understand, but then, perhaps this was a work in progress, or one that had come to a sudden halt as his health declined.

Off to the right, the greenhouse looked quite sorry for itself, abandoned since her mum's passing. The glass was stained by storms and birds and there was a broken pane, its edges jagged, like a predatory mouth waiting to catch small prey. When her mum had been alive, it had been an explosion of colour, filled with tomato, chilli and pepper plants, green peas and beans that had been used in a variety of recipes. Seeing it like this made her chest ache, so she turned instead to the left corner of the garden.

And there it was: the small studio where her mum had spent so much time.

Emma headed towards the outbuilding, taking care not to spill her wine. It was like a miniature version of the cottage, with two windows either side of a wooden door, a chimney on the slate roof and roses climbing its front. Square planters holding the roses stood either side of the door and through the windows she could see that the flowered curtains were still held in place with red ribbon ties as if her mum had just opened them. A memory enveloped her, whisking her back to her childhood, to days spent helping her mum in the studio while her dad sat on a bench outside, perfecting his latest cover version, ready for a gig. Her mum would always hum along as she worked, hulling strawberries and stirring steaming pans of jam, and Emma and Ted would assist, their hands stained and sticky with juice and sugar. She'd loved those times, felt useful and quite grown-up, adored by her parents and younger brother, secure in the knowledge that nothing could ever come between them, that together they were strong. How lucky she had been to have two wonderful people as her mum and dad, how lucky to have them around for most of her adult life. Had she taken that for granted as she got older herself? Believed that they'd always be there for her? Of course, there had been difficulties in her relationship with them before she left Little Bramble for good, and things had never been quite the same – not for her, at least – but she had loved them dearly and treasured her happy memories. Then suddenly her mum was gone and now her dad was ailing. If only she could turn the clock back and tell them how sorry she was and that she'd never meant to hurt them.

She approached the studio cautiously and placed a hand on the door. The wood was rough, but warm, and for a moment she gently rested her forehead against it and closed her eyes. Inside, there would be more memories to assault her senses and she was torn between wanting to go in and allow them to embrace her and wanting to remain outside, to savour the dream that her mum could be in there, beavering away at whatever task she had prioritised for that day, the air filled with the aromas of blackcurrants and elderflowers.

Opening her eyes, she stepped back and finished her wine for courage, then she took hold of the handle and tried to turn it. The handle wouldn't budge. The door was locked. She felt shut out, excluded from the one place she now really wanted to be. The connection she craved from entering the studio was being denied her and frustration made her hot and uncomfortable. Common sense told her that she hadn't been in there for years, so one more day wouldn't hurt. She had to be sensible about this, not impetuous and hasty as she had sometimes been in her youth. *Good things come to those who wait,* her mum had often said, and Emma tried to embrace that mantra now. She would have to look for the key and come back out here in the morning.

Just as she turned to walk away, something caught her eye, a flash of colour too quick to decipher, and she whipped back around and peered through the small square glass panes of the window. All that met her gaze was her own reflection, the interior dark and filled with shadows.

Shrugging, she walked away. Maybe what she had seen had been a moth fluttering against the window, or it could have been a memory of something long since gone, trapped inside the studio, waiting to be found.

'It's a lovely evening,' Connor said, as he walked into the village with Grace. They were going to his mum's for dinner and he had a bottle of wine in one hand, a bunch of flowers in the other.

'It's beautiful. I'm going to miss summer evenings in Little Bramble.' Grace sighed. 'But I'm hoping it will be worth it.'

'Of course it will.' He glanced at her, his beautiful daughter, as she walked alongside him. She was three inches shorter than him but with the platform heels she was wearing, they were almost the same height. 'I don't know how you can walk in those things.'

She laughed. 'Plenty of practice, Dad. I need to be able to walk in anything with my career aspirations.'

'I thought that was left to the models, not the designers.'

'Dad, really? I can hardly plod around in flats all the time while celebs and the like wear my creations, can I? The paps will want a piece of me too.'

'Really?' His stomach rolled over at the thought of Grace being hounded by anyone, especially the paparazzi.

'I'm teasing you, Dad. Who knows if I'm going to be a success? And even if I am, then it's a long way down the road. I need to finish my studies first then get my designs noticed. But the paps *do* like photos of designers and it's great promo for a brand, so I need to ensure that I'm interesting enough to capture their attention.'

He shifted the wine under his arm and wiped his hand on his jeans. 'Just be careful.'

'Dad! I'm twenty-five not five. I do know what I'm doing.'

'There are people out there with no morals at all, Grace. People who will take advantage. I'd hate to see you being exploited or having one of those kiss-and-tell spreads in the tabloids.'

'Who am I going to kiss and tell about?' Her voice rose with incredulity.

'Not *you*. I meant if you kiss someone and they tell on you. It happens a lot, you know. And with phones all having cameras these days, anyone can take a photo or video and then the most private details of your life can be everywhere in minutes.'

'Well, I'll be careful who I kiss, I promise, and I'll stay alert for cameras.'

Connor had a feeling she was humouring him now and suddenly he felt very old.

'Good. And no falling for a Frenchman.'

'What? Why not?'

'You'll end up wanting to stay out there permanently and we'll miss you.'

'Stop worrying, Dad, please. Everything's going to be fine.'

'And make sure you eat properly. None of those faddy diets just to become a stick insect. You're perfect the way you are.'

'Healthy English rose that I am?' She giggled and winked at him.

'You're beautiful and don't you forget that by trying to fit some unhealthy stereotype.'

Connor rubbed the back of a hand over his upper lip, feeling too warm in the balmy air. It was anxiety about

Grace causing it, but even so, it was hard to stop worrying. Grace was young and innocent and there were people out there who could hurt her and steal away her self-confidence. To him she would always be the little girl who wanted to help with his work and who asked to sit on his shoulders so she'd be taller than him and Sadie when they went for a walk. She'd forever be the tiny person asking for one more story before bed, even when her eyelids were drooping and her head leant against his arm, her soft hair falling over his hand as she dropped off to sleep.

They passed the row of shops on one side and the village green on the other. When they reached the church, they veered to the left and his mum's cottage came into sight. It was the place where he'd grown up and as familiar to him as the back of his hand. It represented warmth, love and happy times, even though, whenever he went there, he still half-expected his dad to answer the door smelling of coffee and Old Spice, his fingers coated in ink from the newspapers that he read cover to cover.

His chest squeezed at the thought that his dad wouldn't be there, he'd never be there again, and the familiar wave of grief passed over him. He was at a stage in his life where he was caught between grieving for a parent and being a parent, worrying about his mum and his daughter, coping alone because he had no partner to lean on, yet aware of the strength and resilience that had got him this far. But then, he worried about his mum and his daughter all the time, so surely having another woman in his life would mean that he'd just worry about her too?

'Grace! Connor!'

He froze as the voice he knew so well called to them and then turned slowly.

'Hi, Mum.' Grace smiled as Sadie hurried over to them, her bright pink running gear so tight it was like a second skin, her dyed blonde hair in bunches, her skin lightly tanned.

'Where are you going?' Sadie asked, as if she had no idea.

'To Nan's for dinner. I told you earlier on the phone,' Grace said.

The tiny line between Sadie's brows deepened and her eyes bored into Connor's even as she spoke to Grace.

'Did you? I must have forgotten.'

Connor wiped a hand on his jeans again then gripped the bottle of wine tighter.

'I've been running.' Sadie waved her hands at her outfit.

He nodded, not wanting to encourage her because he knew where this was going.

'I'm starving now.' Sadie's eyes widened in challenge, the thick, false lashes like insect legs against her skin.

He pressed his lips together, hoping this would end here, but Grace said, 'Well, I'm sure Nan's made plenty. Shall I run ahead and check? She probably won't mind another one at the table.'

Sadie grinned. 'That would be wonderful, sweetie. Go and check!'

Connor was about to tell Grace to wait but she'd already turned and slow-jogged away, her platforms making a slapping sound against the pavement, her hair bouncing around her head like a golden halo.

'Sadie . . .' He sucked in a breath. 'This probably isn't a good idea.'

'Connor, I want to spend as much time with our daughter as possible before she leaves. Surely you can understand that, can't you?'

'Of course, but . . .'

'No buts. She's *my* daughter too and I have just as much right to see her as you do.'

'No one's disputing that, Sadie–'

He cut himself off, knowing that they'd had this conversation hundreds of times before and that the outcome would be the same as always. Sadie would never see things his way and he would end up feeling sorry for her and overwhelmed with guilt. It was easier to keep quiet and let the evening take its course. He just hoped she'd be polite to his mum – because the last time she'd invited herself for dinner it hadn't gone well at all.

He started walking again and Sadie trotted along at his side, reminding him of a flamingo in her running gear. A tall skinny flamingo with a very sharp beak . . .

✦

'That was a delicious dinner, Emma.' Greg wiped his mouth with a napkin then sat back in his chair.

'I'm glad you enjoyed it.' She'd read that oily fish could be good for the heart and brain and hoped that introducing more into his diet would help stave off dementia, might even improve his memory and general health.

Emma took the plates to the sink, scraped off the leftovers into the food recycling bin then filled the sink with soapy water.

'Just between us, Dilys is very kind and has brought me many meals but she cooks a lot of casseroles and heavy dishes, Emma. I'm really grateful to her, but it is nice to have something a bit lighter like that salmon. Your mum used to make similar meals.'

He fell silent and Emma turned to look at him. He'd smiled a lot through dinner as they'd talked about the news, the summer fête and how the new village hall had brought a welcome new lease of life to the village. Now his expression had changed and he looked older, sadder.

'You miss Mum a lot, don't you?' She wiped her hands on a towel and went back to the table.

'Dreadfully.' He nodded, his eyes fixed on his glass of water. Emma had offered him wine but he'd declined, so they'd both had water with dinner. 'I still can't believe she's gone.'

'Nor me.' Emma reached for his hand and squeezed it gently, feeling the gnarled knuckles and the veins that protruded from under the skin like fat blue worms. 'I keep expecting to see her.'

'I know what you mean. Sometimes I find myself expecting to see all of you, just like it used to be. I'd get one of my guitars after dinner and play in the garden while you and Ted danced around with your mum. I miss those days so much.' He smiled but his eyes glistened. 'It's so good to have you home, Emma.'

She swallowed hard, emotion welling inside her like a hot spring about to burst from the ground.

'Uh, Dad, have you played any of your guitars recently?'

He shook his head. 'I haven't been able to face going into my music room.'

'Why not?'

'I'm afraid.'

'Oh, Dad, why?'

He coughed, covering his mouth with a hand that curled into a fist. He pressed the fist against his lips until they turned white.

'Dad?'

He closed his eyes for a moment then opened them and lowered his hand before holding both of them out in front of him.

'Look at my hands, Emma.'

She looked at them, taking in the swollen knuckles and protruding veins, the slightly too long nails that appeared yellow in the kitchen light.

'Do they make playing difficult?' Emma asked.

'They ache sometimes and burn a bit. But it's not just that.'

He hung his head and Emma waited, not wanting to push him.

'Since we lost your mum and then Paul, the last member of the band, who passed away in the winter, I've felt so sad every time I've considered playing. Looking at my hands just compounds the problem.'

'That's understandable, Dad, but I also know how much you loved playing. We'll have to speak to the doctor about it. I'm sure we can get you something to ease the stiffness and any discomfort and I suspect that keeping your hands active will probably help.'

In more ways than one, she thought.

'Perhaps.'

'You could play at the village fête, perhaps, and it would be just like old times!' She clapped her hands at the idea. 'Wouldn't that be lovely?'

He smiled at her but she suspected it was a tolerant smile and not one of delight at the idea. Best to leave it for now and see how things went. Playing at the fête might be a bit much if he was feeling emotional about it, but she was sure that it would ultimately help him.

'Tell you what, why don't I get those dishes done then make us some tea and we can have it in the garden?'

'No.' He shook his head and concern filled Emma. Was he afraid of going outside and facing more reminders of his wife?

'No?'

'You wash up and *I'll* make the tea. I'm not an invalid and I can still do things. As you said, staying active might well help me.'

'Sorry, Dad . . . I didn't mean to take over. I'm just worried about you, but if I get a bit overwhelming, let me know.'

'Believe me, Emma, I'm grateful.'

Ten minutes later, they sat on the two-seater garden arbour, nursing mugs of tea. Emma ran a finger over the leaves and flowers that had been carved into the wood, admiring the craftsmanship.

'This is really lovely, Dad. Where did you get it?'

'It was a gift . . . from Connor.'

Emma pulled her hand back from the wood as if she'd been burnt.

'He delivered it a few weeks back. Said that with the weather getting warmer it would be nice for me to sit outside under the shelter, so I won't burn. I have to be honest, though, I haven't used it very often.'

'That was . . . very kind of him.' Emma's neck felt tight, her movements jerky. Were they really going to speak about *him* now, after all this time? How could they even pretend to be normal as they did so? They'd avoided the subject of Connor for so long in order to maintain the peace; it had felt like the only way.

Her dad nodded. 'He's a talented man and very generous. He has his own business now . . . since his dad retired. Has done for years, actually, but I lose track of time. It's called The Lumber Shed and it's based just outside the village in a converted barn. He's done well for himself.'

Her dad looked tense as he spoke, running a thumb over the side of his mug, not meeting her eyes. Was he aware of how difficult this was for her to hear or had his recent ailments made him blinkered on certain topics? Was it an attempt to shed some light on things now before it was too late, to air the things they'd left unsaid for years? Emma was torn between wanting to run back inside and yearning to stay to hear about Connor and his life.

'Do you . . . see much of him?'

Emma sipped her tea, trying to stay calm.

'He comes round once or twice a month, I think. Could be more often, but I definitely see him quite regularly. He's a good lad.'

Emma gripped her mug between both hands now, aware that she was trembling. And why? After all this time, she should be able to hear his name without getting upset, without having a physical reaction. Surely her dad remembered what had happened all those years ago? Emma hated herself for how things had gone, for what she'd done to Connor and then to her parents. She'd taken the love and closeness they shared and dashed it against stony ground as if it hadn't meant a thing to her.

'It's a shame things didn't work out between you two.'

It was as if her dad had read her mind and had voiced her fears.

'Hmmm. Uh . . . Dad? Sometimes things don't work out. It was almost twenty-eight years ago.'

Please don't make me discuss it now.

'It is all in the past, of course.' He took a gulp of tea and sighed. 'What a fabulous cuppa.'

Emma released a long breath, relieved that the subject could be abandoned, for now at least. There was so much pain and sadness that could be dredged up and she didn't think that would be good for either of them right now.

'I was looking around the garden earlier, Dad, and I went out to the studio. The door was locked. Do you know where the key is?'

He furrowed his brows and rubbed his chin. 'No.'

'Do you have any idea where it could be?'

He drained his mug. 'I don't.'

Emma suppressed a sigh of frustration and stared straight ahead, watching a small bird hopping along the grass in search of bugs. She couldn't tell if her dad was being deliberately vague about this. Had he locked the door after his wife had died and thrown the key away, not wanting anyone to disturb her space again, or had he simply forgotten where he'd put the key? She could understand his desire to preserve things exactly the way they had been but she wanted to have a look in the studio and spend some time there. The more she thought about it, the more she wanted to get in there and the more her heart ached to be close to her mum again. If she could just whisper the things she wished she'd said all those years ago, then perhaps she could alleviate some of the guilt she felt, lift some of the burden of knowing that, where her mum was concerned, she'd left it too late.

'Sometimes, Emma,' her dad said, patting her hand, 'things are best left alone.'

He held her gaze, reminding her of the man he'd been when she was growing up: strong, resolute, caring and wise, and she bobbed her head in agreement. She wasn't sure if he was referring to her mum or to her past with Connor or both, but she decided to let it lie for this evening.

There would be time over the coming days to find the key to the studio and the key to forgiveness – although her hopes of finding the latter seemed a far more onerous task.

Chapter 7

'Well, what do you think about my proposal?'

Connor shuddered as an unwelcome memory came to him. Mentions of proposals didn't ever conjure happy thoughts for him.

'Your proposal?' he asked Sadie, buying time, as he carried a small chair he'd just finished sanding across the workshop of The Lumber Shed and handed it to a colleague.

'Yes! My offer to help you with your stall at the fête.'

'Right. Of course.'

He paused in the middle of the workshop and rubbed his face, wishing he could snap his fingers and make Sadie disappear. Not in a bad way, of course, just away from him. Somewhere like Bali or Alaska.

'Look, Sadie, I have a lot to get through with it being Friday. We've an order to finish by the end of tomorrow so it can ship next week. I just . . . the fête is a few weeks away and our stall is already fully manned and–'

Her hand landed on his chest, long pink nails flashing with tiny rhinestones. The image of a flamingo popped into his mind again, although today Sadie was wearing bright purple running gear, a full face of thick make-up and her hair framed her face in tiny sausage curls. She was the same age as him but looked as if she was trying to appear thirty years younger.

'Connor, you can always use an extra pair of hands.' Her fingers tapped lightly on his chest.

'OK.' He nodded. It was easier to just agree and let her do her thing.

She removed her hand then straightened his shirt where it had bunched up under her touch. 'OK.' A smile broke out on her full pink lips and she nodded. 'I'll see you soon.'

'I guess so.' There wasn't much avoiding each other in such a small village really, but there was no point saying that.

As Sadie sashayed out of the workshop, attracting a few admiring glances from some of the male employees, Connor turned and trudged up to his office. When the door was closed behind him, he slumped onto the edge of his desk, tiredness washing over him in a giant wave.

At his mum's three days ago, when Sadie had invited herself for dinner, she'd made a case for helping on The Lumber Shed stall. He'd tried to deflect her by getting Grace to talk about Paris and his mum had joined in, clearly aware of what was happening, but Sadie hadn't let it go. After dinner, when Sadie had gone and Grace had been video calling a friend, Connor had been washing up while his mum tried to talk to him about the situation.

He knew his mum was only trying to help and that she was concerned, but there was so much more to the situation than she knew. Sadie was a complicated person and she always had been. When they'd been at school, she'd been one of the crowd he'd hung around with and she'd been fun, wild and attractive. Connor had liked her but hadn't been romantically interested because he'd only had eyes for one person. Sadie had dated a few of his mates and gone off to university to study nursing, returning as a qualified paediatric nurse. She'd loved her job in a London hospital and spoken enthusiastically about it, but later, when she'd fallen pregnant with Grace, something had changed, and she hadn't wanted to go back to work.

Grace had been an accident as far as Connor was concerned, a broken condom, although he'd never had one regret about her conception since he'd seen the first scan. The image of her tiny limbs, rounded belly, her little turned-up nose as she sucked her thumb, had grabbed hold of his heart and never let go.

Getting involved with Sadie had happened after Connor had been through a tumultuous time and though he felt terrible for admitting it, he hadn't been in the right place to have another relationship. Sadie had come along with her long, soft hair, kissable lips and warm body and he'd fallen into her arms one night after too many beers, needing to feel that he wasn't unlovable, that he wasn't as worthless as he'd felt after Emma had gone. Even now, years later, the old anger flared in his gut as he thought about how weak and useless he'd felt back then. It was as though he'd lost himself, lost control of his actions and floundered as he'd tried to find his way again. If he'd been in his right mind he'd never have slept with Sadie, never have allowed apathy to sweep him along in what she grabbed on to as a relationship, but he'd been so sad and damaged, he'd stopped caring about what happened to him. That was, until Grace was born and she brought a light to his life that restored his strength and belief that there was something worth fighting for again.

He wasn't proud of how he and Sadie had got together, but he had tried hard to make it work – and failed. Life was how it was, had worked out as it had, and nothing would change now. All that mattered was that Grace went off to Paris and began the next stage of her life. Connor would continue to provide for her, to be there for her and his mum, and to live his life in Little Bramble.

Life had once seemed full of good things, of future possibilities, but as he'd aged, his world had narrowed, his hopes and dreams had shrunk, and now he was simply content to see the two women he loved as happy as he could make them. As for Sadie, he didn't want to cause her any pain; and while he couldn't love her, he would do what he could to avoid hurting her. He felt he owed her that at least.

He pushed himself to his feet and took a deep breath. There was work to do and he was the boss, so he'd better set a good example to his employees. He reached for the door handle but it swung open and Sadie stood there, hands on hips, eyes wide.

'I forgot to ask you: I have a new kitchen coming tomorrow and I wondered if you could fit it for me?'

'Fit it?'

'Yes, on Sunday. I know you're working here tomorrow but you're free on Sunday, right?'

He swallowed his dismay. 'Has the old kitchen even been taken out yet?'

Sadie grinned. 'Well, no, but Grace is coming to help too.'

'Right.' He nodded, because what else could he do?

'See you bright and early!'

Sadie padded down the steps and across the workshop as Connor watched her go. Some people would say he was a mug but no one knew how they would react in his situation, if they knew what he did, if they'd been where he had.

'Are you there?' Lucie peered out of Emma's laptop screen, her dark fringe framing her beautiful face, her thin brows meeting above her straight nose.

'Yes, I'm here.' Emma waved at the screen then wondered why she'd done that. Was it part of human conditioning that people felt the need to wave, even at a computer screen?

'Excellent!' Lucie appeared to be wriggling in her seat, her head bobbing from left to right repeatedly.

'Are you all right?' Emma adjusted the angle of her screen. 'You look as if you're going over speed bumps.'

Lucie laughed then lifted her iPad and showed Emma the exercise bike she was sitting on. 'I'm just keeping fit while we chat.'

'You bought one of those super-expensive machines?' Emma shook her head. Lucie had always been a bit of a gym bunny, so it didn't surprise her that she'd bought into the latest exercise craze. More than once in the past few months she'd thought about getting one for her flat but was now glad she hadn't bothered because it would be in London while she was in Little Bramble.

'I did! Well, with things being a bit . . . complicated here at the moment as we wait for results and all that, it seemed like a good plan. I spend so much money on gym member-ships that getting more equipment at home made sense, especially in light of what we're hoping to achieve.'

'When Phoebe does get pregnant and has a baby, you'll need to be home more.' Emma always said *when* rather than *if*, because some superstitious part of her hoped that if they were positive about it happening then it would.

'Exactly!' A sheen of sweat beaded Lucie's upper lip and roses bloomed in her cheeks. 'So . . . how . . . are . . . things . . . with you?'

'Good.' Emma nodded. She had texted Lucie since her return to Little Bramble but they hadn't managed to coor-dinate a chat. However, Lucie often worked from home on Friday afternoons, which was how she'd managed to fit

Emma in today. 'Dad seems OK, if a bit frail, but he said he's glad to have me home and, to be honest, I'm glad to be here.'

'Not bumped into any ghosts from the past yet?' Lucie grimaced into the screen and in spite of her discomfort at the question, Emma had to stifle a giggle.

'No. Well, not really. But I haven't been out that much yet.'

'*Yet* being the operative word, darling. You'll no doubt bump into people soon.'

'I don't even know if they'll recognise me. It's been *years* and with my hair so short and highlighted now, and a few more menopausal pounds around my middle, I look so much older.'

'You *are* older!' Lucie laughed and Emma joined her.

'True.'

'But you look fabulous. However, it's a small village and I doubt people have forgotten what happened. Well, not everyone.'

Emma groaned and covered her face with her hands.

'Where'd you go?' Lucie was bobbing up and down now even more vigorously.

'I'm here. I just felt like hiding. Every time I think about bumping into Connor, his family or his friends my stomach churns. I have to keep reminding myself that I'm here for Dad. He needs me and I'll only be here for a few weeks – months – at most, and then I'll be leaving again.'

'What will happen then?'

'I expect Connor and his family will carry on with their lives.'

'Noooooo! I meant what will happen to your dad?'

Emma stared at Lucie, following a bead of perspiration as it ran down her nose and plopped off the end like a teardrop.

'I'm not sure. I have to take him to a GP appointment next week. His neighbour took him to one before I got here and the GP said give it a fortnight then come back and see how things are. But if he's getting worse, then – then I'm not sure. I'll have to cross that bridge when I get to it.'

'Well, look, we're still plodding along here and have no news yet because we have to wait at least fourteen days after insemination before taking a pregnancy test, and I quite fancy a break in the countryside. How about I come and visit next weekend?'

'Really? Won't Phoebe mind?'

'We're getting on each other's nerves a bit at the moment, to be truthful. It's the tension, I think, so she'll probably be glad to have some space.'

'Check with her then let me know. It would be great if you *could* come. You can stay here, there's plenty of room.'

'Wonderful!'

'How many calories have you burnt?'

Lucie frowned as she peered at the bike. 'What? This has to be faulty.'

'Not many, huh?'

'If I want to burn off that almond croissant I had for brunch, I need to stay on here for another two hours.'

'Oops!'

'It's bloody insane how hard it is to stay in shape,' Lucie growled as she upped her pace.

'What's that, Emma?' Her dad had entered the kitchen and he came and stood behind her. 'Goodness, who's that? I thought you were watching tigers or something with all that grunting and growling.'

'It's Lucie, Dad, she's on her exercise bike.'

'Oh, hello, Lucie!' Her dad leant over her shoulder and waved at the screen. 'Is it hot where you are?'

'It is quite warm, actually, Greg, but I'm still in London.'

'London? Whatever are you doing there? I thought you would be in Scotland.'

'Scotland?' Emma turned around and peered at him. 'Why would Lucie be in Scotland?'

His expression changed and he gazed out of the window. 'Oh . . . uh . . . I thought Lucie lived in Edinburgh.'

'No, Dad, that was . . . never mind, just a different friend.'

'Yes.' He nodded. 'Of course, it was. Goodbye, Lucie. Watch you don't get sunstroke.'

'I will, Greg, thanks.'

Lucie had slowed her pedalling now and was staring into the screen as if she could read Emma's thoughts. Greg filled the kettle then wandered out of the kitchen and Emma grimaced at Lucie.

'It could be nothing, Emma.'

'It could.'

'It's easy for parents to mix up their children's friends and where they live.'

'I know. I'm just hypersensitive at the moment, wondering if it's a normal mistake, an age-related slip or something more serious.'

'That's completely understandable, but he looks all right to me.'

'I can't stand the thought of leaving him here alone again, though, especially if he's . . . changing.'

'Don't beat yourself up, Em. Where's your brother in all of this? It's not just on you, you know.'

Emma did know but it was still difficult. She lived closer to Little Bramble than her brother did – what could he do from Australia? – and she was here now so was the one who could see how her dad was faring. The idea of not being here for him when he needed her most was like a corkscrew in her gut. But could she really consider coming back to Little Bramble long-term? Leaving everything in London behind? She'd be taking a step backwards, leaving the life she'd prioritised all those years ago. But now she and her dad were older and life was changing in ways she'd never imagined. What young person could imagine how life would be nearly thirty years down the line? Things changed; there was no escaping that fact.

Emma's laptop pinged with an incoming email and it snapped her back to the present.

'Look, you need to finish your ride and I need to go through my emails before the weekend in case there's anything urgent, so let me know about next week and we'll speak soon.'

'Sure will. Now take care, my darling, and call if you need me.'

Lucie blew a kiss at the screen then disappeared and Emma's desktop reappeared with her folders of work done, work to do, of quotes and publisher details and names of authors she'd worked with over the years. There were tax folders and banking folders and one for the dictionaries she used and useful links to websites where she could double-check facts.

Opening her emails, she sighed when she saw the number in her inbox. She'd need to go through them and reply to the urgent ones then flag the ones she'd need to get to next week. It wasn't the idea of the work that made her sigh, just that she was struggling to focus on anything other than her dad; and if she was being brutally honest with herself, about Connor and all that had happened before.

But that had been almost thirty years ago and he'd probably long forgotten her and what had happened. After all, she'd seen the Facebook profile of him with a beautiful young woman, who she guessed was his daughter. She'd tried not to look, but because they still had a few mutual friends, his photo sometimes popped up as a friend suggestion. Emma had limited contact with people from her past because she'd wanted to leave it behind. She didn't want to know what they were up to or to hear any village news apart from what her parents told her. Even the few friends from Little Bramble that she'd kept in touch with, she rarely spoke to because it was easier not to, easier to focus on people from her London life and her new world. Besides which, if she didn't interact with Facebook friends regularly, the algorithms soon stopped showing her their news – and that suited her just fine.

A few times, after cocktails or too many glasses of wine, she'd almost clicked on the button to request Connor as a friend, waking the next day with a jolt in case she'd actually gone through with it. She never had, thankfully, but the fact that the temptation had been there had shown her that she was still curious about him and his life, still interested in what and how he was doing. Then, the other profile that came up sometimes as a friend suggestion was Sadie Pierce. Her profile photo was of her, Connor and the young woman in Connor's photo and so Emma had put the clues together. It seemed that Sadie and Connor were a couple and they had a daughter who looked as though she was in her twenties, so presumably they had got together not long after Emma had left. In spite of how Emma had left, the thought that Connor had moved on so quickly had stung. As much as Emma felt bad about what she'd done, sometimes this helped her to justify it. Connor couldn't have loved her as much as he'd claimed to if he'd fallen into bed with someone else so quickly.

Emma's parents had always held back on mentioning Connor and he had become a taboo topic of conversation. After she'd left him as she had, Emma and her parents had fallen out. Throughout her childhood, they'd been incredibly close, even when she was a hormonal teenager, but the way she'd treated Connor had resulted in an enormous argument during which Emma had screamed at them that she had a right to live and behave as she chose, that she didn't want to end up living a boring little life as they had done. She'd wanted more from her future than a lifetime in Little Bramble with the pressures of everyone knowing her business.

The shouting and screaming had been mainly hers, but her parents had been devastated and that had made Emma feel worse, which in turn led to her becoming angrier. Anger felt better than sadness and guilt and so she'd fled the village, leaving Connor and her parents behind. It had taken a few years to feel able to reconnect with her mum and dad properly again. Even then, Emma had never spoken to them about Connor or their argument, and so issues they could have cleared up had remained buried. Then Emma's mum had died without Emma ever having apologised for her part in things, or explaining why she'd behaved as she had. Instead, her mum had gone to her grave believing that Emma would always carry that anger and resentment with her and that was something Emma felt deeply sorry about.

Emma sometimes lived in the past. In those moments when she allowed herself to remember, she hoped that Connor still thought of her too. But didn't men find it easier to move on than women? Emma was probably just a distant memory for him and one he was glad to forget.

Why that thought made something inside her ache she didn't know. She wanted him to be happy and to remember their time fondly and he had clearly moved on and had a beautiful partner and even more beautiful daughter.

It was Emma who had made the decision for them back then and she had only herself to blame.

Chapter 8

After a restless night, she'd woken later than usual to find a gunmetal grey Saturday morning, the windows streaked with rivulets of water, the wind rattling the glass planes in their frames. Before her mum had died, she'd been talking about getting new windows and Emma thought it was definitely something her dad needed to do. Another thing to add to her ever-growing list. However, the one thing she kept thinking about was the key for the studio.

Emma had been searching on and off for the key since she'd asked her dad about it, but she'd had no luck. It was a heavy old thing that had always been attached to a letter D key ring. She'd looked in all the kitchen cupboards, sorting out the remaining post that seemed to be stuffed everywhere, the old magazines and abundance of Tupperware – many pots without lids – as she did so. In the lounge, she'd thrust her hand down behind the sofa cushions and found lots of coins, some pens and a petrified chrysalis that had made her scream, but no key.

She'd pulled all the coats out from under the stairs, screeching when she'd disturbed a nest of woodlice and running up and down the hallway shaking her hands as she tried to get the thought of the tiny grey shells out of her mind. Some of the boots and shoes under the stairs were her mum's, still there, as if waiting for her return. After going through that cupboard, Emma checked under the plant pots on the windowsills and even in the earth of the pot with the giant yucca plant in the corner of the lounge. She just had upstairs left to check now but couldn't exactly rifle through her dad's room, so she was trying to work out how to ask him to do it instead.

Downstairs, she made tea then peered out into the garden, watching the trees being whipped around by the wind, the green leaves fluttering through the air to land on the lawn like biodegradable confetti. Movement from the arbour caught her eye and she went to the back door and opened it to see better.

'Dad! What are you doing?'

She hurried across the patio and reached out her arms but he frowned at her and shrank back. 'Dad, please, it's me, Emma.'

'Emma?'

'Yes.'

'You're not Emma! You're old. My Emma's a young woman with dark hair and a pretty face. She works in London.'

Emma bit the inside of her cheek. He didn't recognise her.

'Dad, it's me. Please come inside. It's cold out here and you're getting wet.'

He looked at the rain as if seeing it for the first time, then nodded and let her help him up and guide him back indoors.

'I thought you were still in bed, Dad. How long have you been outside?'

'I-I don't know.' He was trembling so she encouraged him to sit down then went and grabbed a chenille throw off the sofa and wrapped it round him. 'I think I must have sleepwalked.'

'Oh, Dad!' She hugged him, her heart hammering against her ribs, her breath coming thick and fast. 'We need to get you warm and dry.'

'Are you really Emma?' He frowned, his eyes murky with confusion. 'You sound like her, but you look . . . different.'

'I promise you I'm your daughter. Let's get you upstairs and into a warm bath.'

The cold and stress was clearly not helping him and she hoped with all her heart that getting him warm and relaxed would help him to become more lucid. The alternative was unthinkable.

Upstairs, she sat him on the bottom of his bed then ran a bath. When it was ready, she took him to the bathroom.

'You have a soak and warm up and I'll get you some dry clothes ready. Then we can have some breakfast.'

He nodded, his brows still meeting above his nose. 'I'm sorry. I remember you now, Emma. I just don't know how I got outside.'

'It's OK.' She said the words but didn't believe them for a second.

'I-I'm scared.'

Stroking his cheek, her chest filled with love for him. 'I know, Dad, but you don't need to be. I'm here now. You're going to be fine.'

She pulled the bathroom door after her to give him privacy, leaving it open a crack in case he needed her. It was possible that he'd sleepwalked, of course, and she recalled him doing exactly that when she was younger and her mum cursing him for treading mud from the garden all through the house. It happened when he had a big job on at work and when he caught a nasty bout of flu one winter. This was bound to be frightening and confusing, especially at his age and in light of his recent forgetfulness. She'd make sure to tell the GP on Monday and hopefully they'd be able to find some reassurance and help.

She returned to his room and made the bed, then went to his chest of drawers to look for a fresh pair of pyjamas. When she opened the first drawer, the scent of dried lavender rose into the air and she had to pause for a moment to collect herself. Her mum had loved lavender, growing it in the garden then drying it and using it in all her drawers and cupboards to fragrance clothes and bedding. Smells were so attached to memories and this would always remind her of her mum, as would the aromas of jam bubbling on the stove and cakes and bread baking in the oven.

She set the pair of striped cotton pyjamas on the bed then closed the drawer. As she turned back to the room, her mum's wardrobe caught her eye. When her mum had died, her dad had refused to get rid of her things, saying it was too soon. Emma had understood that, still having a few things from her time with Connor, even after all these years. At Christmas, when Emma had been home, she'd avoided even raising the subject, not wanting to go through her mum's clothes and belongings. Some things were just too hard to do, especially at Christmas. Sometimes it was better to ignore things, to leave them as they were than to delve through them and stir everything up again. Emma had felt this way about emotions over the years and so often did her best to push memories away, to avoid thinking about things that hurt and conversations that would be difficult to have.

But today seemed like a good day to take a look inside the wardrobe. After all, the key could be in there. She approached the wardrobe, a large mahogany affair with ornate brass handles and a lock with a key. It wasn't that she wanted to sort everything out at this point, it was curiosity about the key.

She took hold of the heavy wardrobe key, feeling its cold weight against her palm, then turned it. For a moment, it stuck, so she applied more pressure. The mechanism inside the lock clicked and the door swung open with a creak.

More smells washed over her: lavender, mothballs, old paper and clothes that hadn't been worn in years. It was a strange aroma, not horrid but stale, and beyond that, familiar. It was as if the clothes that her mum had worn over the years held her essence, a scent that was her own, a combination of her and all the things she liked to do.

Emma reached inside and ran her hands over the garments, touching the cool cotton smock tops and the French silk scarves that her mum often wound around her hair, smoothing her fingers over the piles of leggings and T-shirts on the shelves and feeling a longing to see her mum that was so intense it stole her breath away. Grief was so cruel, so powerful, and it hit her hard when she let it in. The temptation to flop to the floor and cry was strong, but Emma had trained herself not to cry over the years and she didn't want to start now when there were things to do.

There was a shelf above the hanging garments and on it sat several shoeboxes. She'd take a peek inside them.

She lifted the shoeboxes down and set them on the bed, then paused, listening for her dad. Water was running, so he must be adding more hot to the bath and would be in there for a bit longer. Lifting the lid off the first box she sighed; inside it was a pair of fancy trainers in her mum's size. They looked as if they hadn't been worn and she realised that they'd probably been a gift from her brother, all the way from Australia, something he'd thought would be a good idea but that her mum hadn't got round to wearing. She put the lid back on then opened the next box. Inside was a pile of letters tied with a pink ribbon. Assuming they were love letters, she put the lid back on the box and set it aside, not wanting to pry too far. The third box contained photos, some black-and-white and some colour, in the pale, bleached shades of photos from the eighties and nineties. Not wanting to stop now, she decided not to go through the photos but to save them for another time.

The final box was her last chance, she thought, as she lifted the lid off and sighed, because inside was her mum's leather-bound recipe book. Her dad must have tucked it away in here – Emma would have expected to find it in the studio or in the kitchen. It had been safely stored, preserved in dry conditions to be discovered again. She lifted it out and opened the cover reverently, emotion creating a haze around her vision as she gazed at the first page.

The paper was aged and stained, well-thumbed and slightly brittle, but she could make out her mum's name and the cottage address, written there in case it was ever lost. But her mum had not lost the recipe book; it had lost her mum.

A noise from the bathroom made her jump and she recognised it as the plug being pulled out, so she quickly closed the book and put all the boxes back in the wardrobe then locked it again. But the book she carried out to the hallway and put it between some other books on the shelf there. She was sure her dad wouldn't mind her looking at it, but she didn't want him to think she'd been going through her mum's things without asking him. She dashed back into the bedroom and spotted something glinting on the carpet, so bent down and picked it up.

It was the key for the studio, its D key ring tied to it with a red ribbon. It must have fallen out of the recipe book. She'd have to tell her dad how she found it, but that could wait until after breakfast because he'd need to eat before he did anything else – she wanted to get his strength up and keep it that way. Besides which, he'd been distressed enough for one morning and she didn't want to add to that, so she pocketed the key, feeling a bit guilty but also relieved that she could now get into the studio.

After breakfast, Emma and her dad went through to the lounge and sat on the sofa together. She was surprised that he didn't go straight to his chair but also glad to be close to him.

The rain had stopped and the sun had come out, offering the promise of a lovely day ahead. She sipped the tea she'd made and gazed at the TV screen, seeing but not absorbing any information from the property programme that her dad was watching. A presenter strolled through a derelict Victorian house, hands folded across his chest as he commented on each room, his high voice squeaking now and then with excitement or mock horror at the grisly features of the property. At intervals, her dad laughed and shook his head, clearly enjoying having a good nose at someone else's mess.

'Makes me think about this place, Emma,' he said during the commercial break. 'Perhaps it needs a good sort out.'

'In what way, Dad?'

'Well, I've kept all your mum's stuff and watching things like this makes me think about how, when I'm gone, everything will be left for you to sort out.'

He was back to himself again, thank goodness.

'Oh . . .' She sat upright.

'I mean, it's not like Ted's here helping, is it?'

'Well, he has a busy life, Dad, and it's a very long way to travel.'

Her dad smiled. 'Isn't it just? You know, I often wondered in the past if he emigrated to Australia to get away from us.'

'No! Of course he didn't.' Emma shook her head vigorously. 'It's just that there were opportunities out there that he might not have had here. Plus, of course, he fell in love with Kylie and didn't want to leave her. Look at Mum and how she left her life in France behind to be with you. Love moves people to make big decisions.'

'Don't get me wrong, Emma, I'm glad he's happy. Kylie is adorable and those children of theirs are just perfect. But I do miss him, and your mum did too.'

'I know.' Emma inclined her head. She had missed her brother over the years but always told herself that he was doing what he needed to do. Just as she'd told herself that she was doing what *she* needed to do. Children had a right to grow up and spread their wings, to move away and live their own lives. It was what good parents wanted for their offspring and she knew that, as far as she'd been concerned, it hadn't been her desire to move away that her parents had disapproved of, just the way she'd gone about it. Perhaps, with hindsight, they hadn't even disapproved, more wanted to check that she was certain about the momentous decision she was making.

As for her brother, Ted had a wonderful quality of life, but from time to time it had crossed her mind that he must miss their parents, and maybe her too. He was five years younger than Emma but as children they'd been close; he'd followed her everywhere as a toddler and she'd often woken to find him in her bed, having padded into her room during the night in need of comfort. She hadn't minded at all, had adored his cuddles and company. But now he was a grown man with three children of his own and a successful estate agency. The little boy he'd once been was long gone – and their closeness. It wasn't that they didn't get on, just that they didn't see each other or speak that often anymore.

'He had to make his own path.' Her dad placed his mug on the side table. 'It's the only way. Oh yes, I was talking about having a clear-out, wasn't I? We should do that while you're home. I haven't felt ready to part with your mum's things but I think that the time has come. I mean, what am I keeping it all for? I can't exactly take it with me, can I? And I hate the thought of you having to sort it when I'm six feet under.'

'Dad! Please stop it. I don't want to think about that.'

'Nor me, but it's going to happen. I'm eighty-four, Emma. Six years off ninety! I can hardly believe it some days when I think about it for any length of time. I still feel like a lad in my head, you know? Like the same boy who had hopes and dreams and wanted to marry your mum and have a family. I was excited about life once upon a time and then the years just sailed past. I look down at these veiny, bumpy old hands and struggle to accept that they're mine.'

'Oh, Dad!' Emma shuffled closer to him and slid her arm around his shoulders. 'I love you so much.'

'I love you too, my girl. More than you will ever know. Being a parent is such a rollercoaster. You love your children and sometimes you want to scream at them or get a refund on them, but more than anything you want them to be happy and healthy and to have a good life. That was all your mum and I ever wanted for you and Ted.'

'I know that, Dad.'

'Do you? We worried so much when you went off to London and we didn't see you for months. Then, when you finally came back, it was just for lunch one day and everything seemed so tense. Your mum really struggled with it and I know she missed you over the years. She said to me many times that it never felt the same after you and Connor split up. It was why, every time we did see you, we never raised the subject again. We were afraid of upsetting you, afraid that you'd cut us off completely and it would have been more than we could bear. We never judged you, Emma. You do know that, don't you?'

Emma swallowed hard. 'You didn't?'

'Of course not! We just wanted you to know that we loved you and were concerned about you. For years, you and Connor were inseparable and then something happened and we struggled to understand what it was.'

'I'm not even sure that I knew myself.' Emma shook her head. 'I thought I did . . . I felt so afraid and so boxed in and I panicked. It wasn't that I didn't love you and Mum and the life you had or the life you gave me – I was always so proud of you both. I feel terrible that Mum thought I hated how she lived.'

Her dad was shaking his head now. 'She didn't think that. Well, for a brief time . . . but she also understood how you felt. As you said, she left France to come here. You don't know this, but she had a relationship before me and he proposed to her. She'd told him she'd think about it during her time in Little Bramble, but she said that when she met me she knew she didn't love him and couldn't return to France to be his wife.'

'She did?'

He nodded. 'Things were different then, of course, but he was the son of friends of her parents and had always liked your mum. She tried to be kind to him but said there was no spark. When she came to England, it was to be her last taste of freedom before settling down. Then we met and sparks flew everywhere.'

'I wish I'd known that years ago, Dad.'

'She wanted to tell you, but raising the subject of Connor was difficult. Then it seemed as though too much time had passed and so the conversation never happened. But your mum understood your feelings and just wanted you to be sure, mainly because we both saw you and Connor together and knew that you loved each other.'

Emma rubbed her eyes with the heels of her hands. Her mum had known and understood and not judged her. If Emma hadn't been so proud and so defensive then they could have talked it through and she would have had less to feel guilty about. But hearing that her mum hadn't blamed her made something inside her shift now and ease, like a massage could loosen a tight shoulder or deft fingers could undo a knotted shoelace.

'I always knew you cared, but I felt that I'd messed up and I was too proud to apologise in case I crumbled. I wanted to be this strong, independent, career woman.'

'You are all three of those things and we're so proud of you for knowing what you wanted and going for it.'

'Thank you. That means a lot.'

'Good.' He patted her hand. 'Gosh, I feel old.'

He held up his hands and gazed at them as if seeing them for the first time. When he turned to her, she saw the tears in his eyes and felt as if her heart would break. She knew exactly what he was talking about, because inside she felt like the girl she'd once been and couldn't believe that she was almost fifty. She too wondered where the years had gone.

'Hey, did you mean it about wanting to get a refund on us?'

He laughed. 'Sometimes.' Then he shook his head. 'Not really. Never, in fact, but it was something your mum and I used to joke about.'

'I think the guarantee has probably expired by now.' She nudged him.

He held up a finger and jabbed it into the air. 'As your mum always said, getting older is a gift and something many people don't get to do. I might wish I could turn the clock back about twenty years, but I did live those years and I am so grateful that I had as long as I did with your mum. We had such good times together and we laughed a lot. Plus, she made me a bit fat with all her delicious baking and those incredible jams and chutneys. I have no regrets. What more can anyone want than that?'

Emma rested her head on his shoulder and held his hand, treasuring being close to him and present in the moment. Over the years, she wasn't sure that she had really listened to him as much as she could have done. She'd always been rushing around, even when speaking to him on the phone, checking her emails or social media platforms while speaking to him; even at Christmas when she'd come home, she'd had one eye on her phone all the time. She'd always been so preoccupied that she hadn't given her dad the time and attention he deserved and that was something she *did* regret. Something she didn't want to do this time. She wanted to give him her full attention so she didn't have any more regrets.

'Will you help me sort your mum's things?' he asked.

She lifted her head and met his gaze.

'Of course I'll help you, Dad. Just tell me when you're ready to begin.'

'Hello, Connor.'

'Oh, hi, Clare.' Connor smiled at Clare Greene where she stood opposite him on the woodland path. 'Sorry, I was miles away then.'

He'd gone round to his mum's early on Saturday afternoon and the dogs had jumped all over him, excited to see him, sniffing around his jeans and boots because he clearly smelt of The Lumber Shed. Toby and Digby had then headed straight back to the lounge to hog the sofas, roaching on their backs with their skinny legs in the air. His mum had been busy cleaning her oven, something he'd offered to do for her but she said she'd rather do herself as hard work was good for the soul. He kind of agreed, because for him hard work was the best way to forget. He'd had a coffee then made the mistake of telling her he was going for a walk and instantly the greyhounds had bounced into the kitchen, Digby dragging his lead from the hallway and dropping it at Connor's feet. So he had taken them along too.

'I know that feeling. I get it too when I walk around here. It's turned into a glorious day, hasn't it?' Clare smiled and he realised that she looked different than when she'd arrived in Little Bramble in the autumn. Her brown hair was a bit shorter and shone with health, her eyes were bright green as if she had absorbed part of the woodland and her cheeks and nose were covered with freckles that he suspected had been enhanced by time outdoors. She looked happy and healthy, whereas when he'd first met her last year she'd looked tired and drawn, as if life hadn't dealt her very good cards.

'It really is,' he replied. 'How's Goliath?'

She looked down at the Great Dane who resembled a small horse at her side and stroked his head. 'He's really well. My new best friend, as I've come to call him.'

'He looks it.'

'How are Toby and Digby?' Clare stepped forwards and held out her hand. The greyhounds both sniffed it then she stroked them. 'They're such beautiful dogs.'

'My mum wouldn't be without them.'

'She talks about the good work that the rescue charity does all the time. In fact, I'm helping her out with her stall at the fête.'

'That's brilliant.' Connor nodded. Goliath was a rescue dog too, adopted by Clare's mum, but since Clare had come to the village, the dog had seemed to adopt her.

'Right, best get on. Sam's working today but has an early finish so we're going to the bistro tonight for dinner.'

'It's lovely there. I took Grace last week and will definitely go back.'

'See you soon!' Clare marched away, her feet moving quickly to keep up with Goliath's large strides, and

Connor walked slowly onwards, letting the dogs have a good sniff of the grass at the sides of the path. Clare was a few years younger than him but he'd known her a little when growing up. His mum had told him that she had come back to Little Bramble after her marriage had broken down and she'd stayed, along with her son Kyle, who was now seeing the veterinary nurse, Magnus Petterson, while Clare was in a relationship with the village vet, Samuel Wilson. It was lovely to see them together, to know that middle-aged people could find love again, even if that wasn't for him. And he was, as he kept telling himself, fine with that.

He strolled on, giving the dogs' leads a gentle tug to get them moving and focused on enjoying the walk, on appreciating the scenery around him and savouring the moment. What could be better than that?

The countryside around Little Bramble was beautiful and the woodland walk was one of his favourites, but he had to admit that it was even better with canine company. The trees were resplendent with green summer leaves, branches reaching into the sky as if to touch the sun. The evergreens were full and lush, the hedgerows brimming with colour and life and the path was wet from the morning's rain, gleaming with reflected sunlight as if the earth itself was glowing. The scent of flora and fauna filled the air that was laced with layers from sweet meadow flowers in nearby fields, the rich peaty earth and the tang of pine. Birds sang all around him, the warble of a blackbird as uplifting as any love song. He felt good, at peace, and grateful to be right where he was.

Suddenly, Digby's ears pricked up and he stared hard at a tree. Connor laughed; when the greyhounds reacted like this, it usually meant that there was a small furry creature about. Digby's bottom lip trembled with excitement, tail arced upwards, and Connor tightened his grip on the lead, not wanting to lose the dog if he tried to chase after whatever it was that he'd spotted.

There was so much joy to be found in time spent with dogs. They lived in the moment, enjoyed what they were doing, and Connor aimed to learn from them. He didn't always succeed, but he was doing the best he could – and right now, he was OK with that.

Chapter 9

Connor woke early on Sunday morning, blinking hard, wondering if he'd left his alarm on by mistake. He'd worked yesterday then enjoyed a lovely long walk with his mum's dogs before coming home and eating a vegetarian lasagne that Grace had made. They'd sat on opposite ends of the sofa and munched on garlic bread, lasagne with a rich tomato and basil sauce and home-made chips. It had been delicious and they'd washed it down with a fruity red wine. He was certainly going to miss evenings like that when Grace was gone.

So why was he awake so early?

He sat up and rubbed his face, pushed his hand back through his hair that was, thankfully, he thought, still quite thick, and reached for his phone.

A text from Sadie had arrived two minutes ago and although the sound had been off, it must have made his phone vibrate. Of course! He'd agreed to go and fit her new kitchen today and she'd sent him a kindly reminder. He grimaced; his own sarcasm was something he didn't need today, not when he had hours of being around Sadie ahead of him.

He slumped onto the pillows, wishing he could go back to sleep and forget for another hour, but there was no way his brain would allow that, so he might as well get up and get on with it. Coffee and a bacon sandwich would probably help.

Emma had gone to get the Sunday papers from the shop, taking the shortcut on the way there, then deciding to head around the village green the long way to get home. It was a perfect morning; the sky was a flawless blue, there wasn't a cloud in sight and the air was warm. She had a spring in her step as she walked and was relieved she'd only worn a light cardigan over her T-shirt because anything else would have been far too warm.

The shop was quiet, only two children buying sweets and an elderly lady wandering the aisles. Aromas of fresh croissants and bread filled the air from the small bakery at the back of the shop, along with the scent of fresh fruit and vegetables from local suppliers. Emma had filled a basket with strawberries and raspberries, adding a carton of thick cream and a bag of crispy croissants. Her mouth had watered as she strolled around thinking about how good the pastries would taste with the red berries. She'd picked up the two newspapers her dad had requested, then a jar of maple-pecan-flavoured coffee.

After she'd paid, she left and strolled around the green, hidden behind her giant sunglasses, feeling quite relaxed. She'd had a better night's sleep following her chat with her dad and it had confirmed to her that being open and honest was always good for the soul. There was still much to sort and much to discuss, and his GP follow-up appointment was tomorrow, but for now she planned on making them a delicious breakfast and trying to relax at home.

She came to a row of small cottages that she knew were over a hundred years old. A green van was parked outside one of them, *The Lumber Shed* written in white on the side with a logo made up of different kinds of trees. The name sparked something in her mind she remembered what her dad had told her.

'That must be Connor's van,' she whispered to herself.

A woman was standing in the front garden of the cottage. Something about her was familiar, but Emma couldn't immediately place her. With fair hair tied back in a shiny ponytail, tight black leggings and a vest top, she had the figure of someone who worked out regularly. She appeared to be directing something just inside her front door and Emma was intrigued, so she slowed her pace even more.

'Not like that!' the woman shouted, waving a manicured hand in the air. Emma saw painted nails flash, bright pink talons in a pointy style. They looked like they'd take your eye out or snap if they hit the computer keyboard.

A tall broad-shouldered man appeared, lugging a heavy object out into the front garden. He set the object down and Emma saw that it was a kitchen cabinet. Then the man stood up straight and stretched.

Emma's breath caught in her throat and she almost dropped her shopping.

It was him!

Older. Looking quite fed-up. But definitely him.

Connor . . .

The name formed on her lips, soundless, but her heart pounded out the syllables, over and over, as she stood there watching him. His hair was grey, his jaw was strong, his brows thick. In jeans and a white T-shirt that clung to his muscular frame, he looked strong and had filled out in the years since she'd last seen him.

He looked good. *Really* good.

'Connor, you've chipped the paint.' The woman in the garden was now running her fingers along the door frame and shaking her head. It hit Emma like a punch to the stomach; that was Sadie.

Connor rubbed his eyes and Emma watched as he seemed to deflate, as if he was carrying a heavy weight upon his shoulders. Her heart went out to him and she had a sudden urge to run to him and tell Sadie to back off. But it wasn't her place to do so and hadn't been for years.

'I'll sort it out later. It'll be fine,' he said.

'Well, it's another job you can do. In fact, the entire hall needs painting so you could do that next weekend.'

Connor sighed and turned slightly so he was looking right at Emma. She crouched down and pretended to be tying her laces. Her cheeks burned and her skin prickled as she wondered if he'd seen her watching him, but when she looked up, he was gone and only Sadie remained in the garden.

Emma stood up and Sadie's eyes fell on her, then she looked her up and down. Emma bristled under the scrutiny, wondering if Sadie would recognise her, but when she shrugged and went back inside, it was clear that she hadn't.

Sadie Pierce had hung around with Emma and Connor's crowd during their time at high school but Emma hadn't known her well. It had been a big group of teenagers, after all. Some had come and gone, spending time with other groups as well, and when some of them had headed off to university, the group dynamics had changed completely. Since Emma had left Little Bramble for London, she hadn't seen anyone she was friendly with as a teen, apart from the handful on Facebook who she rarely checked on.

But Sadie . . . there was something she remembered about the blonde woman, only she couldn't quite put her finger on it right now. She'd gone to university to study biology . . . or was it nursing? Yes, the latter. Was Connor married to her or just in a relationship with her? Sadie's tone had been harsh and Connor's reaction dejected. It wasn't a dynamic that was easy to witness. Were they happy?

A memory returned like a bubble trapped beneath a float in a swimming pool, slowly rolling underneath then up to the surface. Sadie had liked Connor, even back then. She had tried to kiss him at a party one night when Emma had stayed at home studying for her A-levels. Emma hadn't gone to the party because she had an exam on the Monday, but she had told Connor to go, not wanting to ruin his Saturday night. He'd gone but left early and phoned her as soon as he got home, telling her that Sadie Pierce had been drunk on cheap cider and tried to kiss him. He'd promised he hadn't done anything to encourage her and swore he'd pushed her away, but he'd wanted Emma to know in case she heard any rumours. Emma had laughed, knowing she could trust Connor completely and actually felt sorry for Sadie.

But Emma had given up any right to question who Connor spent his time with a long time ago. He'd been her best friend, once, her first love, and they'd been as close as peas in a pod. So much had changed since then and she doubted he'd even recognise her now, let alone want to speak to her if he did. After all, the last words they'd spoken had been harsh and hurtful. His eyes had blazed with anger as she'd tried to explain how she felt and she'd seen the shutters come down as he'd cut her out of his life and his heart.

Connor went back into Sadie's kitchen and surveyed the mess – there was no way he would finish the job this weekend or even next! And the kitchen units she'd had were old and worn from the cupboard doors to the worktops, but could have been given a new lease of life with a lick of paint and a good sanding. However, she had insisted that she wanted it to be completely new. Connor found this confusing when people were meant to be making an effort to conserve and upcycle, but he wasn't about to argue with Sadie about it.

Something bothered him as he worked, removing screws and putting them into a jar. He saved everything and would put all the old units in Sadie's front garden for now then load them onto his van later and take them back to The Lumber Shed, where they'd be sanded and painted, and hopefully find a new home in someone else's kitchen. But it wasn't the idea of waste that was making him tense right now, or the knowledge that Sadie would soon be fluttering around him like a moth to a flame, trying to engage him in conversation or to get him to commit more time to her in one way or another.

When he'd been in the front garden just now, he'd seen a woman on the opposite side of the road. She'd been wearing large sunglasses and had ducked down to tie her laces, but she had reminded him of someone. Her hair had been short and light brown with golden highlights that had caught the sunlight, but her height, her shape, her movements had been as familiar to him as his own.

He had seen Emma, he was sure of it, and if it hadn't been her then she had a doppelgänger roaming the streets of Little Bramble. He dropped another screw into the jar then sat back on his heels. It had been a long time since he'd seen or spoken to Emma. In fact, it had been four years ago, at Dawn's funeral, when he'd last laid eyes on her and she'd still had shoulder-length black hair then, so the pixie cut must be something more recent. He'd attended the funeral out of respect for Dawn and Greg – and for Emma and what they'd once had – but he'd kept his eyes down as much as possible, not wanting to make eye contact with his ex. He'd been aware that seeing her pain at losing her mum would rock him to his core, that it would bring everything back, and he couldn't face that. Instead, he'd crept out of the church as soon as the service was over then headed home alone to lick the wounds that had never fully healed.

Connor knew that Greg had become frail recently, that his memory wasn't what it had been and he'd begun to look out for the older man. He visited him every few weeks and had recently taken him a bench complete with an arbour, a cosy affair that he'd spent a while carving in his own time, wanting to give Greg something nice. Perhaps, if he analysed his feelings, he had wanted to retain some sort of connection with Emma's father, not wanted to let go of the past completely because it had, of course, been the best time of his life. Grace was his world now and seeing her happy made him happy, but it was a different feeling to the one of being completely, utterly and hopelessly in love with someone. Only Emma had ever given him that.

Then snatched that happiness from him in the cruellest of ways. The old anger raised its head and growled deep inside him.

He shook his head and rubbed his hands over his face, feeling their roughness, the slight stiffening of the knuckles that happened sometimes these days. Connor's hands were those of a working man, scarred from years of accidental knocks with his hammer and cut by the sharp blades of Stanley knives and stabbed by splinters. They were big hands and should be clumsy, but he'd always been able to take things and shape them to create beauty, from carving to building and more; he was a craftsman and he loved what he could do. But there was no getting away from the fact that he had not been enough for Emma; she had wanted more than he could give and that still hurt, more than any blow from a hammer, because what man wanted to know that he wasn't enough to keep the woman he loved happy?

And that was why, in spite of all the pain he'd gone through, he'd been torn between feelings for Emma. He'd cared about her happiness and yet been crazed with hurt that she'd turned away from him. She'd had ambitions, a yearning for a different life, and he had never wanted to hold her back, but he'd also believed that they should compromise to ensure they were both happy. Emma had seen things differently as he'd found out in their final argument and Connor had been left hurt, humiliated and damaged beyond repair. In spite of his skills at restoring furniture, he'd been unable to fully restore his once-trusting heart.

'Hi Dad, I'm back.' Emma closed the front door then carried her bag of shopping through to the kitchen. He was sitting at the table with a steaming mug in front of him. 'Ooh, has the kettle just boiled?'

'It has indeed. You want tea?'

'I'll make it.'

'No, let me.'

'OK, thanks. I got your papers, but I also picked up some berries and fresh croissants.'

'Sounds good to me.'

She put the bag of croissants on the table then handed him his papers.

'Thank you, Emma. You're spoiling me.'

'You deserve to be spoiled, Dad.'

She got two plates out of the cupboard, washed the berries then put them in a bowl and set everything out on the table. Her dad had already got the butter and jam from the fridge. When they sat back down, he buttered two croissants and gave one to her.

'Do you want jam?' he asked.

Emma looked at the jar, a supermarket brand that she'd tried before and not been fussy on. It just wasn't as good as her mum's and always disappointed her.

'No, thanks. I'll stick to butter.'

'It's not the same, is it?'

'What?'

'The jam.'

'As Mum's, you mean?'

He nodded. 'I miss her adventurous flavours, as well as how fresh it all tasted. From growing the fruit to making the jam and marmalade, she did it all and it just tasted so much better. Sandwiches were always better with her chutneys too.'

'I miss her inventions.'

'You could always try making some, you know.'

'Me?' Emma laughed.

'Your mum's old recipe book is here somewhere.' He frowned. 'Oh yes . . .' He reached out to the chair next to his and retrieved the book that Emma had found in her mum's cupboard. 'I found this on the shelf on the landing. No idea how it got there.'

Emma grimaced. 'Sorry, Dad. I should have asked but I was looking for the key for the studio when you were in the bath yesterday and I came across that.'

'It's OK. Like I said, we need to sort everything out anyway.'

'We do. I, uh, I have the key too.'

'The studio key?'

She nodded.

'I haven't been inside the studio in years. I just couldn't face being surrounded by her things, seeing what she was working on right before she . . . It's probably a right mess in there.'

'I'll take a look and tell you how it is, then clean it up a bit before you go inside.'

He broke a piece of his croissant and moved it around his plate, sweeping it through melted butter then dropping it again. 'There's no need for that, but I am expecting it to be difficult seeing it all again.'

'We can do it together.' She took hold of his hand.

'I'd like that.' He smiled.

Chapter 10

Emma put a cup of tea and two biscuits in front of her dad then sat at the table. They'd got back from his Monday morning GP appointment ten minutes ago and she was feeling a mixture of relief – his physical examination had gone well; his blood pressure was fine and his heartbeat was strong and he'd actually put on three pounds since she'd returned – but also uneasy because Dr Creek had done a blood test and taken a urine sample. The blood test checked for liver, kidney and thyroid function, diabetes and folate levels, while the urine test was to check for signs of infection and to rule out any other conditions, he'd said. It meant waiting for results and Emma hated waiting.

Her dad's memory function had then been tested with a General Practitioner Assessment of Cognition. He had managed to answer most of the questions, but had become a bit agitated when trying to work out some of the mathematical problems and had struggled with the colour differentiation. Emma had sat rigid in her chair, pressing her nails into her palms, but her dad had given her a small smile after each test, joking that he'd never been good at maths and had always suspected he was colour blind. Dr Creek had said some reassuring things, recommended lots of fluids, a good healthy diet and avoiding stress and asked if Emma would be around for a while. She'd seemed relieved when Emma had said she would be, then told them that she'd be in touch soon with the results from the initial tests.

'That's a good cuppa,' her dad said, bringing her back to the present.

She smiled at him. He did seem quite upbeat, had chatted away on their walk home about how the GP had seemed positive and it could just be his age and it was always worse when he was tired. Emma had squashed her worries down and tried to be positive too.

'When we're done, let's go and take a look at the studio, shall we?'

Emma met his eyes. 'Are you sure you don't want a nap first?'

'No, I'm fine. Better to make a start anyway. Might find something useful in there that we've forgotten about.'

Half an hour later, they were outside the studio. Emma held the key tightly in her right hand, then took hold of her dad's hand with her left one.

'Ready?'

'As I'll ever be.'

She slid the key into the lock and tried to turn it.

Nothing.

She tried again, using two hands, this time pushing while she turned. It didn't seem as if it would give, then suddenly it did with a loud clunk, and the door swung inwards, taking Emma with it. She staggered forwards and put out her hands to break her fall, landing on the stone floor with a *humph*.

'Emma?' Her dad rushed to her side.

She coughed and waved a hand at the dust on the floor, which had puffed up in a cloud when she landed. 'I'm OK,' she croaked. 'It's just very dusty.'

She stood up and they looked around, taking in the familiar sights from the baskets in the middle of the floor that would have held the fruit her mum had picked in the garden, to the old green wellington boots behind the door that she wore for gardening and the rocking chair in the far corner, a patchwork quilt folded over its back. The studio might have been coated in four years' worth of dust, but it didn't smell unpleasant, and as Emma's eyes roamed the room she could see why; there were dried bouquets of herbs and flowers hanging from the ceiling beams, and over in the right-hand corner was a unit piled high with bunches and bunches of dried lavender and roses, tied with twine, no doubt ready for sale at the summer fête the year her mother had died. Seeing the studio like this, with everything exactly as it would have been just before her mum's death, brought a great cloud of sadness that made Emma sway. Her dad placed a hand on her arm.

'Are you all right, angel?' His eyes were red and shiny and her own vision blurred.

'I-I'm OK.' She bit the inside of her cheek and sucked in a few deep breaths, determined not to break down because she didn't know when she'd find the courage to come back in here if she did. 'It's just . . . quite sad.'

'I know.' He wrapped an arm around her shoulders and she leant her head on him, grateful to lose herself in the security of her dad's love for a little while.

Connor drove through the country lanes towards Little Bramble, his windows down, the radio on loud enough to drown out his thoughts. Or so he'd hoped. He'd just delivered a table and chairs and should be feeling happy that he had another satisfied customer, but instead he felt like a dark cloud was hovering above the van and he couldn't seem to escape its shadow.

Nothing dramatic had happened. He'd done half of Sadie's kitchen yesterday, had dinner with his mum and Grace, then fallen asleep as soon as his head hit the pillow, but his dreams had been plagued with images of Emma. Not as she looked now, if that had been her he'd seen yesterday, but as she had looked back then, with her black hair, big brown eyes and peaches-and-cream skin. In the dream they had been cuddling in the large room of the old village hall, then Connor had pulled a diamond ring from his pocket and Emma had turned into a cat, slipped from his arms and made a dash for the door. He'd tried to chase her but the wooden floor had turned into toffee and he'd been stuck, shouting after Emma as she disappeared from the hall and from his life. He'd woken soaked in sweat and blamed that for the wetness on his cheeks, not wanting to admit that it could be anything else.

He'd done well for almost three decades to get on with his life, to put the past behind him and to be a good dad to Grace, but things were changing and he couldn't escape it. There was security in familiarity and he liked knowing where he was, having control of his emotions, being aware of how to avoid feeling when the pain tried to resurface. A therapist would probably have told him to confront those feelings long ago, but he hadn't had therapy and had used his own devices to keep going. When the pain came it wasn't as sharp as it had once been; it was more like toothache, dull and irritating, and he'd been able to use anger to push the hurt away.

But he was bound to see Emma again at some point and he had to accept it. He just wished he didn't feel so vulnerable, because he had never wanted to feel that way ever again. It was as if Emma had returned with a key to his past and had opened the door to everything he had tried so hard to forget.

Emma had sent her dad back into the cottage while she got to work. She'd started by trying to get rid of some of the dust with a damp cloth that she repeatedly rinsed in a bucket of warm soapy water. She hadn't wanted her dad out with her, getting dirty and breathing the dust in. When he'd tried to protest, she'd suggested that he make them some lunch while she made a start. His face had fallen when he'd asked what she wanted to eat and she'd told him to surprise her. He clearly did not feel up to trying to come up with an idea, so she'd suggested a sandwich or cheese on toast.

That had been over an hour ago, but she'd told him to have a sit-down first and to watch his property renovation programme. She suspected he might have nodded off but that wouldn't be a bad thing as the GP had told him to get plenty of rest.

She stood up and stretched out her back. It had been a long time since she'd cleaned like this, if ever in fact, and her back was aching, her neck was stiff and her hands felt raw from scrubbing, but at least the surfaces of the worktops and the Aga were clean now, as was the floor. She'd moved things from one work surface to another as she'd cleaned then moved them back to where her mum had kept them. It was sentimental, wanting to keep things the way they'd been when her mum had worked out here, but it was a way of preserving a part of her mum, of feeling close to her again.

She'd even fantasised as she worked about how it would be to use the studio on a daily basis, to come out here every morning and create just as her mum had done. She could stay on in the village, continue her editing and use her mum's studio to make jams, chutneys and more. It wasn't a horrible idea, and she could even turn the space into a kind of office as well. Being here today with the door and windows open so the fresh air swept away the stuffiness and the birds sang outside was actually quite lovely. There was a table in there that her mum had used as a desk and though it was a bit battered, Emma thought she could clean it up and use it. If she shuffled it round a bit so it was right in front of the window, she'd have a view of the garden and could watch as the seasons changed, observe the birds, the squirrels and the hedgehogs that frequented the garden. It would also mean that she could be there for her dad for as long as he needed her.

She coughed as a dust particle tickled her throat and stepped outside for a moment to clear her airways. It wasn't a terrible idea at all, in fact, it could be workable . . .

Her eyes fell on the arbour and her heart squeezed. There was one problem and it was a big one.

Connor Jones.

How could she live in a village where he still lived? Even if he had forgiven and forgotten, how could she see him every day and not feel like the worst person in the world? It wasn't as if she could tell him that she'd regretted what she'd done almost as soon as it had happened, that she'd have taken it back a thousand times over if she could, that she had cried herself to sleep night after night, thinking about how much she had hurt him.

Was it?

Or could she?

But would that be the whole truth? Because she'd enjoyed her life in London, loved her career in publishing and enjoyed the freedom of her single life. Her regret lay in how she'd hurt Connor and her parents and in wishing she'd done things differently. If she and Connor had met a few years after she'd moved to London, things could have been very different, but then she just hadn't been ready to settle down at the same time as him and it had caused a conflict in her that had grown too big to manage.

The image she'd seen the previous day popped into her mind and she shivered as if a cold wind had just blown over her. He was with Sadie, had a whole other life now. If Emma tried to speak to him and apologise or explain, he'd probably laugh and shake his head, his eyes would fill with confusion and he'd look at her as if she was mad. Wasn't it narcissistic to think that she'd matter to him after so long? To assume that Connor would care one way or the other how she felt now or how she'd felt then? Yes, she had hurt him and she knew it, but they'd been so young and it was such a long time ago. They were both fifty now – well, he was, and she was almost there – so whatever happened in their twenties was way back there in the nineties with the Spice Girls, Blur, Sunny Delight, *Friends*, *Cold Feet* and *The Vicar of Dibley*. Admittedly, she still watched reruns of those TV shows, listened to the music and was sure she'd had some Sunny Delight a few years back, even if it didn't taste how she remembered it, but for Emma and Connor there could be no reruns.

Life moved on, people moved on and the past had to stay in the past.

But that left her wondering . . . could she return to Little Bramble permanently? If Connor wasn't bothered, then why should she be?

After lunch, Emma wanted to head back out to the studio to carry on cleaning, but she needed to get a new mop and bucket and she hoped the village shop would have one, otherwise it would be a trip out of the village tomorrow.

She kissed her dad goodbye but he barely seemed to notice because he'd found an old crossword book of her mum's and was puzzling over one of the clues. Emma hoped it would do him good to try to work it out and not cause any damage to his confidence or his anxiety levels. Surely using as much of the brain as possible would be a good thing, exercising it in the same way as the body?

Emma found herself going the long way, walking past the cottage where she'd seen Connor and Sadie. Had it been deliberate, her subconscious dragging her back there just to try to spot Connor again? Or had it been innocent, a slip of awareness after a busy morning?

The cottage looked empty as she peered across the road at the dark windows, wondering if Connor lived there with

Sadie, if they were happy. She'd had brief relationships with men in London, smart professional men she'd met through work and mutual acquaintances, but it had never come to anything. Sometimes she had let things fizzle out, sometimes they had stopped calling, but Emma had never been sad for long, never cared as much as she'd cared about Connor. She'd tried to tell herself this was because he'd been her first love, her best friend, and that he'd always have a special place in her heart because of that. She suspected that something in her psyche had refused to open up to anyone else because she'd hurt Connor so much that she felt she didn't deserve to love again. Thinking about it now, after seeing him again, she wondered if she'd been unable to love anyone else the way she loved Connor because he'd been special and what they'd had was unique. It would make sense, after all. And so her career had been her lover, her online life a substitute for a partner, her social media platforms the children she created, tended and watched over.

When she reached the site of the new village hall, Emma slowed her pace, noticing that the front door was open. Her dad had been meant to perform there at the Christmas show but the weather had been dreadful as the worst snowstorm in years covered Little Bramble in high snow drifts and caused a power cut. The show hadn't gone ahead in its intended format but from what Dilys had told her, the villagers involved had pulled together to salvage what they could of the evening. Knowing that had given her a warm feeling at the time and a sense of nostalgia had swept over her because Little Bramble had been a good place to grow up. The village had always felt safe and she'd been lucky to have such wonderful parents and a lovely home, as well as, when she reached her teenage years, a gorgeous boyfriend. Connor had been gorgeous inside and out, such a kind and attentive partner, at a time when many teenage boys would be too cool to show they cared. He had always stood out from the rest and not just because of his height, but because he held himself with an air of quiet confidence. He hadn't needed the approval of his friends to act on something; he'd happily gone his own way and that had made him a natural-born leader for many of the others. Emma had been proud to be the one he'd wanted and she'd wanted him just as much, had loved him just as much.

Emma fancied a peek at the new hall so she climbed the steps and walked inside. She was greeted by the slightly chalky aroma of fresh paint, along with smells of baking and coffee. The hall was clearly well used and this was confirmed by the noticeboard in the entrance hall which boasted an impressive range of classes from bread-making to yoga to tai chi and crochet. A large poster advertising the fête took up half the board, confirming it as the event of the summer.

She wandered through a doorway into a large room with a stage and piano under a cover. Tables had been set up at the far end of the room in a U shape and a woman was standing behind one, cutting something with a pair of scissors while a younger man sat at a table scrolling through his mobile phone.

'Hello,' Emma said, but neither looked up because her voice was swallowed up by the space. She tried again. 'Hello there!'

'Oh, hello.' The woman smiled at her and Emma realised that she looked familiar. She was around Emma's age, possibly a bit younger, with bright green eyes, high cheekbones and shiny brown hair. 'Can I help you?'

'Uhhh . . . I'm not sure, actually.' Emma approached the tables then stood there feeling awkward and a bit shy. 'I saw that the door was open and I wanted to have a nose, to be honest.'

'Well, that's absolutely fine. Are you staying in the village, then?' the woman replied.

'I am. With my dad, Greg Patrick.'

'Oh, I know Greg! So you must be Emma.' The woman held out a hand. 'I'm Clare Greene. I was at school with your brother Ted.'

Emma frowned, recognising the name.

'And I helped run the Christmas show. Your dad auditioned for it but couldn't make the actual thing.'

'Of course! And yes, I do recall you being friends with Ted, but that was a very long time ago.'

'Indeed it was.'

They shook hands and Emma relaxed, relieved to find such a warm welcome, though what she had expected on entering she wasn't sure. Had she thought she'd tell someone her name and be chased away by an angry mob carrying pitchforks and calling her a monster?

'This is my son, Kyle.'

The handsome young man seemed to snap out of a trance. He trained bright green eyes the same colour as his mum's on Emma and nodded a head of thick dark hair.

'Nice to meet you.' Kyle shook Emma's hand.

'Likewise,' Emma said.

'Are you back in the village for a visit or here for longer?' Clare asked, then she chuckled. 'I should know better than to ask that question, because when I came back last year that's all anyone seemed to ask me. Some people do just come to visit, of course.'

Emma smiled. 'I've come home for a bit because Dad's been . . . a bit under the weather.'

Clare's brows furrowed. 'I'm sorry to hear that.'

'He wasn't 100 per cent before Christmas.' Emma sighed. 'He kept forgetting the words to the song he wanted to sing at the show.'

'Oh yes.' Clare inclined her head. 'But we all forget things. Kyle gets so cross at me because I'm always singing the wrong lyrics to songs.'

'I do.' Kyle's eyes had widened. 'She has a terrible memory and makes lyrics up, I swear. I don't know how many times I've told her that Starship's city was not *built on sausage rolls* and Queen were not *kicking their cat all over the place*.'

Emma giggled, aware that she'd sung a few wrong lyrics herself over the years.

'Is your dad OK, though?' Genuine concern filled Clare's eyes. 'He's a lovely man and I know my mum thinks a lot of him.'

'He had some tests earlier at the GP surgery and when we get the results back we'll know if he needs anything else. I'm going to stay around for a while to see how things go.'

'We spend our lives raising our children then caring for our parents,' Clare said. 'If we're lucky, that is.'

'Well . . . I don't have children and lived quite a care-free life in London. I've only ever had to worry about myself. I worked in publishing – I still do, but now I'm self-employed.'

'I bet that's amazing.' Kyle stood up now, his interest apparently piqued. 'Do you meet any famous authors?'

'Lots.' Emma laughed. 'But, at the end of the day, they're just people.'

'There are so many authors I'd love to meet.' Kyle's eyes shone and his cheeks flushed. 'Do you have lots of signed first editions of books and go out for drinks with the likes of Stephen Fry and J. K. Rowling?'

'Kyle!' Clare was staring at her son, her eyebrows raised.

'Sorry.' Kyle gave a small shrug. 'I get carried away sometimes. It's the *actor* in me, I think. I want to know as much as possible to get details for my roles.'

'Some people would call that nosy,' Clare said to her son.

'That's OK.' Emma shook her head. 'My life in London was, in many ways, quite wonderful.' A pang of something hit her then and her breath caught in her throat. She'd only been in Little Bramble for two and a half weeks but she did kind of miss her flat and some things about her life in London. It had been home for a long time and she was used to being there, to having her own space decorated and furnished exactly as she wanted it. But then she also liked being home in the cosy cottage with its memories and ghosts from the past; it was comforting, and she felt needed, which was something she hadn't felt in a long time.

'Well, Emma, if you're going to be here for a while, we have the village fête coming up three weeks on Saturday. We'd love for as many of the villagers as possible to be involved in it and if you are around, your help would be appreciated.' Clare held out a leaflet advertising the fête.

'It's OK, we have a leaflet at home.'

'Would you be interested?' Clare asked. 'It's going to be a lovely event. We have lots of stalls and a bouncy castle and a crepe stall booked.'

'It sounds wonderful, but I'm not sure what I could do.' Emma looked around the hall as if searching for an answer.

'Do you make anything? You could sell something you've made or help out on another stall, offer your editorial services in the raffle?' Clare held out her hands. 'Anything, really.'

'I'll have a think.' Emma looked at the table in front of Clare and her eyes fell on the colourful card and ribbon. 'You're making bunting?'

'Yes. Got to have bunting at a fête.'

'I agree with that.' Her mum used to make bunting and labels and lid covers for her jars of jam, marmalade and chutney.

Of course!

'I could, I suppose, have a stall selling jams and marmalades? Chutneys too,' she said, her heart racing as the words left her lips.

'That would be amazing!' Clare nodded.

'My mum, Dawn, used to run the jam stall. I used to help her make things sometimes, so I'm sure I could manage.'

'Of course she did. Do you know, I've only been back since October and before that I didn't visit as often as I should have done, and I've forgotten a lot over the years. I'm still getting to know people again and being hijacked by memories when I walk around the village. Poor Kyle and Sam have to hear my frequent exclamations when I recall something new. The memories of my dad are really special.'

Emma waited, wondering if Clare wanted to say more.

'He passed away over a decade ago but some days I still feel like I'll open the door to Mum's cottage and find him waiting there.'

'You and me both.' Emma gave a wry smile.

Clare nodded. 'It's hard losing a parent.'

'Mum!' It was Kyle's turn to interrupt with a frown. 'I'm sure we can steer this conversation towards something a bit lighter. It must be your age making you so maudlin all the time.'

Clare started to giggle and Emma joined in. Kyle was right. What was it about being middle-aged that set you talking about death? Though it was nice to speak to someone who was around the same age as her and who understood.

'Look, I don't suppose you fancy a coffee, do you?' Clare asked. 'I'm going to make some for us and we have some delicious cookies that Kyle made. He's bad for my waistline, this son of mine, but he does bake like a professional.'

Emma was about to accept then she remembered why she was there.

'I would love to, but I need to get back for Dad. I only came out to see if I could buy a mop and bucket.'

'I doubt you'll get these in the village shop.' Clare shook her head. 'However, there are several in the kitchen cupboard here so why don't you borrow a set?'

'Really?' Emma asked.

'Yes, it'll be fine.'

'Is it OK if I borrow it for a few days?'

'Of course.'

'I'm clearing out my mum's old studio so it might get quite dirty but if it seems beyond salvaging, I'll buy a new one to replace it.'

'No worries at all. Come with me.'

Clare led Emma through to the kitchen area where the cupboard boasted a selection of mops and buckets that Clare said had been donated by a local cleaning supplies firm.

Back in the hallway, Emma thanked Clare for what could have been the hundredth time.

'Honestly, it's fine. Just have a think about the fête and let me know because we'd love to have you involved.'

They exchanged numbers and Emma headed back out into the sunshine, a big smile on her face, a mop and bucket in her hands and a lightness in her heart. Clare was very warm and friendly and Emma hoped to get to know her better. They'd grown up in the same village but barely exchanged more than a few words when they were younger, as often happened with children when they were different ages. Being an adult levelled the playing field and Emma knew all too well that having friends was a gift worth treasuring. Especially friends who'd been through similar experiences. Clare had told her that she'd only come back to Little Bramble to visit but had ended up falling in love with the village – and with the handsome vet, Samuel Wilson – and Emma thought that if Clare could do it, then there was a chance for her too.

To fall back in love with the village, that was, not with any handsome men. Emma had no intention of looking for love or even accidentally bumping into it on the village green. She just wanted to make sure her dad was OK, and she had a feeling that staying around would be one way, probably the best way, to do exactly that.

'Dad?' Emma peered into the lounge but he wasn't there. 'Are you in the kitchen?' She winced, realising that he might have gone for a nap and she wouldn't want to disturb him.

In the kitchen she set down the mop and bucket and frowned at the open back door. She stepped out into the garden and looked around. He wasn't sitting in the arbour or within sight so he must be further along the garden. Her heart jolted. What if he'd wandered off in a daze and forgotten who he was or something? You read about things like that happening to older people. He had, after all, been found at the bus stop just after dawn one morning. Granted, he'd seemed a bit better since Emma arrived and her company was clearly benefitting him but she'd gone out and left him alone. He could have slipped and . . .

She hurried through the arch of trees and towards her mum's studio and exhaled noisily when she saw that the door was open.

'There you are!'

She burst through the doorway, then paused. He was facing away and his shoulders were shaking.

'Dad?'

He turned agonisingly slowly, his hands clenched over his chest, his face grey.

'Oh God, Dad. What is it? Your heart?'

He shook his head and she noticed the tears on his cheeks, the way his lower lip was trembling.

'What happened?' She reached for him and gently took his hands. He nodded to his side and she looked past him.

'Did it break?'

'I-I sat on it and started to rock and . . .'

'Hey, it's OK.' She rubbed his arms gently, murmured soothing words as she surveyed the damage. 'That rocking chair was pretty old.'

She patted his back as she eyed the broken chair.

'I bought her that rocking chair when she was pregnant with you. She kept saying that she wanted one to nurse the baby in and that was all I could afford at the time.' His hand shook as he pointed at it. 'And now I've broken it.'

'Dad, it's been out here for four years in the cold and damp. And before that it was very well used.'

'It won't be used again.'

Emma stared at the chair, worried that he might be right, then something occurred to her.

'Didn't you say that Connor has a furniture making business?'

'It's an upcycling business.' Her dad sniffed.

'Well, I could take this chair to him and see if he can fix it.' The thought of going to Connor's place of work and asking him for a favour made her stomach churn but the alternative, seeing her dad this upset, was worse. If she needed to face her past in its most palpable form, then she would do.

'Do you think he'll be able to?' The hope in her dad's voice broke her heart.

'I don't see why not. He was always good with his hands . . .' She realised what she'd said then shrugged it away; her dad would never make that link. 'I mean, he was always good at making and fixing things. If anyone can put this chair back together it's him.'

'He's a good lad, isn't he?'

She nodded, hoping her face wasn't betraying the whirlwind of emotions that the thought of going to see Connor had aroused. Who would put themselves in a situation where they had to face the person they'd loved in the past, the person they'd abandoned at a very important time, the person they'd once loved more than anyone, unless it was for a very good reason? She just had to hope that Connor, the man she'd respected and adored, would be understanding.

Chapter 11

Connor was adding a lick of varnish to a chair leg when he heard a car pull up. The gravel yard outside the converted barn announced every arrival better than a guard dog. He checked the clock on the wall and saw that it was just after ten, so he doubted it would be his mum bringing lunch. He felt better today and suspected that yesterday's low mood had been something of the Monday blues – at least, he preferred to attribute it to that.

Jay Sutter, a twenty-something employee who Connor had employed a few months back, after he'd moved to Little Bramble to live with his girlfriend, waved a hand at him from the doorway of the reception area. Connor couldn't see who had arrived as the reception was separated from the main workshop by screens.

'Lady here to see you, boss.'

'Me?'

'Yeah.' Jay nodded. 'Asked for you even though I said I could help her.'

Connor put the brush down on the tin lid then wiped his hands on a cloth. It couldn't be anyone he knew because Jay would have invited them through, so it must be a potential customer.

'Cheers, Jay.' He patted the younger man on the back as he passed him then walked around the screens and through to the small reception area. Standing there, her back to him as she gazed out of the glass doors, was a woman with short brown hair flecked with blonde. She was wearing loose jeans and plimsolls with a grey T-shirt. 'Hello, can I help you?'

She turned and it was as if an earthquake had hit the barn. Connor actually gasped and staggered.

Dark brown eyes he knew so well.

Heart-shaped face.

Full, kissable lips.

But different hair, hair he'd seen the other day. It was short and framed her face like a halo as it caught the light that shone through the doors.

But this was no angel.

Her pupils dilated as her eyes met his and his heart seemed to somersault, then a whole load of different emotions coursed through him: hurt, betrayal, anger, love, need, desire, sadness and, finally, the feeling that trumped all the others and settled in his gut like bile, awkwardness. Once upon a time he'd known this woman better than anyone else, but that was a long, long time ago and they'd both more than doubled in age since then.

'Hello, Connor.' Her eyes scanned his face and he noticed that her hands were entwined in front of her as if

151

she was holding herself together. He felt like grabbing hold of a chair to support himself.

The voice, so familiar and unheard for years, sent him hurtling back to the last time they'd spoken. He'd arranged to meet her at Greg and Dawn's cottage, needed to see her face to face to ask why she'd abandoned him on the day of their engagement party, why she'd accepted his proposal if she didn't want to marry him, why she'd let them plan the party and start to plan the wedding if she didn't want any of it. Her replies had been stuttered and he'd grown angry, had used that anger to bury his distress and she'd become angry too, shouted at him that she'd never wanted what he did and had felt backed into a corner. She needed a life of her own, not to marry the only man she'd ever been with and before she'd seen any of the world. Her parents had come to try and calm things down and Emma had shouted at them too, told them they'd made her feel like she'd let them down because she didn't want to settle for a boring life in a small village as they had. Emma had been furious and her parents had seemed broken-hearted. Connor had fled then, unable to listen to any more of it because the woman standing in front of him had not been the Emma he'd known and loved. He'd never have proposed if he'd suspected she didn't feel the same way he did.

'Emma?' It emerged as a question.

'Yes. It's me.' She raised a hand to her hair and touched it self-consciously. 'I know I look a bit different but then it's been a while.'

'You've come back?'

'I'm staying with Dad for a while. He's been . . . under the weather.'

'Right. Yes. I'd heard he wasn't as well as he could be.'

Euphemisms to avoid saying the actual words out loud, to escape having to give Greg's recent behaviour a label. There had been rumours in the village that Greg Patrick was suffering from the early signs of dementia, news that had left Connor torn. He wanted to be there for the man who'd once been so good to him, but he also didn't want to overstep the mark and interfere where he wasn't supposed to.

'He said you visit him sometimes and I wanted to thank you for that.'

Connor shook his head. 'It's fine. I care about your dad.'

'He cares about you too.'

Connor blew out his cheeks to try to ease the tension inside.

'I've come because I have a favour to ask.'

She looked down and he followed her gaze. Her white plimsolls were so small, reminding him of her size 4 feet with their tiny stubby toes. He used to tease her about those toes, kiss them and tickle her feet to make her giggle. Her feet shifted as if she was aware of his thoughts and he raised his eyes.

'You want a favour?' His voice was cold. For years he'd imagined what he'd say to her, how he'd tell her that she was cruel and heartless, that people like her didn't deserve to be loved as he'd loved her. He'd imagined making her cry, wanted to see her hurt in the same way she'd hurt him. But now that she was here, everything felt different because they were, in reality, strangers.

'I hate to ask, but it's for my dad.'

'What do you want, Emma?'

'I was sorting out my mum's studio and my dad went in there and sat on her old rocking chair. It broke . . . well, the back came off it, and I wondered if it could be fixed? Obviously, I'll pay whatever it costs . . . I mean, I don't expect you to do this for free but I'd be so grateful if you could take a look.'

'Where is it?'

'In the car.'

He could turn her away, tell her to get lost and never come back, but it just wasn't who he was, not who his mum and dad had raised him to be.

'Let's go and have a look.'

Relief crossed her face and she led the way out to the car and opened the boot. The chair was in three pieces. Connor lifted them out one by one and checked the joins in the wood and the condition of it.

'It clearly got damp in the studio, but I'll clean it up and see if I can put it back together. I might need to add or replace a few pieces but essentially it'll be the same chair. Is that OK?'

'That would be amazing.'

'Help me carry it inside and I'll take your details.'

He picked up two pieces of the chair and left the smallest one for Emma. In the workshop they set the pieces down and he pulled out his phone.

'What's your number?'

'Oh . . .' Her eyes widened. 'I can never remember my own. Hold on.'

She pulled a phone from her jeans pocket and dialled his number when he gave it to her. Then he saved her number in his contacts. The significance of the moment wasn't lost on him; for the first time in years, he had Emma Patrick's number in his phone and he felt the weight of it in his pocket, as if he'd discovered a hidden treasure that could rock his whole world.

And yet, it was nothing more than the number of a woman who wanted him to do a job.

'Thank you.' She nodded. 'Dad will be delighted if you can fix the chair. If not, though, no worries. We appreciate you trying.'

He stared at her, absorbing every detail. He didn't want her to go just yet, wanted her to keep standing there so he could reassure himself that it was really her. Her perfume was different than the one she used to wear, more expensive and mature, but beneath it was her own unique scent and it made a part of him that he'd suppressed for what felt like a lifetime want to rise to the surface and rejoice.

'Well . . . I'll take a look at this and let you know if it's fixable.'

She held his gaze and opened her mouth as if she wanted to say more, but then she pressed her lips together so hard they went white and shook her head gently.

As she walked away and disappeared behind the reception screens, Connor's legs weakened and he had to lock his knees to stop himself sinking to the floor. Emma Patrick was back in Little Bramble and it seemed that it wasn't a fleeting visit, so he'd have to get used to seeing her around. The thought made his heart ache. He'd managed to bury his anger because he hadn't seen her every day, hadn't heard her voice and had known she was far away living the life she'd chosen. She'd been the person who made his heart soar and then the one who'd humiliated him more than anyone. He was torn between wanting space to process seeing her again and yearning to talk to her and find out more about her life now.

How would he manage now she was back? How would he hold it all together and keep the Connor who'd loved Emma buried?

Only time would tell.

Emma's hand shook as she turned the key in the ignition. She glanced behind her, wondering if anyone had seen her error but the car park outside the converted barn was empty. She felt clumsy, her mind and body disjointed as if she'd experienced a terrible shock.

Voices ran through her head. There had been so much shouting – most of it hers. Not today, but back then when she'd met Connor for one last conversation. She'd felt suffocated for some time and needed space, time to breathe, but Connor hadn't understood that when she'd tried to raise the subject, then he'd proposed and she'd felt obliged to accept, too cowardly – or at least too young and inexperienced – to speak to him about what she really wanted. It was easier to take the ring and to arrange the party and to smile at her parents' delight and at Zoe's delight while wondering how she would stay in Little Bramble and be the person they all wanted her to be. But the fear of disappointing and hurting them all created intense conflict within her and culminated, ironically, in her hurting them more than she'd have done if she'd dealt with things differently.

She pressed her hands to her ears and took some deep breaths, looked around her to ground herself in the moment.

On the outside of the barn was a large sign in the same colours and style as the one she'd seen on the van. This was Connor's business and her dad had been right; he was doing well. It had been what he wanted all those years ago and he'd achieved his dream. That thought comforted her, even though she was still shaking from their interaction. She'd expected him to be all sorts of things, but calm and polite hadn't been one of them and she was so grateful that he'd behaved so civilly. Emma didn't feel that she deserved to be treated well but she would have found animosity from

Connor very difficult to deal with. And yet, it would have been something she believed she deserved.

Now she had to go home and wait to see if he could fix the chair. She'd given him her number, something she'd never imagined doing again, and there was something reassuring about knowing he could reach her if he needed to.

Up close in the workshop, surrounded by the smells of sawdust and varnish, she'd been able to see his Adam's apple bob as he swallowed, the hairs that poked out above the collar of his T-shirt, the breadth of his shoulders. He'd always been taller than her but now he was broad and masculine, the man grown from the boy she'd known and loved.

An urge had stirred in her, in spite of her nerves, a desire to step forward and rest her forehead on his chest as she used to do, to breathe him in and feel safe again. Connor had always made her feel safe, had been her port through many teenage storms – and yet it hadn't been enough. Not back then when the world seemed so inviting, when life offered places to go and things to see and do, and she'd decided she wanted to be independent, to spread her wings and sample what was on offer. It was as if her younger self had thought she couldn't have both security *and* freedom, that she had to choose between them and so she had done. Not without being nudged, because Connor had been in their relationship too and he had wanted more from her than she'd been able to give at that time. So she'd left and he'd stayed. Life had taught her many things since then and she wished she could return to speak to her younger self to share her wisdom, but that was the problem with hindsight; it didn't offer second chances, only lessons learnt.

Emma took a deep breath and drove out of the car park, leaving behind her a trail of dust in the gravel.

Chapter 12

'Emma?' Her dad wandered into the studio and looked around. 'Oh, well done!'

'Hi, Dad. Looking good, right?'

'It certainly is.'

After returning from her encounter with Connor, Emma had been filled with nervous energy so she'd pulled on rubber gloves, grabbed the mop and bucket and come out to the studio. She'd removed the first layers of dust and tidied the other day, but now she was doing a thorough deep clean, keen to make the most of the relief that physical activity offered.

She had scoured the top of the Aga and all the compartments, making sure that it was fit for use again. Scrubbing, cleaning and sorting definitely had the benefits that some of the celebrity cleaning gurus had built their careers on and Emma was glad to have a distraction. She'd also spoken to a local window fitter and had arranged for him to come round the next day to give her a quote for some new windows in the cottage, because now that she'd had a good look, it was obvious that the old ones had to go. She didn't think they'd survive another winter.

'Oops!' Her dad shook his head.

'What is it?' She went to his side and peered at him.

'I was so impressed when I came in here that I forgot to tell you that you have a visitor. Well, two visitors, actually.'

Emma's stomach somersaulted. 'Visitors?'

Was it Connor? Had he come to shout at her after all, as he often did in her dreams? When she woke from those dreams she often found her cheeks and pillow wet, her heart racing. But then, if it was Connor, who was the second visitor?

'Yes, it's . . . uh . . .' Her dad frowned. 'Clare! Yes, Clare Greene.'

'Oh . . . right.'

Emma swallowed her disappointment – it seemed there was a part of her that *did* want to see Connor again. 'Did you leave her inside?'

'She's in the kitchen with that enormous dog of hers. I didn't bring her out here because I wasn't sure you'd want anyone to see the studio yet.'

'I think it's a bit more presentable now, Dad.'

He smiled. 'It's wonderful. Your mum would be delighted.'

'I don't know about that. After my initial reluctance to change anything at all from when Mum was here, I've moved some of the cupboards around because I didn't

161

think they worked as they were. Mum had her system but there was a lot of space wasted.'

'Probably because she was always using things then ordering more. She was perpetually in motion. And as for the deliveries we'd get once she discovered how to order jars and the like online!' He tutted affectionately.

'I think we'd better get back inside, Dad, don't you? It's a bit rude to leave Clare waiting.'

'Oh yes! Come on.'

In the kitchen, Clare was standing by the dresser, peering at photographs of Emma and her parents, her dog sitting at her side like a large statue. Clare greeted them with a big smile as she walked through the back door.

'Hello, Clare.' Emma went to her and kissed both her cheeks in the way she would greet an old friend. At Clare's side the dog wriggled and emitted a low whine.

'Behave, Goliath. Sorry, he's just eager to say hello too. I hope you don't mind me popping in but I wanted to bring you some more information about the fête and a little welcome back to the village gift.'

She held out an envelope and a bottle of rosé wine.

'Thank you. That's really kind.' Emma took the envelope and the bottle, which had clearly come straight from a fridge as it was cold and had beads of condensation on the glass.

'And hello, Goliath.'

The Great Dane wagged his tail and it made a swishing sound against the floor tiles.

'There's a list of stalls in the envelope and information about availability and what other stalls we'd like to have this year. Basically, I have an ulterior motive as I thought . . . well, *hoped* you might really be interested in taking a stall.'

'I'll take a look.'

'That sounds exciting.' Emma's dad rubbed his hands. 'Plus it means that you'll be staying a bit longer if you do take a stall.'

Emma nodded at him, an urge to wrap him up in cotton wool and keep him safe from worry and harm sweeping over her again. She was overwhelmed by a need to speak to someone, to share her thoughts and feelings before she popped like a balloon.

'Clare, I don't suppose you fancy staying for a bit and opening this wine, do you? It's a lovely afternoon and we could sit in the garden.'

'I'd love to.'

'You don't have plans?'

'Nothing that can't wait and, to be honest, I've been so busy lately with planning the fête and my job at the local stables that an afternoon in the garden with wine sounds idyllic. As long as you don't mind Goliath staying too?'

'He's very welcome.' Emma went to the cupboard and got out three wine glasses. 'Does he need some water?'

'That would be lovely. But I'll give it to him outside because he can be messy when he drinks and he'll turn the kitchen floor into one big puddle.'

'Dad, are you having a glass?'

'None for me, thank you.' Her dad shook his head. 'I want to get back to that crossword book.' He patted his pocket where his mobile phone was. 'I found a great website with some . . . helpful hints.'

'Helpful hints?' Emma frowned.

'Yes, you know . . . you type in the clue and it helps you.'

'I see.' Emma nodded as she put the third wine glass back in the cupboard. 'Sounds good.'

'I don't use it for *all* the clues, just the ones I get really stuck on.' He winked and Emma's shoulders relaxed a bit. He was teasing her.

'Shall we go outside then?' She handed Clare a glass and a bowl of water for Goliath then they headed into the garden.

The arbour looked inviting but Emma felt like having some sunshine on her face, so they went further down the garden and sat on the picnic bench near the greenhouse. Clare placed the bowl of water under the bench to keep it cool then unclipped Goliath's lead from his harness and he started to wander around, sniffing the grass.

'Will he be OK?' Emma asked, her eyes on the giant dog and his long, wagging tail.

'As long as the garden's enclosed.'

'It is. He won't be able to get out unless he can climb trees.'

'He would love that!' Clare laughed. 'He'd definitely catch the squirrels then, but what he'd do with them once he caught them I have no idea. Probably just lick them. He's such a big softy.'

'He seems lovely.'

Emma poured some wine into the glasses, then took a sip of hers.

'This is delicious.'

'One of my favourites.'

The wine had aromas of vanilla and roses and flavours of strawberries and watermelon. It was perfect for a sunny day. There was a gentle breeze that toyed with Emma's hair and brushed against her skin. After an emotionally difficult morning and busy afternoon, she had needed this more than she realised.

'How are you finding it being back in the village?' Clare asked.

'I'm glad to be back for Dad but there are some things about Little Bramble that I'd rather not revisit.'

'I think everyone goes through that when they return to their childhood home. I avoided coming back here other than for brief visits – and I had more than one reason for that. Look, you don't have to tell me what's bothering you because you barely know me, but I just wanted to let you know that I understand. Life can be tough.'

Clare's clear green eyes were filled with understanding and Emma found herself wanting to talk to her. Clare was right, they hardly knew each other but sometimes it helped to speak to someone who didn't know you and who had no prejudices towards you.

'I'm worried people in Little Bramble will judge me.'

Clare tilted her head. 'Why would they judge you?'

'Why wouldn't they?'

'Maybe we should address who "they" are first?' Clare's eyes crinkled at the corners.

'I know, it sounds dramatic, doesn't it? But I left here almost twenty-eight years ago after hurting someone I really cared about – and because I've avoided coming back for longer than a few days at a time, I think part of me feels as if the past is still very much alive here.'

'People do move on.'

'I know . . . and that's the thing. People who would have been around back then will have passed away, like my mum, or moved away and there will be new people here who know nothing about what happened, but for me–'

'It's still raw.'

'Yes! Exactly that. I didn't think it was, as I had a whole new life in London, but when I come back here? Well, it's as if time has stood still.'

'For you?'

'Yes.'

'I can understand that. But I'm willing to bet that you'll be one of the only people who cares about what happened.'

'Except for him and his mum.'

'So it's a man then?' Clare sipped her wine. 'I'm not prying, Emma, not at all. However, I think I might know what you're referring to.'

166

Emma slapped her hand against her forehead. 'Of course you do. You were friends with my brother.'

'I was – and I knew about you and Connor splitting up just before your engagement party but don't know any gory details.'

'And the details *were* gory.' Emma grimaced.

'It was a very long time ago and I'm sure few people will remember now. The ones who do will be you and Connor, along with your close family members. It won't matter to anyone else as it's none of their business. Whatever the reasons were for you splitting up, that's your affair. Love is complicated and it makes us do things we never thought we would, feel things so deeply that we barely know what to do for the best.'

'Thank you.' Emma hoped Clare was right, but found it hard to believe that she wouldn't be a subject for local gossip. Clare seemed to know that she'd split up with Connor but not the specifics so perhaps it was the same for other people too.

'Have you seen him since your return?'

'This morning. I had to go to his workshop and ask him for a favour.'

'Ouch!' Clare winced. 'How did it go?'

'Awkwardly.'

'But you did it.'

'I did.'

'Well, that's half the battle over, surely? He didn't shout at you or beat his chest, tug at his hair and cry?'

Emma met Clare's eyes and saw that she was teasing her.

'No, thank goodness. That would have been truly awful. He was very cool and calm. If he had shouted at me, been mean, even, I think I'd have felt better.'

'So you're punishing yourself, then?'

'Do you think so?'

'Definitely. And I bet every time you've thought about what happened over the years you've experienced a similar heartache.'

Emma nodded, her throat tightening so much it hurt.

'You are a human being, not a machine, Emma. You probably have made mistakes over the years, but doesn't everyone? I'm sure you didn't hurt anyone deliberately and surely the lack of intent there has to count for something? You made your decision for a reason – and at the time, that reason might have been the only thing driving you forwards. How we feel changes all the time, especially as we age and gain experience of life, but you have to be kind to yourself and let this go.'

Emma swallowed some more wine. 'I know that there's a lot of sense in your advice, but I can only wish it was that easy.'

'It won't happen overnight, and you'll probably need to see him again to become accustomed to it, but if you've both moved on, then things will get better.'

Emma sighed and hugged herself. Clare was right, but since she'd seen Connor she'd felt all mixed up again and as if she'd been catapulted back in time. She wanted to ask

Clare about Connor and Sadie but felt it would be too much too soon – and she didn't want to seem nosy, so she swallowed the questions and tried to think about other things.

At that moment Goliath came over to the bench and gazed up at Emma, then he laid his head on her lap. She put out a hand and ran it over his soft head, wondering what was going on inside it.

'Have *you* moved on, Emma?'

'I . . . I really don't know.'

Chapter 13

When he walked into the workshop the next morning and saw the rocking chair out the back with the completed jobs to be collected or delivered, Connor experienced a flash of pride. It looked amazing now it was fixed up. He had worked on it in the late afternoon and all evening on Tuesday, feeling the need to get the job done. Usually, he had a queue of jobs and liked to do them in order, but something about this one meant that he had to prioritise it. It was, he mused, as if fixing the chair might fix something inside him. Or perhaps he just wanted it done so he didn't have to keep thinking about Emma.

He loaded the rocking chair into his van, sent Emma a text to let her know he was on his way, then drove it to Greg's cottage, knowing that if he waited until later to do it he wouldn't have any peace of mind all day – like an anxious teenager before an important exam.

Emma paced up and down the garden, clenching and unclenching her hands. When she'd taken the chair to Connor yesterday, she hadn't expected it to be ready so soon, had thought it would likely take him a few weeks, but he'd sent a text to say it was done and he was on his way to her.

Connor was coming here, to the cottage, after all the time that had passed! Years ago, they'd spent a lot of time together in her parents' cottage, watching TV, playing games, eating meals and reading, talking about the future and what they wanted to achieve. Her parents had taken Connor into their home and family, accepting that because Emma loved him they would too. When it had become clear, early on in their relationship, that it looked likely to become serious, Emma's mum had taken her aside and spoken to her quietly about love and other elements of a relationship. Fifteen-year-old Emma had squirmed and tried to get away, but she'd taken the advice on board. She and Connor had got to know each other, had progressed things slowly, and along the way had fallen in love. It had been sweet, then intense and passionate, but they had laughed a lot and been such good friends. She'd thought it would last forever, not imagined for a moment that her feelings would change.

Along with her parents, Connor had encouraged her to go to university in London, where she'd studied English Literature then done a post-grad in publishing. She had commuted because it was only forty minutes from the

Surrey village by train and she knew she'd save a lot of money by not living in London during those four years. While in London, she had fallen in love with the city, had loved the vibrancy, the nightlife, the architecture and being in the centre of things. Coming back to Little Bramble each day had become a bit of a chore, especially as she started to get to know people in the publishing industry in her last year, and she'd found herself changing in ways she'd never thought she would. She still loved Connor but found she had hopes and dreams for their future that didn't involve staying in Little Bramble for the rest of their lives . . . When she had graduated, aged twenty-two, sensing that she was on the cusp of an exciting career, Connor had proposed and everything had been turned upside down.

She heard a car pull up on the street outside and hurried inside the cottage, checking her appearance in the hall mirror before answering the door. Her eyes were bright, her cheeks pink and she looked younger than she'd done for years. Perhaps it was the country air or perhaps the anxiety she was feeling had brought the flush to her cheeks, but something inside her had changed since she'd been home. Taking a deep breath, she opened the door.

Connor had carried the rocking chair up to the front door then set it down, knocked and waited. He was jolted back in time to when he used to come here every day and, in the later years of his relationship with Emma, to stay overnight. He'd always received a warm welcome from Dawn and Greg and had enjoyed their easy-going natures, their happy acceptance of him and enthusiastic conversation about his dreams of expanding his dad's business and one day getting a bigger workshop. What he had found most wonderful of all was how they had trusted him with their daughter, never made him feel on edge or awkward and, as a father, Connor now knew how challenging that must have been. Grace had brought a few young men home over the years and Connor had been civil towards them, but he'd also had to control his urge to talk to them about being respect-ful towards his baby girl and making sure they never hurt her. None of them had lasted long. Grace was twenty-five, three years older than he'd been when he'd proposed to Emma, and she seemed so young, far too young to get mar-ried and commit to one person. But at just twenty-two he had thought he was mature enough to get married and have a family, to commit to one person for the rest of his life. Had times changed that much or was it just that he'd been immature and too keen to settle down at such a young age? Even now, he was sure he'd still be with Emma if she hadn't left, couldn't imagine not loving her and being happy shar-ing his life with her.

The door opened and there she was, the woman who had rocked his world. Rosy cheeks, full lips, shiny hair and pretty face with eyes he had loved to gaze into for hours.

'Connor, come on in.' Emma stood back and he picked up the rocking chair and carefully carried it inside.

'Where do you want this?'

'Uh . . . let me check.' She stuck her head around the lounge door. 'Dad, Connor's here with a surprise for you.'

Greg came to the door and smiled at Connor. 'Hello, lad, good to see you.'

'Always a pleasure, Greg.'

'You've fixed it.' Greg clapped his hands together. 'Thank you so much!'

'It was easy . . . just needed a carpenter's touch. And I have all the right tools at The Lumber Shed.' Connor shrugged, feeling embarrassed by Greg's praise. After all, Greg had been an engineer and a DIY expert. He could probably have fixed the chair himself a few years ago, so Connor was conscious of not wanting to make the older man feel in any way inadequate. He knew that Greg's gnarled hands didn't work as well as they used to, that his grip had weakened – something Greg had also explained as a reason for why he no longer played his guitars – and that it would be a difficult thing about ageing that any man would have struggled to accept.

'Where do you want it, Dad?' Emma asked.

'Out in the studio where it belongs, of course.'

Emma met Connor's eyes. 'You can leave it here and I'll take it out later.'

'No, I'll carry it out. Don't want you bumping it against something and undoing all my hard work.' He flashed her a brief smile.

'Of course. This way then. Although you know that, of course.' Emma tutted at herself then led him through the kitchen and out into the garden.

'Cup of tea, Connor?' Greg called from the back door. Connor didn't want one but didn't like to say no.

'Yes please, Greg.'

When they reached the studio, Emma paused outside.

'Thank you so much, Connor.'

'It's fine, honestly.'

'How much do I owe you?'

'Nothing.'

'But I want to pay you.' She pulled some notes from her pocket.

'No. It was easy to fix.'

'I have to give you some–'

'I said it's fine, Emma! For goodness' sake, just leave it, OK?'

Her eyes widened and she blanched.

'OK. Thanks.'

'Where shall I put it?'

'Next to the table, please.'

He carried it inside, trying to ignore the guilt that was gnawing at his insides. He hadn't meant to be sharp but there was no way he'd have taken a penny from her. It just didn't seem right, and besides which, it was for Greg.

'There you go. Perfect.' He stood there and admired how the chair looked and Emma came and stood at his side.

'It looks wonderful.'

'So does this place,' he said, looking around.

'I wanted to tidy it up a bit. No one had been in here since Mum . . .'

'It was very sad that your mum passed away so suddenly.'

'Your dad, too.'

Silence fell in the workshop and only the sounds from outside filled the air: birds singing in happy oblivion, a tractor on a distant field rumbling across the land and music coming from a car as it passed on the street.

Connor's heart was beating so hard he was surprised Emma couldn't hear it. Being so close to her and completely alone like this, her scent invading his nostrils, her warmth just centimetres away was doing all kinds of crazy things to his mind and he could feel rationality slipping away. He was no longer Connor the responsible businessman and father, no longer a fifty-year-old man with joints that creaked and salt-and-pepper hair. He was back to being Connor, untouched by time and pain, a man who cared about this woman and wanted to be with her. It was as if the past twenty-eight years had never happened.

'Connor . . . Th-this is . . . quite strange.' Emma startled him from his thoughts and he gulped in a deep breath as if snatched from a dream. He turned to meet her eyes and saw that they were glistening.

This woman could be his undoing all over again . . .

'It *is* strange,' Connor said, his voice husky. He rubbed at his neck and Emma watched him, afraid to blink in case he disappeared.

Being out here alone with him had hit Emma hard. Yesterday, there had been other people at The Lumber Shed but here, surrounded by trees and bushes and the thick stone walls, it was as if they were isolated from the world, as if time had stood still.

They had fallen quiet and something crackled in the air between them: things left unsaid, things left undone.

'So . . . you've tidied all this up, but for what purpose?'

'I'm sorry?'

'Well, what's the point in doing all this if you're going to leave?'

'Oh. Uh . . . I'm here and I wanted to keep busy and I thought I'd clean this up because it was Mum's. There's so much of her here and I hadn't been out here for years so when I found the key and saw the state of the place, it made me really sad.'

He stared at her, his face expressionless, something in his eyes altering.

'I've also thought that it'll be hard to leave Dad now, with him finding things difficult, and so I'm considering . . . uh . . . perhaps staying for longer. Also, there's the village fête coming up and I actually had thoughts that I could use Mum's studio and some of the fruit and veg from the garden and make some chutneys and jams and have a stall and . . . and . . .' She was babbling nervously now, because Connor staring at her was unnerving. He had never looked at her like that before, well, just the once, and that was not long after she had done what she had done.

'What about your job?'

'I work for myself now. Have done for a while. I can work from home.'

His brows furrowed for a moment and she wanted to reach out to him, to undo the hurt she'd caused. But that was impossible.

'Well . . . that's just great, isn't it, Emma? Just great. Well bloody done. After everything, you're going to come home to Little Bramble?'

'No. I mean, I don't know. Perhaps. And just for my dad because he needs me. I didn't say permanently . . . it's just that I don't know what to do for the best. I'm not even sure I *will* stay longer but I have to give it some thought.'

'You do that, Emma, because your dad's a good man and he deserves to have people who love him around.'

Emma felt very small and sad standing next to Connor She had hoped he would be over what had happened but it seemed that some of his pain still simmered just below the surface and her return had affected him. If only she could do something to help make things better.

'I'm going to leave now, Emma, before I say something I'll regret. I feel so angry with you that I can't stand to look at you.' He went to the door then paused. 'But you know what? I have to say this: it's a damned shame you didn't decide to stay all those years ago because you'd have saved a lot of people from a lot of pain.'

His voice cracked on the final word, then he opened his mouth as if to say more before shaking his head and stomping away, leaving Emma alone with only the ghosts of what might have been to torment her.

Chapter 14

Connor slammed the front door behind him and kicked off his boots then threw his keys on the floor. His whole body was trembling and he felt terrible. He rarely got angry, never showed it if he did, because he knew that anger got him nowhere. And yet being around Emma had brought the old raw anger back, along with a fierce attraction that still burned inside him and he didn't know how to deal with any of it.

'Dad?' Grace was at the top of the stairs. 'What's wrong?'

She padded down the stairs towards him in her socks and yoga gear, her face a mask of concern.

He sucked in a deep breath and tried to pull himself together. The thought of his daughter seeing him like this was dreadful. In all the years he'd had to deal with Sadie's nonsense, he'd never once allowed anger to get the better of him.

'Come and sit down and I'll get you some water.'

Grace took his hand and led him through to the kitchen then pressed him into a chair while she got a glass and filled it. She handed it to him.

'Is that OK or do you need something stronger?'

'This is fine.'

He gulped the water down then set the glass on the table.

'Is it Mum? Has she gone too far this time?'

Grace pulled a chair up next to his and sat down, taking his hand.

'I know she's hard work sometimes and I'd be lying if I said she didn't frustrate *me* but I always take deep breaths and try to let what she says float over my head. She doesn't mean half of it, I'm sure, and it's just not worth getting into arguments over. I know I used to argue back when I was younger but you taught me to stay calm and I'm so glad you did, because losing your temper gets you nowhere. I can't control other people – but I can control my reactions to them.'

Connor looked into his daughter's eyes and forced a small smile to his lips. She was wrong about the source of his anger, but right about how he should deal with it.

'It's not your mum.'

Grace nodded. 'That's a relief. But then who upset you? You're always so cool and calm.'

He shook his head. 'It doesn't matter.'

'It does to me. You're upset and I love you and I want to help.'

He sighed, wishing he could head up to bed and hide under the duvet, forget about everything until the morning.

'Please, Dad. I might be able to help you know?'

He cleared his throat and took her hand between both of his.

'I guess you're old enough now.'

'Old enough for what?'

'To hear about my past.'

'Before Mum?'

He nodded. 'Before your mum and I got together, there was someone else.'

'I know.'

'You know?'

'Kind of. I've seen photos at Nanna's from when you were younger.'

'Oh. I didn't know that.'

'She didn't show me them deliberately, but I asked to see some of your childhood photos and she showed me where the photograph albums were and I just went through them all. Your cute baby ones are there too and your teenage ones and those from your early twenties. There were lots of you with a really pretty woman with long, dark hair and so I asked Nanna who she was.'

'What did she tell you?'

'Just that she was called Emma, that she's the daughter of Greg and Dawn Patrick, and she was a close friend of yours for years. When I was younger that made sense, but as I got older, I realised that "close friend" could be a substitute for girlfriend.'

'You never said anything.'

Grace shrugged. 'What would be the point? Most people have other partners before they settle down.'

'I suppose they do.'

'Could you imagine if I'd settled down with some of my old boyfriends?' She giggled and rolled her eyes and Connor found himself smiling. She was right; none of the boys she'd dated growing up had seemed like they'd be right for her long-term.

'Emma was very special to me. My first love. We were together for years and then she went off to university and got a job in publishing. I was so proud of her – but also a bit jealous. I felt left behind and I was afraid she'd find someone more interesting and successful and leave me. I really loved her and wanted her to be happy in whatever she did, but I also wanted her with me. She, however, wanted to live in London, be at the heart of publishing.'

'Oh, Dad!' Grace squeezed his hand. 'I wish I could go back and give the old you a hug, but can you imagine how *she* must have felt?'

'I even proposed to her. I thought that if we got married she might feel differently.'

'How old were you?'

'Twenty-two.'

'Bloody hell, Dad, that's insane! You were younger than I am now and the last thing I want until I'm at least thirty is to get married.'

'Thirty, eh?'

'Yes. And even *that* seems young.'

'I'd prefer you to wait until you're forty at least.'

She tapped his arm. 'What happened when you proposed?'

'Emma accepted and we started to plan a party as well as to discuss a wedding.'

'Wow! Were your parents happy?'

'They were. It was a bit different back then and we'd been together for years and everyone got on so well. It seemed like the natural step.'

'Terrifying!' Grace's eyes widened.

'Why?'

'Well, there you were, so young and in love, but Emma had career aspirations and then you proposed. She must have been so torn. Couldn't you have gone to London with her?'

'I didn't want to. I had plans for my business here, based on expanding Dad's – and you know me, I'm not really a city dweller, am I?'

She shook her head. 'You like trees and fields and plenty of sky.'

'Exactly.'

'So you split up?'

'Emma didn't turn up to our engagement party. It was the worst night of my life.'

Grace gazed at him and her eyes filled with tears. 'That's so sad.'

'I was very sad, but then also very angry.'

They sat together for a few minutes as Connor tried to work out how to explain his feelings to Grace. She wiped at her cheeks as tears escaped and he passed her a tissue from the box on the table.

'Why are you telling me this now?' Grace asked eventually.

'Emma's back in the village.'

'Oh.'

'Her dad isn't well and he needs her here. I wasn't expecting to see her, although I knew deep down that one day she'd be back.'

'You haven't seen her at all since then?'

'She came back for her mum's funeral four years ago and for things like Christmas and so on, but I've managed to avoid her.'

'You never looked her up on social media? You know, to check out her profile, find out if she's still hot?' She nudged him, clearly trying to lighten the mood.

'Never. You know what I'm like with Facebook; I have a profile because of my business page and never check the actual timelines or notifications. Your mother used to do all that and even had my password for a while, so she used to post photos on my page. I had to change my password when she kept posting old photos of me and her together because people kept asking if we were back together.'

'Yikes!'

'Anyway, I'm struggling a bit with my anger towards Emma.'

'That's understandable, Dad. You loved her but she rejected you. You must have been devastated.' Her mouth dropped open and her eyebrows rose. 'Is *that* why you and Mum got together?'

Connor froze. How could she have guessed that?

'It is, isn't it? Mum was your rebound relationship. Now it all makes perfect sense!'

'It does?'

'You two were never suited and everyone knows that a rebound relationship isn't a good idea.'

'Do they?' Connor's heart was pounding and he felt nauseous.

'Yes!' Grace nodded furiously. 'And anger is a natural defence mechanism when you've been hurt. It's a way of building a protective layer around yourself and probably feels a lot better than sadness.'

'It does.' He'd thought this so many times.

'So don't blame yourself, Dad. You went through a lot. But, you know what?'

'What?'

'I don't think you should blame Emma, either. She had ambition and drive and wanted to find herself. Would you blame me for wanting freedom now to discover the world, to follow my career? Yes, she was wrong to hurt you as she did. And yes, she could have done things more gently, or even spoken to you and you could have found a way through things together. But you were both very young and how many people in their early twenties have that much common sense? It's all about strong emotions and passion and acting on impulse. If it had happened later in life, you'd have dealt with it differently, been more likely to compromise. Sounds to me like you were both too pig-headed and wanted your own way.'

Connor didn't know what to say. Grace had her sights set on her career and her future and she'd never wanted to settle down. In many ways, she reminded him of Emma and how focused she had been on her career goals. It was ironic, he knew, that while in Emma he had found this single-mindedness difficult to accept when it had impinged upon their relationship, with his daughter he was glad of it because he wanted her to achieve her dreams before she even *thought* about settling down. Where had this incredibly wise and wonderful woman come from? She was also 100 per cent right. He wouldn't blame Grace for any of those things, would do his best to support and advise her, and so, looking back, how could he blame twenty-two-year-old Emma? She'd been younger than his daughter was now.

'Thank you, Grace,' he said when he could speak.

'No problem, Dad. I'm just glad I'm still here to help you. Imagine if this had happened a few weeks or months down the line. You'd have had to deal with it all on your own – and from the looks of things you'd be in a right old pickle.'

She stood up and gave him a hug then filled the kettle.

'You need a mug of tea and a slice of cake. It will make you feel better and help you think straight.'

He nodded, keen to go along with whatever his daughter suggested. At the moment, it seemed, she really did know best.

187

Emma stood in the studio, hugging herself after Connor stormed off, trembling, her heart racing. Tears had burned her eyes but she'd refused to let them fall. This was not the time for weakness. The anger Connor had displayed during their final meeting all those years ago clearly still burned hot.

But as sad as that made her, she also felt a sense of relief because she'd always expected him to react that way if they ever spoke again. His initial calm at The Lumber Shed had surprised her, so the anger was, in some ways, easier to handle, because it seemed like a more normal reaction.

Rather than stand in the studio feeling sorry for herself, she decided to get busy, so put her trainers on and headed to the village shop to pick up some lemons and bags of sugar, then returned home and put on an old T-shirt and shorts and went outside.

In the studio, she located the large plastic bowls her mum had used for fruit and took them out to the garden, filling them with all the strawberries, raspberries and redcurrants she could find. She washed them under the outside tap then strained them well then let them dry in the sun.

Back in the studio, she set her mum's equipment on the worktop and stared at it, hands on hips. She'd seen her mum do this so many times, helped her when she was a child, but she'd never done it alone and suddenly it felt daunting. But she was forty-nine, a capable woman, and she could do anything she put her mind to, couldn't she?

Besides which, she needed to keep busy to forget about Connor and the worries about her dad.

She picked her mum's recipe book up off the table and flicked through the pages to find a basic strawberry jam recipe. The flickering of the pages sent a shiver down her spine. Every recipe inside had been handwritten by her mum and used by her and that made them even more special. The strawberry jam recipe looked straightforward enough, so she'd give it a go.

She brought the bowls of strawberries inside then patted them dry with some kitchen roll and hulled them, taking her time, enjoying their sweet scent and popping the smaller ones into her mouth as she worked. They really were the delicious taste of summer: fresh, sweet and organic.

When the strawberries were ready, she tossed through 750g of the sugar then set them aside. The recipe said to do this for at least twelve hours, so she'd have to continue tomorrow.

Turning the pages of the book, she found the recipe for raspberry jam. This one she could get on with. First, she needed to sterilise the jars and put a small plate into the freezer to chill.

Half an hour later, after another cup of tea and a quick chat with her dad, she tipped half the raspberries into a large pan then added the juice of a lemon and mashed it all up with a stainless-steel potato masher. When it was pulpy, she placed it on the Aga hotplate and let it cook for five minutes. This wasn't so bad, she thought, and as long as she followed the recipe step by step, she should be fine.

The next step involved pressing the pulp through a sieve, discarding the seeds and putting the juice and berries back on the heat with the sugar and the rest of the raspberries. She hummed as she worked, a Carpenters' medley, feeling quite happy with herself that she was doing so well. She brought the jam to the boil, keeping an eye on it, then a noise from the garden caught her attention.

'Emma?'

'Yes, Dad?'

She went to the open doorway and smiled at him.

'I can't find my glasses. Have you seen them?'

'They're on your head, Dad.'

He reached up and patted the glasses then rolled his eyes. 'I was reading, then I went to the lavatory, and when I returned to the lounge I couldn't find them anywhere.'

'Easily done.'

'What's that smell?' He grimaced. 'Is something burning?'

'Damn it!' Emma turned and ran into the studio, grabbed the pan and moved it off the heat but it was too late; the jam had boiled over and sickly-sweet smoke filled the air while dark red jam congealed on the top of the Aga.

'Burnt the jam, did you?' Her dad was right behind her, peering at the damage.

'It was going so well!'

'Don't worry, it happened to your mum endless times. All it takes is a momentary distraction and the jam can boil over and burn. Takes ages to clean it off the pan and Aga top too.'

'Thanks, Dad!'

He chuckled. 'I'll give you a hand if you like. I have lots of experience. Used to clean up after your mum all the time. She was a good cook but she was terribly messy.'

'Really? I don't remember that.'

'Oh yes.' He squeezed her shoulder.

'That's funny. I never knew that about her.'

'She had me there to tidy up after her so I guess you never saw the chaos she could leave behind.'

'You were such a good team.'

'We were.'

'But how on earth will you get this off?'

'Vinegar and baking soda. Works like a charm.'

He turned and ambled out of the studio and Emma shook her head. She was learning new things about her dad every day and he was surprising her in many wonderful ways. It was like getting to know him all over again, but as an adult this time, and she was grateful for the opportunity because he was an incredible person.

The day passed in a blur of jam-making, from the first disaster that her dad had miraculously managed to clean off the top of the Aga and the pan, to another three better attempts that had resulted in ten jars of raspberry jam and eight jars of redcurrant. Emma was proud of what she'd achieved and her dad seemed excited about the idea of having home-made jam on toast for breakfast again.

Jars safely stored in the cupboards of the studio, Emma cleaned up then checked on the strawberries that she intended using the next day. She had plenty of jars left because her mum always kept them to reuse and Dilys and a few other neighbours had brought their used jars round too. It was, Emma realised, an early form of neighbourhood recycling and pride in her mum filled her heart. There was a lot to be learnt from older generations – it was a shame that it often took getting older for people to realise it, she thought ruefully.

When she fell into bed that night, following a long soak in the bath, she was exhausted and sank into a deep sleep, images of sweet red fruits floating through her mind along with thoughts of the stall she could have at the village fête.

Chapter 15

Emma got up extra early the next day to make the strawberry jam then showered and made her way to the train station. It had been nearly three weeks since she'd arrived at Little Bramble Station herself, but it felt like months. There had certainly been some ups and downs and she knew that she wasn't the same person she'd been when she'd arrived, but in spite of it all, she was glad to be home. It wasn't the first time Lucie had been to Little Bramble, so she knew what to expect of the small country village, and Emma was looking forward to her friend joining them and having her moral support.

As Lucie stepped off the train, it was like a scene from a movie that played out in slow motion: a gentle breeze caught the skirt of her scarlet midi dress and swirled it around her legs, her red toenails were framed by gold gladiator sandals and her blue-black hair shone in the sunlight. People turned to stare at her, mouths open, clearly wondering if she was a model or celebrity.

For as long as Emma had known her, Lucie had been showered with male attention, but shrugged it off like a silk shawl that she let float to the ground untended. She did that now, seemingly oblivious to the admiring glances, as she donned large sunglasses and walked straight towards Emma, one arm thrown wide for a hug as the other dragged her Louis Vuitton suitcase behind.

'Emma, darling, so good to see you!'

They hugged, double-cheek kissed, then Lucie stepped back and peered at Emma over the top of her glasses.

'How are things?'

'Things are OK. Not perfect, but OK.'

Even if Emma was worried about her dad and sad that Connor had been angry yesterday, she was still glad to see Lucie. In fact, it was as if a refreshing sea breeze had come to Little Bramble with the train and she felt a touch of her London life washing over her, reminding her that she was an adult, in control and capable of running her own life. It was so easy to drift back towards the girl she had been years ago and to forget that she had forged a whole life since then.

She held out her hand. 'Let me pull your case for you.'

Lucie cocked an eyebrow. 'What, and let me waste the chance to weight bear while we walk back to yours? Not a chance, doll! I have guns to tone.'

She hooked her free arm through Emma's and they strolled back to the cottage together. Something about having Lucie with her made Emma feel more confident, more self-assured. Lucie knew the adult version of her, had been her friend for over twenty years. She hadn't been there when Emma had done what she had to Connor, hadn't seen the devastation she left in her wake when she first moved to London – and even when Emma had told her, Lucie hadn't judged her for it. Lucie was Emma's support network, just as Emma was for Lucie. They had each other's backs and she believed they always would.

'How d'you feel about being back?' Lucie asked as they walked.

'Not bad. It's nice being here for Dad and I can see how much it means to him to have me here. He seems to pick up a bit with company, as well as good food and plenty of tea and water. Dehydration can make his symptoms worse so I'm keeping an eye on his fluid intake.'

'And have you . . . you know . . . bumped into anyone else?'

'Yes.'

'Really?' Lucie stopped suddenly, causing Emma to sway before she found her balance. 'You've seen Connor? And how is he?'

Emma swallowed. 'He's . . . angry.'

'At you?' Lucie frowned.

'Yes.'

'Well, he has no right to be angry. It was a whole adult life ago.'

'He kind of does have the right and we haven't exactly been in contact over the years, so he hasn't had the chance to vent.'

Lucie blew upwards and her short fringe parted, revealing her smooth forehead.

'I understand that he might have some things he wants to say, but he shouldn't still be holding on to anger like that. It's really bad for his health.'

'Try telling him that. Anyway, he did me a favour, he fixed Mum's rocking chair.'

'He fixed it for you?'

'Yes.'

'Still good with his hands?' She waggled her eyebrows then gave an exaggerated wink.

'He has a successful carpentry business now. He's done well for himself.'

'And so have you.' Lucie squeezed Emma's arm.

'I know. In different ways. But he seemed OK with seeing me then he got a bit angry when he asked if I intended on staying in the village. I said I might, to which he responded that I could have avoided hurting a lot of people if I'd stayed years ago!'

'Ouch!' Lucie grimaced. 'Seems like he's still hurting.'

'And that makes me feel awful. How can I be the source of all that pain? I must be such a terrible person.'

'Oh, honey, you're not responsible for that. You made a decision that you thought was for the best, but you never meant to hurt anyone. Imagine if you'd stayed, got married and had children and then a few years down the line decided that you couldn't live like that? More people would have been hurt – or worse, you'd have lived a half-life, unhappy and unfulfilled. We do things when we do them for reasons that seem right. You have to forgive yourself and move on.'

Emma stared into Lucie's eyes, drawing strength from her friend. She knew Lucie was right because if she had stayed and pretended everything was fine, it could have all imploded further down the line and she and Connor might have ended up resenting each other even more than he already did her. There was no way of turning back the clock, anyway. There was only the here and now.

'I know.' She nodded.

'How did he look?' Lucie's eyes widened with interest.

'Really good, actually.'

'What, good for a middle-aged man or good hot?'

Emma laughed. 'Lucie!'

'Oh, come on, surely you were interested in finding out?'

'OK, he's hot. Always was.'

'Then there's still a spark? All hope is not lost then.'

'What?' Emma spluttered. 'I'm not about to try to win him back.'

'Emma, I have known you for a long time and I know that you still have feelings for that man.'

'He's with someone.' Her stomach lurched as she thought of seeing Connor and Sadie together.

'Is he? Are you sure?'

'Well . . . no, but I saw them together outside a cottage in the village and she had a thing for him growing up and–'

She held back on telling Lucie about the Facebook photos she'd seen. It was her secret shame and she didn't want anyone to know about it.

'And nothing. If he's still hurting then he still has feelings for you.'

'I'm a forty-nine-year-old woman not the fifteen-year-old girl he fell in love with or the twenty-two-year-old who hurt him. There's been a lot of water under the bridge since then. We're different people now. I think he also has a grown-up daughter.'

'I see.' Lucie nodded. 'So you've both moved on, but . . . first love never dies.'

'How would you know?'

'I know.' Lucie winked. 'I'll tell you about it sometime.'

'I'm intrigued.'

'Come on, let's get to Greg's because I need caffeine and to wash the train off my hands and face. Even though there was aircon, I still feel sticky.'

'Thank you for coming.'

'I'm delighted to be here and if I can help you and Connor find a way through this sorry mess, then I'll feel a whole lot better leaving you here. Not that there's anything wrong with Little Bramble, you know, as far as country villages go, it's very sweet but it's not for me.'

'You wait.'

'Until what?'

'You'll change your mind when you want somewhere for the little one.'

'Don't you start! You sound just like Phoebe. Oh God, and just thinking about that makes me feel queasy. It's too early to do a test yet but she's desperate to. I'm glad I've come away for a bit of space because the tension is driving me crazy. Being at home is like walking a tight-rope in stilettos.'

'It sounds tough. Phoebe didn't mind you coming?'

'Not at all. She practically kicked me out the door. She's as tense as I am and can't even have a glass of wine to take the edge off, poor love.'

'Well, *you* can while you're here and I'm sure some time out will help both of you.'

'I hope so, darling, I really do. And it's a BIG yes to wine!'

They giggled as they made their way through the village and Emma found herself picturing a future different to the one she'd had in mind, one where she could live in Surrey with her dad and where Lucie and Phoebe could raise a child locally with Emma as an honorary aunt. Perhaps it was being on the cusp of fifty, or perhaps it was being back in the village, but something inside her was definitely changing – or was it evolving? Whichever, she didn't seem to mind.

Connor had barely slept. He felt so awful about the way he'd spoken to Emma, especially since Grace had made him consider Emma's perspective in more detail. He was also having trouble accepting that he still felt angry. Years had passed and they'd both moved on. If Emma had stayed in Little Bramble, then he wouldn't have had Grace, might not have thrown himself into his business and made it so successful. Things could have been very different and he'd have missed out on a lot. As might Emma. Life had taken the course it had and he needed to let go of the past. He would go through what he had a thousand times to have Grace and, in a strange way, Emma was responsible for that. If she hadn't left, then he wouldn't have fallen into Sadie's arms and he'd have missed out on being a father to such a wonderful human being.

Every cloud had a silver lining and Grace was a sparkling one, with stars and rainbows. He had learnt so much about himself and about people through becoming a father and he got so much enjoyment out of being around Grace. Even though he'd not loved Sadie as he'd wanted to, moments like that first time he held Grace in his arms and she blinked her grey eyes at him were some of the best of his life. Rocking her to sleep in the early hours of the morning when Sadie was exhausted from trying to breastfeed had been special times for him and his daughter and pushing her on the swings at the park on sunny days while she asked him questions that made him laugh were etched on his mind like sunbeams. Later, taking photos as she twirled in her graduation outfit then threw her mortarboard high in the air, had brought tears of joy to his eyes.

Whatever he had lost when Emma walked out of his life had been replaced by a love that was far more straightforward, far easier to understand, far more than he had ever wished for. It was a very different kind of love.

Connor had thought to have both types of love, as both husband and father, when he'd dreamt of a future with Emma, hoped that one day they'd share children that they'd love and adore, young people they would send out into the world. It hadn't happened that way but he would never have any regrets because Grace was perfect. His love for his daughter was strong, pure and enduring. He had to remember this when his old feelings about Emma tried to cloud his mind, to affect his judgement. Grace was everything.

He felt a need to go to see Emma and apologise. He didn't want her feeling awkward now she was back in the village because Greg needed her and Connor could not be the reason she left again. She had every right to stay in Little Bramble and he had to be an adult about it.

He'd have a quick shave and shower then pop to the shop and pick something up to drop off at Greg's as an apology. Wasn't it sunflowers she used to like? And dark chocolate? No. They would seem too romantic, given their history. He'd get a bottle of wine for her and Greg to enjoy together. That was a safer idea. A gift like that would show her that there were no hard feelings and he was fine about everything. *Absolutely fine.*

He jogged upstairs to the bathroom, trying to push away the sensation of anticipation in his belly at the thought of seeing Emma again. Grown-up Emma, with her cute hair, her womanly shape and her beautiful eyes. The woman who had slipped into the place that had belonged to the girl . . .

'Well, this is a delicious lunch, Greg.' Lucie smiled across the table at Emma's father.

'It's nothing fancy.' He shrugged but Emma could see the glow in his cheeks and how he sat up a bit straighter at the compliment. 'Just mashed potato with cheese and tomatoes on top.'

'The tomatoes are yummy. They have so much flavour.'

'Grown in the garden,' Emma said, picturing the tomato plants in the raised bed outside of the greenhouse that had grown in the nearly three weeks since she'd arrived. She hadn't recognised the plants at first but the sunny days had boosted their growth and the small yellow flowers had given way to red tomatoes. The raised beds were rich with things that could be eaten or would soon be ready to eat and she knew now that it was because Dilys had helped her dad. One morning, as they'd sat on the bench sipping tea and eating hot buttered toast, he'd told her that Dilys had said it would be good for him to spend some time in the garden, though his hands made it harder than it used to be.

Lucie had nearly cleared her plate and Emma was a bit surprised to see her friend wolfing down the carbs and cheese. She was always so body conscious that she was usually very careful about what she ate, but perhaps the country air had hit her already and increased her appetite.

Lucie caught Emma watching her and waved her fork at her plate. 'I'm on holiday, so I'm giving the diet a rest as well.'

'Glad to hear it.' Emma smiled.

'You girls and your diets!' Greg shook his head. 'Not an ounce of fat on either of you. Don't you know by now that men like a few curves to snuggle up to?'

Emma coughed as a piece of tomato lodged in her throat and Lucie patted her back.

'Dad, that may or may not be the case, but Lucie couldn't care less about what men think.'

He put his fork down, his brow furrowed. 'Oh . . . of course. I'm sorry, Lucie, I forgot for a minute there. I should have said that many men *and* women like women with curves.' He chuckled and colour filled his cheeks. 'I do forget sometimes. Apologies.'

'Not at all, Greg. It's fine, honestly.' Lucie sipped her water.

Once Lucie had helped herself to seconds and they'd finished eating, Emma took the plates to the sink and ran the hot tap.

'There's a cracking movie on TV this afternoon on that Netflix thingy Emma got for me,' said Greg.

'It's fab, isn't it?' Emma said. 'So much choice.'

'Incredible. I could sit there all day in front of it.'

'You do know that you can watch the films at any time though, Dad? That's the point, it's available when you want to watch it.'

'Is it now?' He frowned. 'Well, that's clever, isn't it? Your mum would have been delighted with that. Do you remember when you were little, Emma? We had just three TV channels through the seventies.' He shook his head and released a long sigh.

Emma started to wash up.

'And some of the programmes were just brilliant. Remember *Are You Being Served*, *Blake's Seven* and *Crossroads*, Emma?'

'I do, Dad.'

'I remember *Crossroads*,' Lucie said. 'And what about *Grange Hill*? That was a good series.'

'I loved *Grange Hill*.' Emma nodded, thinking about how Connor had loved it too.

'And your mum's favourite of the eighties was *Dempsey and Makepeace*. I think she had a secret crush on Michael Brandon.' He chuckled.

'Yes, and not so secret!' Emma smiled, enjoying listening to her dad reminiscing. Surely it must be good for him to talk about memories, to remember happy times? The thought that when he was here alone, he'd have had no one to speak to about these things made her feel sad and strengthened her resolve to stay around for longer.

'What film's on Netflix?' Lucie asked.

'Uhhh . . . something about an apocalypse and a search for a cure, I think,' Greg said.

Emma's mind flashed back to her thoughts that night as she wandered around Tesco Extra in her pyjamas. It felt like such a long time ago.

'Sounds good to me.' Lucie got up. 'How about I make some tea and we can take the packets of biscuits Phoebe sent for you and have an afternoon in front of the TV?'

'Biscuits and tea sounds perfect.' Emma's dad clapped his hands.

Emma turned back to the sink and ran the brush over the plate in her hand. Seeing her dad looking forward to something like that served as a reminder of how lonely he must have been since her mum had died. Hell, she'd seen the adverts on TV about how many elderly people were affected by loneliness and isolation, and yet she'd ignored the fact that her dad was probably feeling that way. She'd comforted herself that he was a member of a friendly community, not living in a high-rise flat where he'd struggle to climb the stairs, or face the risk of being mugged every time he went through the front door. People in Little Bramble looked out for their neighbours and the elderly always had someone to call on them. But even so, her dad wasn't the type of person to impose upon anyone and she knew that if any of his neighbours had asked if he needed help, he'd have insisted that he was fine. Greg Patrick was a proud and independent man and he would hate to put on anyone.

Half an hour later, they were in the lounge, curtains drawn against the afternoon sunshine, TV on with tea and biscuits in front of them. Emma and Lucie sat on the sofa, feet curled up under them, while her dad sat in his armchair and Emma felt herself really relaxing. There was nothing to do this afternoon other than sit, binge-watch TV and eat the delicious biscuits that Phoebe had sent with Lucie.

So when the doorbell rang, Emma jumped in surprised and almost spilt her tea.

Connor stood on Emma's doorstep for the second time in two days with his stomach churning and his heart pounding. He moved the bottle of white wine from one hand to the other and wiped his palm on his jeans then swapped hands and repeated the process.

He stepped back as the door opened and held up the wine almost like a shield as Emma stood there gazing up at him.

'Connor.' The colour drained from her cheeks. 'I-I wasn't expecting you.'

'No. No, you weren't.' He licked his lips. 'I came to apologise.'

She frowned then ran a hand over her hair. 'Oh?'

'Yes . . . for . . . uh . . . yesterday. I was out of line and I didn't mean to be so rude.'

She shook her head. 'It's fine, honestly. You had every right to say what you did.'

'I had *no* right. What happened was a very long time ago and we don't even know each other anymore. I shouldn't have let old feelings come to the surface like that.'

'Maybe I deserved it.'

'Not after all this time. If you hadn't gone like you did, I wouldn't have ended up living the life I am now and I have to be grateful for that.'

Something that looked like hurt flickered over her features and confusion filled him. What had he said that could possibly hurt her?

'You're grateful?'

'I wasn't back then . . . but I have so much to be grateful for and some of it is because we split up. So . . .' He extended his arm so the wine was closer to her. 'This is for you and Greg.'

'Thank you.' She took the wine and held it with both hands.

'Anyway . . .' He glanced behind her, seeing someone loitering in the shadows of the hallway. A woman with a dark bob and what looked like a large chocolate chip cookie in her hand. 'I'll see you around.'

'OK.'

Emma nodded then stepped back and closed the door, leaving Connor feeling a bit lost. But then, what had he expected to happen? He'd been so rude the previous day, and Emma had every right to be perplexed at his arrival with wine in hand. They were strangers to each other now. He'd thought they had known each other so well but now, thinking about it with the advantage of hindsight, he wondered if they really had.

After all, if he'd known her as well as he'd thought he did, then he'd have anticipated that a big engagement party was not what she wanted or needed, would have read her hesitation when he'd proposed more clearly, have taken note of it rather than ignored it because he didn't want to think for a second that she might not want to get married, had another life entirely in her sights and that the idea of staying in this country village with him for the rest of their lives held no appeal for her. He'd chosen to be blind back then because he had an image of the life *he* wanted in his head and he'd been guilty of not listening to her properly, of not reading her reactions and understanding that the futures they wanted were not the same.

He turned and trudged away, his shoulders slumped and his feet so heavy it was hard to lift them. Not only did he feel bad for his actions in the past, he was also aware that he was still very attracted to Emma, that she still had a hold over his heart, a hold he'd believed she'd destroyed a long time ago. It seemed that letting go of the one who got away wasn't as easy as he might want it to be.

Chapter 16

'Where are we going again?' Lucie asked as she checked her appearance in the hall mirror then applied more peachy lip gloss.

'The King's Arms.' Emma slid her arms into the sleeves of her denim jacket. It was a warm evening but would be cooler later when they walked home and she needed to get out for a few hours. After seeing Connor again, she'd been all churned up but had done her best to hide it from Lucie and her dad. Connor's anger she had understood and even felt she deserved, but his apology, the emotion in his eyes when he'd stood on her doorstep and handed her the wine, had almost been her undoing. How could she still have a fondness for him after so long? Or was it more than a fondness? It was as if she had kidded herself that she didn't care about him anymore when, in reality, her feelings for him had been on hold and now that she'd seen him, been near him again, she was unsettled and off-kilter.

'Not the Red Squirrel?'

'We can go there if you like but I fancied the King tonight.'

Lucie laughed. 'That sounds funny. You fancied the king.'

Emma rolled her eyes, grateful for the distraction that Lucie offered. 'Ha! Yes, very amusing. Are you ready?'

'Think so.'

Lucie smoothed down her glossy bob then smiled. 'Let's go.'

Emma stuck her head through the doorway into the lounge. 'You sure you don't need anything else now, Dilys?'

'I'm positive, Emma. You two have a lovely evening.'

Emma looked at her dad and smiled. He was OK; she could leave him here and not feel guilty. She'd only be gone a few hours at most. He had a cup of tea in his hand and was nibbling on a chocolate brownie that Lucie had made that afternoon. His eyes were glued to the TV screen while he watched a documentary about canoeing along the Ardèche.

'Now that's something I'd like to do,' he said to no one in particular then sipped his tea. 'It looks incredibly relaxing, doesn't it, Dilys?'

'Oh, it does, Greg.' Dilys sat on the sofa, hands folded over her ample bosom. 'Shall we book for next summer and we can get in some of that cliff jumping too?'

Greg chuckled. 'Absolutely! It looks like such fun, doesn't it? Although a few of the people who were standing on the rocks as the cameraman passed seemed to be wearing very small trunks.'

Dilys let out a loud snort. 'Greg, you are funny! They're naked.'

'Naked?' He raised his eyebrows and sat forwards, his eyes now glued to the TV. 'How is that allowed?'

'It's permitted in France.'

'Well, I say.' He shook his head. 'So we don't even need to pack our swimwear?'

'I certainly will, Greg. I'll be wearing a Victorian onesie.'

'Not your birthday suit?' They laughed together and Emma's heart lifted.

'See you later, Dad.'

He waved without removing his gaze from the TV. 'Have fun, girls.'

'Thanks, Dilys.' She gave her a thumbs up and Dilys returned it. When she'd arrived earlier, Dilys had told Emma that she thought Greg seemed a lot perkier and it was music to Emma's ears.

Emma closed the front door and followed Lucie out onto the pavement.

'I wish he'd wanted to come,' she said.

'I know.' Lucie nodded. 'But it looked like he was enjoying himself. If I'm honest, even more so once he knew there were naked people on the TV.'

Emma giggled. 'Stop it! That is not something anyone wants to think about when it involves their parents. I mean, he's eighty-four. But no, apart from when he played with his band, he never was one for going out that much. Occasionally, he'd enjoy a quiet pint or two with a friend or bandmate, but most of the time he preferred to stay in with Mum, watch TV and take it easy.'

'We're all different.' Lucie shrugged. 'And at his age, he should do exactly what he wants. Besides which, I think Dilys was glad to have him to herself for a few hours.'

'She's been a good friend and neighbour to him. If she hadn't been there . . .' Emma's voice wavered.

'Don't beat yourself up.' Lucie took her arm. 'Yes, Dilys is lovely and yes, thank goodness that she was there but you're home now and Greg's lucky to have you.'

'Do you really think so, Lucie? I feel like I've let him down.'

'Well, you haven't, so there!' Lucie poked out her tongue. 'And we're only going to be gone for a few hours, so let's go and let our hair down a bit, shall we? My life has been one round after another of hormone injections, healthy eating and mood swings, so I'm glad to have the chance to go to a cosy country pub and drink wine with my bestie.'

Emma frowned. 'You weren't taking the fertility drugs, having to abstain from alcohol or suffering the mood swings. That was all Phoebe, wasn't it?'

'Well, in theory, yes, but I stopped drinking out of sympathy – apart from the odd vino or cocktail when I was with you, and yes, she was the one taking the drugs, but I was there with her for the rest of it.' She waved a hand as if to dismiss it all. 'I love Phoebe with all of my heart. She's the best thing that's ever happened to me and I hope with everything I am that the test is positive. However, just for tonight and the sake of my sanity, I want to forget about it. I am away with you and we need this time together.'

'Then let's away to the pub and don't spare the horses!'

Emma made a conscious effort to let go of her worries about her dad and her thoughts about Connor and to focus on having some fun with Lucie. Sometimes, letting go, even if just for a brief time, was the only way to survive.

Connor stood at the bar, bottle of beer in one hand, the other tucked into his pocket. He couldn't believe it was here: Grace's last night in Little Bramble before she left for her new life in Paris. He'd arranged with Sadie for Grace to arrive after seven so he could get everything organised. His mum was there along with Sadie's parents and a few of Grace's local friends. They'd kept the gathering small because they didn't want Grace to be overwhelmed. This was about giving her a good send-off and not making her feel emotional or guilty. He hoped Sadie would remember that too.

'The buffet is ready in the back room,' his mum said as she came and stood next to him. 'Is this mine?' She pointed at the gin and tonic on the bar.

'It is indeed.'

'Thanks, love.' She took a sip. 'Perfect!' Then she frowned. 'What's wrong?'

'Sorry?'

'You're scowling.'

213

'Am I?'

'You are. Is it because Grace is leaving tomorrow?'

His stomach flipped and he set his beer down on the bar, worried he'd squeeze the bottle too tight and it would shatter in his grip.

'I'm going to miss her, obviously, but I want her to go . . . to get away from here and never let anything hold her back.' The irony of his words wasn't lost on him. He'd thought more about what had happened between him and Emma all those years ago and preparing for Grace's departure was bringing a lot back.

'There's something else on your mind, isn't there?' His mum placed a cool hand on his arm. 'I've thought so for a few days now. It's clear today that this is about more than Grace.'

Just then, the pub door opened and he tensed, ready to greet Grace and Sadie, but it wasn't them. Instead, it was a very familiar face.

'Oh!' His mum squeezed his arm. 'Now I get it.'

Emma had been laughing all the way there but as she entered the pub and her eyes fell on Connor and his mother Zoe, the smile dropped from her lips and she froze. Lucie was right behind her and she crashed into her, sending Emma staggering forwards, arms flailing. She managed to stop herself falling flat on her face but not before she'd done a good impression of an aeroplane and bit the tip of her tongue, tasting blood.

'Emma!' Lucie grabbed her shoulders and pulled her backwards into a hug. 'Are you OK? I'm so sorry, I didn't realise that you'd stopped.'

'I'm fine.' Emma touched her tongue tentatively against her front teeth. 'Just bit my tongue.'

'You need a strong drink to take the pain away.' Lucie pulled her purse from her bag. 'My treat.'

Lucie marched towards the bar, oblivious to the two people standing staring at them as if they had two heads apiece.

'Come on, Em!'

Emma dragged in a deep breath then followed her friend, lowering her gaze from Connor and Zoe and instead moving it to Lucie's hair, trying to focus on how the bob was inverted with stylish shorter layers at the back that showed off Lucie's slender neck, trying to ignore the thudding of her heart and the sweat that slicked her palms.

When she reached Lucie's side, she raised her eyes to look at Connor and his mother. He offered a small, polite smile, but Zoe glared at Emma as if she'd just farted loudly, blamed Zoe then laughed about it. Of course, when they'd been teenagers, that had been one of Connor's tricks, not Emma's, and she'd always been mortified as he farted in the hallway then blamed Emma, leaving her worried that his parents thought she was really quite bad-mannered and suffered from chronic flatulence.

'Hello, Emma.' Zoe stepped around Lucie, glass in one hand, the other holding her bag. 'Long time no see.'

'Hello, Zoe.' Emma inclined her head. 'Connor.'

'Hi.' He smiled but his eyes were filled with worry.

Emma glanced at the glass in Zoe's hand, wondering if she was about to throw it over her head. She wouldn't have blamed her, but she wasn't looking forward to it. Who would?

'Nice to see you.' Zoe's face moved into what could have been a smile, but her eyes and her voice were ice-cold and Emma actually shivered in spite of the warm evening.

'You too.' Emma nodded then watched as Zoe stalked around her and Lucie and towards the double doors that led to the function room.

'Everything OK?' Connor asked.

'I think so.' Emma's eyes followed his mother. 'But if looks could kill . . .'

He gave a wry laugh. 'She's just surprised to see you. She'll come around.'

The doors opened again and Connor turned quickly to see who'd entered.

'Better go.'

Emma watched as he hurried over to the two women who'd just entered. One was about twenty-something, very pretty and well dressed – the other was Sadie.

'What was all that about?' Lucie asked as she handed Emma a glass.

'Ancient feuds.' Emma shrugged, conscious of Sadie's eyes boring into her.

'Looks like the older of the two women who's just come in is as keen on you as the one who stormed away.'

Emma met Lucie's gaze and nodded. 'You can never escape the past, right?'

'I suppose not.' Lucie raised her glass. 'But you can move on and show them that you're a good person who's simply trying to live her life.'

They clinked glasses, then Emma sipped her drink, hoping the alcohol would make her feel braver. She had to fight the urge to down the double gin with clementine tonic in one and order for another. In fact, she'd like to request a line of shots then throw them back one after the other until the alcohol numbed the anxiety completely.

She glanced at Sadie and saw how her hand rested familiarly on Connor's arm, her body turned towards him possessively.

He's hers now.

What was that awful feeling? Was it *jealousy*? After all this time?

'Let's go and find a table and you can tell me why those two women seem to have it in for you. As well as why that very hot silver fox was gazing at you like you'd just promised him a snog at closing time.'

'What?' Emma laughed in spite of how anxious she felt.

'Oh yes . . . he looked like he wanted to walk you home and stop along the way to take you passionately in the hydrangea outside the pub.'

'Actually, Lucie, that was–'

'Oh no! That's not Connor?' Lucie's eyes were filled with horror.

'It is.'

Lucie cringed. 'Sorry. Didn't realise or I wouldn't have made that joke.'

'It's fine. At least one of us is able to maintain a sense of humour this evening.'

'Come on, let's go and sit down before we fall down. I don't know about you but I suddenly feel exhausted.'

Lucie led them to the table near the window and Emma tried not to let the way that Zoe had glared at her bring her down, tried not to care that Sadie had looked as though she was about to rush across the pub and rip Emma's hair out then wrestle her to the floor. Tried not to look again at the younger woman who resembled Sadie but who had something of Connor about her too. That must be his daughter – and seeing the three of them together for the first time was more difficult than she'd imagined it could be. She knew it could have been her standing there instead of Sadie. She could have had what Sadie had now.

*

'Thanks so much for this, Dad.' Grace beamed up at him in the function room.

'It's not much really, but we wanted to give you a bit of a send-off.' He wrapped an arm around her shoulders and smiled.

'It's perfect.'

'How're you feeling?' He watched her face carefully, wanting to absorb every detail from the chickenpox scar just above her left eyebrow to the tiny mole on her right earlobe. She was his baby girl and she was leaving. His life was going to be a whole lot emptier with her gone, but he was delighted that she was following her dreams.

'I'm really excited, Dad, but I am going to miss you so much. Mum, too.'

Grace hugged him with one arm, the other hand holding her glass of champagne. His mum had insisted on ordering a few bottles to celebrate her beloved grandchild's departure.

'We'll miss you, but you're doing the right thing, Grace. It will be an amazing time for you.'

She nodded but he noticed that she was chewing at her bottom lip. 'I'm a bit worried about how Mum's going to manage though.'

'She'll be fine. Your mum is tougher than she looks.' He swallowed hard, knowing that Sadie was tough but not convinced that she'd be fine at all.

'Are you sure?'

'Of course I am.'

'She said she might come and visit me.'

Connor stiffened. Sadie had already expressed her desire to go and see Grace in Paris? Why couldn't she let their daughter have some time alone, away from the pressures that Sadie brought with her?

'It's fine, Dad. I suggested it actually. Not right away, of course, I want to settle in first, but I do think that getting away from the village and her parents and the same old faces might actually be a positive move for Mum.'

Connor let Grace's words sink in and found himself agreeing. 'You're very wise, Grace.'

His daughter giggled. 'Thanks, Dad. I guess I take after my old man.'

He laughed and kissed the top of her head. 'Hey, you, less of the old!'

'So that was Connor.'

'Yup.'

'I know I've been here before but hadn't seen him because your visits home were fleeting and I've seen a few photos of him at your dad's, but he was late teens and early twenties then and not the handsome, mature chap I just laid eyes on.'

'How did you see photos?'

Lucie bit her bottom lip. 'There were some in your dad's music room in a drawer. He showed them to me once when he was showing off his guitars. Your mum was still around then.'

'I didn't know that.'

'He probably didn't want to upset you by letting you know he had kept them. You were in most of them too.'

Emma hadn't been aware that her dad had kept photos of her and Connor but then Connor had been a part of their family and it would have been sad to just throw all the photos away, to pretend all that time hadn't happened. Keen to push the thought away, she asked, 'What did you call him?'

'A silver fox.'

She liked Connor's grey hair but wondered what he thought of hers now it was short and light brown with gold highlights. Did he look at her and see her age or did he see the woman beneath it all, the one whose heart still beat hard with emotion, who still had hopes and dreams, who had done things she was proud of and some she regretted? Her well was deep. She looked like a woman who had lived, these days, no longer young with smooth skin and a firm, youthful body, but someone rich with life experience and knowledge. Not that she disliked her body now. It was softer, curvier, but still hers. Everything worked and she'd been lucky to have good health, with not so much as an appendix removal, but still, she was older, she had changed physically and mentally. But it was silly to wonder what Connor thought of her changed appearance. None of it mattered because Connor was with Sadie and so whatever niggling feelings Emma might be having were irrelevant.

'What is it?' Lucie was peering at her, concern etched on her features.

Emma realised that she was hugging herself, the pain in her chest caused by a sense of loss as it sunk in exactly how she and Connor had changed and how life had taken them along different paths.

'Just . . . remembering.'

Lucie reached for Emma's hand. 'I've got you.'

'Thanks. I just feel a bit adrift, getting used to being home, adjusting to the new norm.'

'There are plenty of ghosts here for you, I know, but at least now you finally have the chance to put them to rest.'

Emma downed the rest of her drink then stood up. 'You're right; and that's exactly what I'm going to do. Life is about moving on but it's also about learning lessons, reflecting and making the most of what you have. We're all perfectly imperfect.'

'I couldn't agree more. Our imperfections are what make us human. And it's always about making the most of what you have.'

'Let's drink to that. I'll get the next round in.'

At the bar, Emma waited while the barmaid served another customer, running her eyes over all the bottles, smiling as she recalled trying different spirits in here after she turned eighteen. There had been some good nights spent with Connor and their friends, filled with laughter and love, youthful exuberance and endless optimism. In some ways, it felt like a thousand years ago and yet . . . she also felt that if she closed her eyes she would be able to slip right back to the past and be right there with Connor.

'Falling asleep at the bar?' The whisper at her ear made a shiver run down her spine and she opened her eyes to find him smiling at her. He was so close she could smell his cologne and the warm scent of his skin, see the yellow flecks at the centre of his green eyes and two tiny hairs on his cheek that he'd missed while shaving. His brows and eyelashes were still dark though, framing eyes she'd gazed into many times.

'Oh! No . . . I was just remembering.'

'Anything pleasant?'

She gave a small laugh, knowing that trying to explain what she'd just been thinking would tie her up in knots.

'I've just come to get some more champagne. I can't believe how much they've got through in there.' He nodded at the function room.

'Celebrating something?'

'Yes. My daughter, Grace, is off to Paris tomorrow.'

Emma opened her mouth then closed it again, not sure which question to ask first. Instead she went for the easy option because she was fairly certain she already knew the answer.

'You have a daughter?'

'Grace. She's twenty-five. She's off to Paris to complete a post-grad course in fashion.'

Emma's mouth had gone dry and she struggled to swallow. 'Congrats.'

'On having a daughter or the fact that she's off to Paris?'

'Both. All of it. It's wonderful!' Emma was aware that her tone had become shrill and she nodded when the barmaid held up the glasses and asked if she wanted the same again. As soon as the drinks were served, she grabbed hers and gulped half of it down.

'Thirsty, eh?' Connor's eyebrows had risen up his forehead.

'Very. But . . . uh . . . congrats anyway. Is Grace yours and Sadie's?'

'Yes. I think you saw them come in together.'

'Lovely. Congrats,' she said again, unable to form any other words.

Emma smiled, feeling as though her teeth would crack because she was pressing them so tightly together, then she hurried back to the table, her legs stiff as wooden boards.

'What on earth is wrong, Emma?' Lucie stood up and took the drinks from her.

'Nothing.'

'You look like a ventriloquist's dummy, all wide eyes and forced smile.'

'Sit down. Don't look suspicious.'

'Why would I look suspicious? You're the one who looks unhinged right now.'

Emma glanced over at the bar. Connor was staring at them.

'He's still watching.'

'I saw you speaking to Connor but then you turned like someone had set a stick of dynamite under you and scuttled back over here.'

'I just had it confirmed that–'

'Don't look now but he's coming over.' Lucie froze as if they were playing musical statues and the tune had stopped.

'*What?*'

'Shhh. Now. Behind y—'

'Emma?'

She turned stiffly to find Connor standing next to her elbow.

'I just thought that it would be nice if you and . . .?' He smiled at Lucie.

'Lucie.'

'Hello, Lucie.' He shook her hand. 'I thought that it would be nice if you and Lucie came and joined us.'

'J-joined you?' Emma grabbed her drink and drained the glass.

'Yes. Well, with Grace heading off tomorrow there won't be another chance for you to meet for a while and I know Mum was a bit frosty earlier, but she does . . . *did* . . . *does* . . . like you. You and Mum always got on and what happened was all a long time ago and we should really all let bygones be bygones if you're staying in the village. Even if just for a bit and–'

'We'd love to join you.' It was Lucie who cut him off and Emma glanced at her, hoping to send a message with her eyes that this was not the reply she'd wanted to give to Connor.

'Great. Well, I'm going to grab the champagne from the bar and I'll see you in the function room?'

'Sure.' Emma grimaced as she turned back to Lucie. When Connor had gone, she muttered, 'Why did you agree to that?'

'I thought it would be a good plan. Like ripping off a plaster. Get the pain over and done with quickly, you know?'

'A plaster? More like tugging out stitches after major surgery. I just found out that the party they're having in the function room is a bon voyage for his twenty-something daughter.'

'He has a daughter?'

'Yes! With Sadie.'

'Is Sadie the woman you think he's with? The one who was glaring at you?'

'That's right. She was kind of a – a love rival, for want of a better description. She always liked Connor growing up and evidently made a move on him after I'd gone.'

'Ahhh . . .' Lucie's eyes were wide now and her cheeks had turned pink. 'Are you OK about this?'

Emma shrugged. 'How can I not be? It's not even any of my business. I'm surprised that neither of my parents ever told me what had happened with Connor after I left, but then, whenever I came home or they came to see me, Connor was the one topic we avoided like the plague.'

'They knew you'd find it hard.'

'And we had to avoid discussing him or we'd never have been able to have a relationship.'

'Because of the argument after you did the runaway fiancée thing?'

'Exactly.'

'Is he married to Sadie, then?'

'I don't know. I didn't notice a ring, so perhaps they're just living together.'

'How old is she?'

'Sadie?'

'No, the daughter!'

'Twenty-five.'

'Wow!'

'Older than I was when *I* left. It also means that they got together around three years after I left. No, sooner actually, because Sadie would have had to get pregnant so factor in nine months and that would whittle it down to just over two years for the conception so I'm guessing they got together a bit sooner than that.'

'Emma, don't overthink this. You'll drive yourself mad. You were gone, he was probably lonely and sad. Things like that happen all the time. And it wasn't all that soon after you left, really, was it?'

Emma nodded. Lucie was right. But the thought that Connor had got together with Sadie, had slept with her and had a child with her, still hurt. She hadn't looked at another man for much longer than two years after leaving, hadn't been interested in as much as dating. But even as the thoughts swirled in her mind, she knew she had no right to think them. She had left and Connor had been hurt. Why shouldn't he have sought solace in another woman's arms? In fact, perhaps Sadie had been the woman he'd needed all along and Emma had never been right for him.

'It seems like you still have feelings for him,' Lucie said.

Emma sighed. 'Oh, Lucie, I'm so confused right now by what I'm feeling.'

'Do you want to join them or sneak off home?'

'If we go straight home, I'll feel terrible and just dwell on it all night. Connor's right; we do need to be adult about this and accept that this is how our lives are now. So let's go and say hello then I'll know I've done the right thing.'

'Deal.'

'But let's get it over with – because if we don't, I might lose my nerve.'

Connor had filled everyone's glasses again by the time Emma and Lucie entered the function room. He poured champagne into two clean glasses then carried them over, Grace at his side.

'Thanks for coming in.' He handed Emma and Lucie the champagne. 'This is my daughter, Grace, and Grace, this is Emma, an old friend of mine, and her friend, Lucie, from London.'

'Hello, Grace. It's lovely to meet you.' Emma smiled.

'Likewise,' Grace replied, smiling. They shook hands then Grace and Lucie did too.

In spite of her smile, Emma looked uncomfortable, standing with her back rigid and curling her short hair over a fingertip. When it was long, she used to do that when she was nervous or anxious and he could see that she hadn't lost the habit even though her hair was so much shorter now.

'We meet again.' His mum had appeared at his side, staring hard at Emma. He watched as Emma's cheeks coloured and the urge to wrap a protective arm around her shoulders filled him.

'I invited Emma and Lucie to join us. I want her to meet Grace before she heads off.'

His mum cocked an eyebrow at him.

'It's OK . . . we can leave.' Emma took Lucie's arm and turned to go.

'No! Please stay.' Connor nudged his mum.

Grace was frowning, seeming a bit confused by what was going on.

'Yes . . . please stay, Emma. Connor wants you to.' His mum nodded. 'And anyway, it's good to see you. You look well.'

'Thank you.' Emma looked from Zoe to Connor, her eyes wary. This was tough for her and his mum could be hard on people if she felt they'd wronged her or her family, but if Emma was staying in the village, he wanted there to be some sort of ceasefire between them all. He didn't want to feel awkward every time he opened the front door.

'So, how have you been?' Zoe asked Emma.

Connor felt that it might be better to let them talk, so he sent out a silent wish that his mum would be kind, then he took Grace's arm.

'Time for some speeches?' he asked.

'If you must.' Grace grinned, flashing the straight white teeth that had taken expensive braces to straighten. Connor had thought the way the front two were slightly crooked was cute, but Sadie had insisted that it would bother their daughter later on. Now, after several glasses of champagne, Grace's eyes were bright, her cheeks flushed. She was beautiful, young and excited about life. It lifted his heart. 'Then you can tell me why you and your old friend, Emma, were all stiff and awkward around each other.'

He nodded then led her to the corner of the room where there was a small raised platform, then used a key to gently tap on the side of his glass and looked around at the expectant faces.

'Good evening and thanks for coming. This is a small gathering because that's what Grace wanted and we're all here for the same reason – to say bon voyage to our beautiful girl.' He smiled at Grace. 'I'm sorry, I keep saying girl, but Grace is a young woman now. My little girl has morphed into a sweet, kind, caring, intelligent, talented, beautiful woman, inside and out, and I couldn't be prouder of her than I am already. I feel extremely lucky to be able to call this incredible woman my daughter and I know that Sadie feels the same, as do her grandparents about being able to call her their granddaughter. If my dad were here, he'd be singing your praises to anyone who would listen, Grace.' Connor cleared his throat, emotion making his voice gravelly.

'Thanks, Dad.' Grace raised her glass and clinked it against his and suddenly, Sadie was there too, sliding her hand around Connor's waist and standing between him and Grace as if they were a proper family.

'Good luck to you as you head to Paris to follow your dreams. We'll miss you but be happy because you are doing what you've always wanted to do,' Connor said, trying to ignore that Sadie was gazing up at him possessively and to focus on his daughter instead.

Glasses were raised and clinked, and *cheers* echoed around the room. Connor looked around, taking in the faces of friends and family, his eyes lingering a second too long upon Emma. She held his gaze and he was transported back in time to a different occasion when they'd been in this very room, giggling as they shared a bottle of fizz, drinking straight from the bottle and kissing between sips as they tasted the champagne on each other's lips, celebrating her turning eighteen. Then, a few years later, there had been more champagne as they toasted her acceptance of his proposal and he'd thought they were about to embark upon their life together. But just months after the proposal, the journey had been cut short and Emma had walked out of his life.

Now she was back. But in what capacity?

Sadie kissed Grace on the cheek then did the same to Connor and walked away to speak to her parents and Connor was left alone with Grace.

'Dad? Thank you again.' She hugged him tight and he realised that everyone had gone back to talking, eating and drinking. When she leant back, she met his eyes. 'Are you OK?'

'Yes. Of course. I mean . . . I'll miss you but I'm OK.'

She shook her head. 'No, it's not that. I meant . . . what I said earlier about you and Emma and the way you were just staring at her. Who is she?'

He glanced over her shoulder, but Emma was looking in the other direction, standing with some of Grace's friends, nodding as Lucie chatted away.

'That's *her*.'

'*The* Emma?'

'Yes.'

'The one that got away?'

He hung his head.

'Ahhh . . . it all makes sense now.'

She took his chin in a hand and raised his head slowly, then held his gaze.

'Dad . . . I might be going away, but I'm worried about you. I want you and Mum to be happy. You really do have to give yourself a chance to find someone, *whoever* that is.'

'I don't need anyone, I'm quite happy as I–'

'Yeah, yeah, I know all that. I also know you've stayed single because of me, and to a certain extent because of Mum, and obviously I know about your history with Emma now, but you *can* have a life of your own.'

'I'm OK.'

'I know, but I would like to know you have someone to love you.'

'I have you, Grace.'

'I'm not going to be here, Dad. Look, just think about giving love a chance, please? For me?'

'I'll think about it.' He coughed, embarrassed that Grace was speaking to him about love and relationships.

'Try not to live in fear. You only get the one life.'

'I know, so I'll try.'

'That's all a daughter can ask.'

She hugged him again and he wondered how he was going to cope without her.

As they were leaving, Emma looked across the function room to where Connor was standing speaking to some of Grace's guests. He'd given a lovely and moving speech about his daughter and she could see what a wonderful father he must be. It triggered a flicker of pride in her, seeing him like that, as if she'd known all along that he had many good qualities and would have a good life.

'Ready?' Lucie asked as she drained her champagne.

'Yes.' Emma nodded, but as she turned her head she saw Sadie slinking over to Connor and wrapping her arms around his waist, smiling up at him as she did so. It wasn't the first time Sadie had done that this evening but Emma still found it odd witnessing it, as if something wasn't quite right. 'I'm ready.'

Suddenly, Sadie stared right at her, her eyebrows raised as if in question. Emma blinked hard then smiled and nodded, before turning away. Sadie was making her claim on Connor clear, as if she felt that Emma needed to see it and

Emma felt like a teenager, filled with unease and something else. Was it jealousy? Or just plain awkwardness?

Lucie grabbed her hand and they headed out, Emma determined not to look back because, if she did, she worried about what else she might see.

Chapter 17

Connor shifted in the driver's seat of his van. He turned the radio down then turned it up again, but it failed to provide an adequate distraction from the woman sobbing in the passenger seat.

'It'll be OK, Sadie,' he said for what felt like the fiftieth time since they'd left Grace at Gatwick airport.

'No . . . it . . . won't.' She howled into a tissue, her shoulders shaking, and Connor felt terrible for her. He was struggling himself after hugging his daughter for the last time in what would be months, but he'd done his best to be strong for Grace and for Sadie. The last thing he wanted was for Grace to feel bad for leaving when she was about to start her new adventure.

Connor reached over and gently but quickly patted Sadie's hand then returned his to the steering wheel. He wasn't sure what to do to make Sadie feel better. She had, thankfully, held back the tears until they'd walked out of the airport but since then she'd been inconsolable.

'It's all your fault!' She sat up and glared at him. He could see how red her face was from the corner of his eye but he kept his gaze fixed to the road ahead.

'OK . . .'

'It is! If you'd been a normal man, I'd have support now but no! And now my daughter's gone and I have no one!'

'Sadie, please, that's not true. You have your parents, your friends, Grace . . . and I'm here for you. You know that.'

'As a friend!' She spat and he suppressed the urge to wipe his cheek. 'A bloody friend. You know I want and need more than that.'

Connor sighed. He did know and he had tried, but something was missing from their relationship. There was no spark and they had nothing in common except Grace. He hated to think about it now, but Sadie had pursued him relentlessly while he'd been incredibly vulnerable. She'd been there all the time after Emma left, inviting him out, pouring him drinks, turning up at work with cakes and tickets for concerts. Of course, he hadn't been defenceless, had been a grown man, perfectly capable of declining her attentions, but she had worn him down. It had taken over two years for him to give in, but he'd been so low and nothing had seemed to be getting better. Then, one night, he just wanted to be held. Life and sadness had reduced him to such a low point that he didn't know where to turn. And when he'd finally succumbed to Sadie's efforts to get him into bed, she'd got pregnant almost immediately.

And then, of course, Connor had felt that he should do the right thing, the responsible thing, and be there for the woman who was carrying his child. He had tried so hard to love Sadie, but his heart had still been with Emma, in spite of his attempts to hate and forget her. He'd been in love with Emma for so long that it was as if he was incapable of loving another woman. The burden of guilt sat heavily on his shoulders because Sadie was right; she *did* deserve a man who would love her as she deserved to be loved. People made mistakes all the time, especially when they were vulnerable, and Connor had been vulnerable and so, in her own way, had Sadie. She'd been searching for something and thought she'd found it in Connor, but she'd tried to shoehorn him into being what she wanted him to be rather than accepting him for what he was and, of course, that was never going to work.

He could never wish that time away, though, because it had resulted in Grace and she was the best thing in his life.

'You need to be kind to yourself now, Sadie,' he said as they pulled up outside her cottage. 'Give yourself time to come to terms with Grace leaving, but please . . . don't put any pressure on her when she phones.'

'I don't know what type of person you think I am, Connor. I would never do that to Grace.'

'She mentioned that you're going to go and stay with her.'

'I am. I need a holiday and Paris sounds wonderful. I might even find myself a gorgeous Frenchman,' she said, raising an eyebrow and pouting.

'You might.' He nodded.

'Doesn't that bother you?'

'Why would it?' He rubbed the back of his neck. 'I want you to be happy, Sadie, and if that means finding someone to love, then yes, I want that for you.'

'You're not jealous?'

He shook his head then winced as she got out of the van and slammed the door. She began marching away then stopped, spun on her heel, turned back to the van and hammered on the window. Connor lowered it, steeling himself for her wrath. This wasn't the first time this had happened.

'You've lost me now, Connor. For good! I'm done with you.'

'Sadie, please, let this go.'

She scowled at him then puffed out her cheeks.

'Fine. Fine by me.'

She turned and stormed up the path and into her cottage, leaving Connor gripping the steering wheel, wondering what he could do to make things better for her. But he was at a loss, because they had lived like this for a long time and it seemed that he was never able to do the right thing, was, in fact, unable to help Sadie.

It had not just been his love for Emma that had prevented him from loving Sadie though, or even their difference. Things had happened that he would never want to admit to anyone about his time with her, things he would never want Grace to know about. Sadie had always loved attention and about a year after Grace was born he'd found out that she had been seeing another man before they had got together and had started seeing him again. Connor should have been angry, but his main concern was for Grace, to be there to protect and care for her, so when Sadie had insisted it was over, he had tried to let it go. He suspected that the affair had been rekindled several times over the years as there were periods when Sadie acted strangely, became more distant, and yet he found it hard to blame her because he knew in his heart that he could never fully commit to her either and it was one of the things that convinced him, eventually, when Grace was fifteen, that it was time to call it a day. Sadie had never forgiven him and he had hoped she would be able to commit fully to the other man, but then he found out from a mutual friend that the other man had been married with children and had never intended on leaving his wife for Sadie.

As he drove away, it was Sadie's anger and sadness that dominated his thoughts, not his daughter's delight at heading off to Paris, and when Connor found himself outside his mum's cottage rather than his own, he realised he'd driven there on autopilot.

'Mum?' he called as he let himself inside with the key she insisted he keep. 'It's only me.'

There was a loud bark then another and he was rushed by the greyhounds, squashed against the wall of the narrow hallway as they bounded around him, wagging their long tails.

'Hey, Digby and Toby. Good to see you.'

They fussed around him, his worries slipping away as he rubbed their pointy heads and tickled under their chins.

'Connor?' his mum called from the lounge. 'Come on through.'

'I will when I can get past the canine welcome!' He laughed as the dogs kept turning in circles, tails wagging, eyes bright with joy.

He shuffled along between the dogs, trying not to step on any paws, and entered the lounge.

'Everything go all right?' she asked, looking up from the coffee table that was covered in pieces of colourful cloth.

'As well as could be expected.' He perched on the sofa and Digby jumped up next to him and curled up with his pointy head on Connor's lap while Toby took the sheep-skin rug in front of the hearth.

'Sadie create a drama, did she?'

'Well, not at the airport but she was very emotional on the journey home.'

His mum shook her head. 'Oh dear. At least she didn't upset Grace.'

'True.'

'And how are *you* doing?'

He rubbed his palms on his jeans then stroked Digby's silky head. 'I'm all right. I'm going to miss Grace but this is right for her.'

'Yes, it is. I miss her already, but we have to think of the glorious future ahead of her.'

He nodded. 'What are you making?'

His mum moved a triangle of cloth on top of another and pinned it in place. 'Some bunting for the fête.'

'Nice.' He frowned as he peered at the bunting. 'What material is that?'

His mum laughed. 'Anything and everything I could get my hands on.'

'But isn't that a pair of my old boxers?'

'It is!' His mum held up a triangle of stripy material and waved it in the air. 'Some of your old things were still in boxes in the attic and I thought I'd just as well make use of them.'

'And that bit there. Is that from a pair of jeans?'

'Yes. An old pair of mine that I wore a lot over the years. Basically, Connor, I've used whatever spare bits of material I could find. Better than throwing them in the bin and them ending up in landfill. This way they can be reused every year for the fête.'

'Good idea.' He smiled, but knew that whenever he looked at the bunting he'd remember some of it was made out of his old underwear. And everyone would see it!

'So what's up?' she asked as she sat back on her heels.

'What do you mean?'

'Well, I love seeing you, obviously, but you've come here so I'm guessing you want company, food or a chat.'

'Am I that transparent?'

His mum set the bunting down, then stood up and came to sit next to him.

'Only to your old mum.'

'I didn't mean to come here, to be honest, but found myself outside so I must need to speak to you. I guess that Grace leaving has brought a few things back.'

'As would seeing Emma,' she said wisely.

'Yes.'

'And how do you feel about that?'

'It's not straightforward.'

'Of course not.' She placed a hand over his and squeezed gently. 'But as they say these days, it's OK not to be OK.'

He met her eyes.

'When I was younger, we were encouraged to hide feelings, not to show what could be seen as weakness or vulnerability and I still find myself thinking that way at times. However, I also know that feelings are complex and do change. I could see a mile off how you feel about Emma when I saw you together.'

'*I'm* not even sure how I feel.'

'You care for her – and she still cares for you.'

'You think so?'

She nodded. 'It would be a heartless person who could spend such an important stage of their life with someone and feel nothing when they saw them again after almost thirty years. There's an historical connection there.'

Connor rubbed his face roughly then sank back on the cushions. 'I just wish it could all be simpler, Mum.'

'I know, my darling. But life is never simple. Don't rush anything, don't be hard on yourself, just take each day as it comes. What's meant to be will be.'

He gave a wry laugh. 'That old cliché!'

'It helps to have some faith in the universe from time to time. Even if it is a bit clichéd, who cares? Whatever helps us through.'

'Grace said something last night and it got me thinking.'

'Did she?'

'She said that I need to think about my own happiness for a change.'

'And she was right.'

'She also said that I should give love a chance. But I'm scared, Mum. I mean, I think I have a – a connection with Emma, but as much as I sometimes think I want to pursue it . . . it terrifies me.'

His mum nodded. 'Life is short, though, so follow your heart if you can. I'm not saying that Emma is the only love you'll ever have and it may well be that what you had with her is long gone, but I would like to see you happy with someone again. You're a lovely man and I'm so proud of you.'

'Thanks, Mum.'

She squeezed his hand again then stood up.

'Come on, let's take these dogs for a walk. I need to stretch my legs and the boys have been pestering me to go out for the past hour.'

Connor nodded then followed his mum and the greyhounds out into the hallway. A walk would do him good too.

'The heart wants what it wants, Connor,' his mum said as she opened the front door, seemingly reading his mind as she was wont to do. 'Start listening to yours.'

Chapter 18

Emma sniffed appreciatively as she walked into the kitchen. She was cooking a roast dinner for her dad and Lucie and the cottage smelt like it used to when she was growing up. She had a free-range chicken from the local farm shop in the Aga along with roast potatoes and mixed root vegetables and she'd picked some peas and carrots from the garden.

She'd spent the previous day with Lucie, weeding and digging the raised beds that were still tangled with weeds, and they'd found a pleasing amount of fresh fruit and veg in them and in some of the pots. Each time they'd found something that was edible and not a weed, they'd cheered for joy as if they'd discovered gold.

Her back had ached and the muscles in her arms had burned last night as she'd sunk into a deep bath, but it had been worth it just to see how much better the garden looked. Lucie had enjoyed it too, covering her manicure with thick gardening gloves and donning a sunhat as she'd got stuck in. Emma's dad had come outside with glasses of ice-cold water from time to time, commenting on how hard they were working and reminding them that he wished he could help more. Emma had told him to sit in the shade and take it easy. He'd agreed, but only when she accepted his offer of fish and chips for supper.

Emma had picked up their supper in the village, then the three of them had sat in the garden, eating the salty chips and fluffy beer-battered cod off the paper and washing the food down with cloudy lemonade with condensation on the cans. It had been perfect.

Now, as she opened the Aga door and basted the chicken then the root vegetables and potatoes, she thought about how her mum and dad had done the same things over the years. There had always been good food on the table, plenty of fresh fruit and veg, delicious chutneys and jams and bread and cakes. There had been music and love and laughter, and Ted and Emma had both been healthy, happy children. She knew she'd grown up in a wonderful family home and that not everyone was as lucky as she had been. She really had no reason not to have a healthy adult relationship herself, but after being so serious with Connor so early on, something had changed. If only she'd taken some time instead of running away, had given them both some space to try to work things out. Her immaturity had led her to act impulsively and that had created one big, fat mess.

She stood up and wiped her hands on a tea towel then gazed out of the window. If she'd stayed with Connor, would she have been here to spend more time with her parents, been able to treasure her mum's last days before losing her so suddenly? She could have been a source of support for her dad. Perhaps she'd have had children with Connor and they'd have made their grandad smile when he was low. Life was so rich and varied and Emma had enjoyed hers – but had she missed out on what could have been?

She sighed, long and low.

'What're you sighing about?' Lucie picked up the potato peeler and peered at it.

'Be careful with that, it's sharp.'

'Yes, Mum.' Lucie winked. 'So?'

'I was just thinking about how I've changed over the years and how what I wanted twenty years ago is not the same as what I want now.'

'Of course it's not. If we stayed stagnant, the clubs would be overcrowded with geriatrics competing with vicenarians for the barman's attention.'

'Can you imagine!' Emma cringed. 'I find clubs exhausting now on the rare occasions I can be bothered to go; worst of all is how some of the youngsters glare at me as if I have no right to be there. I was dancing way before they were even conceived!'

Lucie shrugged. 'They're not my favourite place to be anymore either. Give me a good movie or boxset and a cuddle on the sofa any day. And have you heard that some young men now have competitions to "grab a granny"?'

'They what?'

Lucie nodded. 'Happened to a woman I work with who was recently divorced. Some twenty-four-year-old guy asked for her social media handles so he could follow her and she was quite flattered. The next day, he sent her a rude picture on Snapchat.'

'Of what?'

'His penis.'

'No!'

'A dick pic.' Lucie shuddered dramatically. 'Anyway, she was so shocked that she screenshotted it and the app notified the guy.'

'What did he do?'

'He messaged her asking if she liked what she saw.'

Emma grimaced. 'I hope she blocked him.'

'She did, but he messaged her again on a different platform and said he was only after her so he could say he'd shagged an oldie.'

'How old is she?'

'Forty-six.'

'That's still young!'

'I know, but to them we seem ancient.'

'How did we get so old, Lucie?'

'Who's old?' Her dad entered the kitchen and went to the fridge.

'Don't eat anything now, Dad, dinner won't be long.'

'I was looking for some wine, actually.' He brandished a bottle of rosé.

'Excellent idea.' Lucie got three glasses out of the cupboard. 'Shall we have a glass in the garden before lunch?'

The three of them headed outside into the sunny morning and Emma smiled; getting older wasn't so bad at all. As long as you didn't talk to young men in clubs, it seemed.

Over lunch, Lucie raised the subject of Emma's dad's guitars, asking if he still played. Emma had cringed inwardly, wondering how he'd react. Initially, he'd talked about his hands making playing difficult but then he'd said he'd like to have a go that afternoon.

The three of them had gone into the small music room off the lounge and gazed around at the guitar cases. They looked a bit like sarcophagi in an Egyptian tomb.

Emma had watched her dad carefully, wondering how he felt as he ran a hand over the dusty cases then picked up a music book and flicked through the pages.

'It's difficult,' he said, 'knowing that the rest of the band are all gone. This is a big chunk of my life in here and I'm almost afraid of stirring it all up.'

Emma wrapped an arm around his shoulders. 'You don't need to play, Dad. Perhaps you should wait a while.'

He shook his head. 'I'll try.'

He opened the nearest case and lifted out his favourite acoustic guitar, a Gibson 1974 Hummingbird. He slid the strap over his head and ran a thumb over the strings, then winced. 'Needs tuning.'

'Can I help with that, Greg?' Lucie asked.

'Have you tuned a guitar before?'

'No.' She wrinkled her nose. 'But I'm sure there's a video on YouTube that'll teach me how.'

'I'll see if I can do it. Now I'm here I'd just as well.'

'You sure, Dad?' Emma asked.

He met her gaze. 'I'm sure.'

Emma stood there awkwardly, not sure what to do, uncertain if her dad wanted some space.

'Why don't you two go and get some air and leave an old man to tune up his instruments?'

'OK, Dad.'

Emma and Lucie left the music room; Emma wasn't sure if she was doing the right thing or not, but she knew she had to respect his wishes.

'There's a lot of fruit here,' Lucie said as she perched on the windowsill of the garden studio.

'I know. My mum used to have more and manage to use it all.'

There were strawberry plants with rapidly ripening fruit in containers, rambling raspberry and blackcurrant bushes off to the side of the studio, and apple and pear trees that were all now heavy with fruit that would be harvested in the autumn. The recent sunshine and occasional showers had created perfect conditions for the fruit to grow and the garden was rich with life.

The afternoon was warm and Emma was sitting on the grass, full of chicken dinner, the wine and sunshine making her feel relaxed. Bees drifted from flower to flower drunk on pollen, birds sang in the trees and a plane soared high overhead, leaving a contrail behind like a frizzy white tail. The air was fragrant with honeysuckle and the combined effect was making Emma sleepy.

She lay back, feeling the grass tickling at her arms and feet, the earth supporting her body as she let go. Her eyelids were heavy, her lips parted, her hands splayed at her sides. Lucie came and lay next to her and they gazed up at the sky, watching as the occasional white cloud drifted across the endless blue.

'It's really beautiful here,' Lucie said. 'I could see myself living somewhere like this.'

'I thought you couldn't imagine living in a village?' Emma teased. 'I do think it would suit you and Phoebe, though.'

'Yes, and we need to find somewhere to raise our family.'

Emma pushed herself up on her elbow and peered at her friend.

'Are you saying what I think you're saying?'

Lucie nodded and a tear rolled from the corner of her eye and ran down her cheek then dropped onto the grass.

'Phoebe FaceTimed just now when I was in the loo. I was letting it sink in before I said anything. She told me she didn't feel right this morning, so she did the test early . . . in spite of being told by the clinic to wait. I had a feeling she might. Anyway, it seems that our last trip to the clinic worked.'

'That's brilliant news!' Emma leant over and hugged Lucie but her friend started to shake. 'What is it?'

They sat up and Lucie wiped her eyes with the back of a hand.

'We've been wanting this for so long and now it's happened, now it's real, I'm terrified.'

'But why?'

'What if it goes wrong? What if we lose the baby? Surely that would be worse than not getting pregnant at all?' Lucie plucked at the grass, sprinkling it into a pile. 'And I'm forty-six. What was I *thinking*?'

'Hey, you're fit and healthy. And so is Phoebe. Plus, she's only thirty-five. You can do this.'

Lucie's bottom lip wobbled. 'Really?'

'I'm sure everyone has some worries when they get pregnant, Lucie. It's perfectly natural, but everything will be fine – and I'll be there for you through it all.'

Lucie took a deep breath then met Emma's eyes. 'Thank you. But you might be here and I'll be in London – or it might even be the other way round!'

'That's not far, Lucie.'

Lucie smiled. 'I need to bring Phoebe here so she can see the village for herself.'

'Then do that, and she can see how lovely it is.'

'I will.'

They lay back down then, holding hands, and Emma closed her eyes. If Lucie and Phoebe could find somewhere to live in the village and Emma stayed, then it would only be work she'd need to sort out and she could do the majority of that online, commuting for meetings and events.

This could work, if she just took a chance.

The next morning, Emma walked with Lucie to the station so her friend could catch the early train back to London, then she spent the rest of the day making jam, enjoying being productive and counting up the jars she'd filled so far. There was certainly enough there for a stall at the fête and the idea had grown in its appeal, as had her sense of achievement at everything she'd made.

Stepping out of the studio into the cool evening air, Emma was suddenly aware of how hot and sticky she felt. The idea of a bath or shower straight away didn't appeal but stretching her legs did, so she would go for a walk before washing up and making some dinner.

After asking if her dad wanted to accompany her – he didn't because one of his programmes was about to begin – she set off towards the woodland path. The evening was beautiful, the sky a pinky-purple and the aromas of flowers and freshly cut grass filled the air as she passed cottage gardens with perfectly green lawns, filled with trees and summer blooms.

She walked past the King's Head and the new bistro and headed along the path, enjoying the gentle cooling breeze on her hot skin and the scents of the earth that permeated the air. One of the best things about Little Bramble was how easy it was to escape into nature. Just a short walk and she could be surrounded by trees and hedgerows, by fields and endless sky. There was a deep connection to nature out here and it grounded her, gave her that sense of wholeness that she sometimes missed in London when she was so far away from the great expanses of greenery that Little Bramble offered.

Emma was lost in her thoughts, at one with her surroundings, when she was suddenly conscious of the sound of feet approaching from behind. She turned and laughed because there were two greyhounds trotting towards her, their ears up, tails wagging.

'Hello!' She held out her hands as the dogs reached her and sniffed at her palms, their pointy noses cool and wet. 'Where did you two come from?'

'Toby! Digby! There you are. I'm so sorry, they don't usually run off like that but they picked up your scent and . . . Oh, Emma!'

'Zoe.' Emma inclined her head. 'You have lovely dogs.'

'They're rescues, both of them, and absolutely wonderful companions.'

Emma crouched down and the dogs sniffed at her face, her ears, her hair. 'I can see that.' She rubbed their silky heads, giggling as their cold noses tickled her skin.

'They like you.' Zoe had reached them now and she stood in front of Emma. 'Dogs can tell if someone has a good heart.'

Emma stood up but kept stroking the greyhounds.

'Uh . . . thank you, I think.' Emma chewed at the inside of her cheek. Was Connor's mother being nice to her? Was this a trick? She expected her at any moment to snap at her and tell her how awful she was for hurting her son.

'Walk with us?' Zoe asked.

'Y-yes. That'd be nice.' But would it?

'Come on, boys, let's go.' Zoe waved her arms and the dogs set off again but didn't go too far ahead, occasionally stopping to sniff a patch of grass or a tree.

'How's your dad?'

'He's OK, thanks. He seems glad to have me home and I think it's helping him.'

'I'm sure it is. He's probably enjoying the company.'

'He's even started tinkering with some of his guitars again, so I'm hoping that's a good sign.'

'It certainly sounds positive.'

They fell silent for a bit, watching as the dogs trotted along, taking cues from each other.

'How long have you had the dogs?'

'Two years.'

'They seem so happy and confident.'

'They weren't like that to begin with.'

'No?'

'When greyhounds come to charities as rescues they're often injured or too old for the racetrack. In fact, some have horrendous injuries and if it wasn't for charities like the one I work with, the dogs would have to be euthanised. Sometimes, if they haven't been doing well in races, they're abandoned by the breeders because they won't earn any money. The poor things are basically used, then forgotten about when they no longer carry any financial value.'

'That's so sad.'

'I know. When I adopted Digby, he was very timid. The day I went to collect him, I saw Toby and just had to adopt him too. From birth, greyhounds live with other dogs so they can miss that canine companionship, even if they have humans around, and I knew this so it made sense to bring them both home. They're great friends and seem happy having each other around.'

'They're lovely. I couldn't have a dog in my flat but if I stay here with Dad, it's something I'd consider.'

'You might stay on, then?'

'I'm not completely sure, but the more time I spend with Dad, the more I see him getting stronger. It might continue now, even if I left, because he's on the right path, but I've done some reading and I know that he could decline again quickly.'

'Have you heard of therapy dogs?'

'I think so. Don't they use them for children with autism?'

'Dogs can help people with all sorts of conditions. Say, for example, dementia.'

'Really?'

'There have been studies about it. Dogs and other animals can help reduce the effects of dementia, like anxiety and agitation, loneliness and depression. They aid the creation of endorphins and help lower blood pressure. If someone with severe dementia is struggling to articulate themselves, an animal can help them to interact in a non-threatening way.'

'That's incredible.'

'Isn't it? So just having a dog around could work wonders for someone like your dad.'

Emma frowned as she thought about it. Would getting a dog be a good thing for her dad? Caring for another creature that would depend upon him but also love him unconditionally and be there all the time for him? But she couldn't get him a dog then leave, so it would mean that she'd have to be there too.

'Something to think about.' Zoe smiled. 'But not a decision to be taken lightly. Dogs, especially rescue dogs, come with a whole range of needs and issues, but caring for them can be incredibly rewarding. My two get me out twice a day, rain or shine, and they keep me going on days when my own loneliness becomes overwhelming.'

'You get lonely?' Emma watched Zoe, the woman she'd once thought of as a mother-in-law, who'd always been strong, capable and warm.

'Oh yes. I know I have Connor and Grace, though she's off in Paris now and goodness knows when she'll come home again, but I do miss my John terribly.'

'He was a lovely man.'

'He adored you.'

'Zoe, I'm so sorry.'

Emma stopped walking and wrung her hands together in front of her.

'Sorry?'

'Yes!' Everything that had been bubbling inside her since her return to Little Bramble suddenly rose in her throat then surged from her like a river bursting its banks. 'For everything that happened. I never meant to hurt any of you. I loved you like my own family. I hurt not just you, John and Connor but my own parents as well. I caused everyone so much pain. My mum, my poor lovely mum, never got to hear an apology and I regret that so much. But – but I was young and confused and . . . Look, I know I can't take any of it back but I'm so dreadfully sorry for . . . for everything.'

Zoe placed a hand on Emma's arm and gazed at her. Seconds of silence felt like days, then Zoe shook her head.

'Emma, you were very young. John and I loved you as if you were one of our own. Obviously, Connor was our son and so we had to be there for him, but had you come to us for help and advice, we would have been there for you, too. You and Connor were together for such a long time and then suddenly you were gone. It was like having a piece of our life ripped away.'

Emma covered her mouth with both hands and mumbled through her fingers, 'I really am sorry.'

'No, sweetheart, don't be. It happened a long time ago and while it was very sad and painful, life moved on. People moved on. It's what happens. I can't deny that I was sad, then angry then bewildered, but I had to support Connor through it. John and I wished that things had worked out differently, that you and Connor had at least been able to talk things through and find a way to stay together, but it was, ultimately, between you and him. It wasn't up to us to interfere. So please don't be harsh on yourself. Connor is fine and you are fine. He's a father and we have Grace. We would never change that.'

Emma nodded. 'Thank you for being so kind.' Her voice emerged as a squeak. 'I don't know where that all came from. I've been managing things since I came back but seeing you and being here in the middle of so much beauty just got to me.' She was trembling, emotion flooding through her after years of suppressing it.

Zoe nodded. 'That's understandable.'

They started to walk again, and Emma pushed her hands through her hair, overwhelmed but also incredibly relieved to have unburdened and to know that Zoe and John hadn't hated her. Hearing that they'd been hurt was tough, but there was no hatred or resentment and that, at least, she could be thankful for.

'So you're a proud grandmother?'

'Very proud indeed. Grace is a wonderful young woman and I'm excited to see how she gets on in Paris.' Zoe whistled and the greyhounds rushed back to her. She gave them a small treat each and stroked their heads then they jogged ahead again. 'It's good to practise recall often just to remind them that I'm here. There are lots of squirrels in these woods and greyhounds are trained to chase small furries. Now, Emma, tell me about you and what you've been up to this . . . what is it . . .? Almost thirty years?'

So Emma did. And they walked and talked and with each step, she felt another thread of her anxiety slip away on the summer breeze. She was finally facing things she had worried about for years.

Chapter 19

The next few days passed with Emma making more jam and chutney in her mum's studio, finishing off the editing job she'd been working on, and spending time with her dad. He asked her a few times every day if she wanted to go back to London, worried that she would be missing out, but every time she told him she was fine right where she was. And it was true. The longer she stayed, the less she wanted to leave. She'd checked her emails through the week and had several jobs lined up for the following few months, and instead of being alone in her flat, now she had company through the day and a beautiful garden to enjoy. It wasn't bad at all.

Her dad's blood tests had come back clear. Dr Creek had told Emma that, should she have concerns about her dad, to take him back to the surgery and they could consider further tests. This would likely involve a brain scan, something that made Emma's stomach churn. She'd told

Dr Creek that her dad had seemed a lot better since her arrival and the doctor had said that was a positive sign, gently adding that Greg's forgetfulness could have been down to factors such as age, loneliness and not looking after himself properly.

Following the call with the GP, Emma had video-called her brother and told him the news and he'd actually broken down on camera. He'd told her how frustrating it was being so far away and that he wished he could be there to help, so she'd done her best to reassure him and, after they'd spoken, she got her dad and the three of them had chatted for over an hour, the time difference forgotten. Ted got his family on the video too so they could all share their news. It had been a long time since Emma and Ted had shared more than a text or a brief phone call and seeing her brother's wife and children and how happy they were, as well as witnessing the joy it brought her dad when he spoke to them, filled her with happiness. It was something she planned on arranging more often to help everyone stay in touch. Her dad even went and got one of his guitars and played the Eagles' 'Peaceful Easy Feeling'. His fingers stumbled over some of the chords and he forgot a few of the lyrics, but overall he did well and his family applauded afterwards. It was heart-warming to see her dad revitalised by the music and she intended encouraging him to keep playing regularly.

'I'm not sure I have enough fruit, Dad,' Emma said one morning as they sat on the bench in the garden, drinking tea. 'I think I need more strawberries because I've used all the ripe ones from the garden and I found a recipe online for strawberry and prosecco jam.'

'That sounds delightful.'

'I might go strawberry picking. You want to come?'

'When?'

'Tomorrow? We could take a picnic lunch and make a day of it.'

'Your mum loved strawberry picking.'

'I remember.'

'And prosecco.'

'She did.'

'Are you sure you don't need to get back to London?'

'Dad! I told you yesterday that I want to stay. Please try not to worry.'

'I'm your dad, Emma. It's my job to worry about you.'

'But I really am happy here . . .'

'Just not for good?'

'For the time being, at least, and possibly longer. I'm really enjoying staying with you and it's such a beautiful summer we're having. Right now, it would be uncomfortably hot in London, so it's a relief to be in the countryside.'

'Good, good.' He patted her hand. 'And it's positive, isn't it, about the test results?'

She caught the uncertainty in his voice. He was understandably scared of being diagnosed with dementia. 'Yes, Dad, very good news.'

'When your mum died, I struggled. Dilys was fabulous, but it wasn't the same. Your mum and I, we plodded along together so well. She was my best friend and I had a purpose when she was here, a reason to look after myself because she needed me. But when she . . . was gone . . . I'm ashamed to say I didn't care what happened to me anymore.'

Emma watched his face, her heart pounding at the pain in his eyes. 'You don't need to be ashamed, Dad.'

'But I still had you and your brother and you didn't deserve to have a father who let himself go. I should have been strong for you two.'

'Mum was your world. We were far away, living our own lives. It's understandable that you struggled.'

'I let things go, didn't take care of myself properly and that hasn't helped with my mental health. Don't they say something like . . . if you don't use it, you lose it?'

Emma smiled in spite of the seriousness of the conversation. 'In certain contexts, yes.'

'Well, I stopped doing crosswords, stopped reading, stopped being positive or thinking about the future. I neglected myself completely.'

'Oh, Dad!'

'It seemed a waste to cook just for myself and some days I'd barely eat at all. I lost my appetite and felt so tired and low all the time.'

'That probably didn't help.'

'I'm so sorry, Emma, but I think I was letting go.' His watery eyes held hers and her throat constricted. 'I was giving up on life.'

'And we can't have that, can we?'

'But I don't want to be a burden, ever, Emma. I can't bear the thought of you staying because you feel you have to look after me. I promise that if you do go back to London, I'll look after myself. I won't sink so low again.'

'Dad!' She shuffled closer to him and hugged him tightly. 'Don't. Please don't. I love you and you'll never be a burden. In fact, I want to stay here with you – I don't want to go back to London. I want to make jam and chutney and watch Netflix and listen to you play your guitars and walk the woodland path and listen to the birds singing when I wake up. I want to stay here, Dad. Permanently.'

There. She'd said it. And it was true. She didn't want to waste a single moment of time that she could be spending with her dear old dad.

She kissed his smooth cheek that smelt like shaving soap and Old Spice. In a white and blue checked shirt and navy trousers, he looked so much better than he had when she'd first come home. He was eating well and drinking plenty of water and tea and it was all helping him, but he was eighty-four and if he didn't look after himself, he could easily decline. Emma wasn't about to let that happen.

'Do you fancy a walk?' she asked when she felt able to stop hugging him.

'That would be lovely. Where are we going?'

'I had a text earlier from Clare to say they're meeting at the village hall this afternoon to discuss fête arrangements.'

'Are you definitely going to have a stall at the fête then?'

'I think so – we'll have a heck of a lot of jam to eat if we don't sell some of it!'

'I don't mind eating a lot of jam.'

'You can have some, but we have to watch your sugar intake too.'

She nudged him and he laughed softly. He might want to be independent and strong and not be a burden on his children but she could also see that he, like most people, wanted to be loved, to know that someone was looking out for him. And there was nothing wrong with that at all.

'I'll grab a few jars of jam and we can take them with us and see if they're happy with us selling them.'

'Us?'

She stood up and held out her hand.

'Yes, Dad. You don't think I'm going to run the stall alone, do you? I need your numerical skills or I'll end up in a right old pickle.'

'Mmm, pickles. You could make some pickles as well as chutneys . . .'

'One thing at a time, Dad!' She winked at him then he let her help him up and they went to the studio to select some jam and chutney.

Connor was driving back to The Lumber Shed after dropping off a coffee table for a client in the village when he saw two familiar figures approaching the village hall. He slowed his van, then stopped at the pedestrian crossing for them.

Emma was chatting away to her dad but she looked up to wave her thanks and started when she saw it was Connor. He raised his hand and nodded at her and she waved then smiled. Greg waved too, a big grin on his face.

For a moment, Emma paused there, one hand tucked into Greg's arm, the other in the air, as if she didn't know what to do next, then Greg said something to her and they started to walk again.

Connor understood why Emma had paused, because he felt as if he should get out and speak to them, but they were at a crossing in the middle of the village and so surely waving was sufficient.

And suddenly the moment was over and Emma and Greg had reached the other side of the road and there was nothing for Connor to do other than to get going.

As he drove away, though, he glanced in the rear-view mirror. Emma was watching him go and he felt lighter than he had done since Grace had left.

Emma and her dad walked into the main room of the village hall. She was still trying to push the image of Connor at the crossing from her mind. Sitting in his van he looked so handsome and familiar and she'd frozen for a moment, feeling as if she should stop and speak to him. Her heart had raced and her cheeks had flushed, but thankfully, her dad had nudged her and told her that they should cross the road and not keep poor Connor waiting there. Of course, he'd been right, but even so, she knew it would take some getting used to seeing Connor around the village and not speaking to him every time their paths crossed.

Bringing her focus back to her current surroundings, she was surprised to see how many people were gathered there. Tables had been set out around the room and some people were sitting working on things while others went around with notepads ticking off items on lists. There was a wonderful feeling of community and Emma felt warm at the thought of becoming a part of it once more.

'It's busy.' Emma's dad took her arm and she nodded.

They moved through the room and Emma scanned the faces, then spotted Clare at a table in the far corner with Kyle and Zoe.

'There! Let's go over and see Zoe.'

She led her dad over and Zoe waved when she spotted them.

'Greg!' Zoe got up and came around the table and hugged Emma's dad.

'Lovely to see you, Zoe. It's been a while.'

'I'm so sorry.' Zoe shook her head. 'Things have been manic.'

'No problem. You look very well, young lady.'

'You look well too, Greg.'

He chuckled. 'I've had some lovely news.'

'Do you want to share it?' Zoe asked.

Greg smiled. 'Emma has decided to stay in the village permanently.'

Zoe's eyebrows raised. 'That's wonderful news!'

'I think so!' He nodded.

'Come and tell me all about your plans.' Zoe hooked her arm through Greg's with the familiarity of old friends.

While her dad chatted to Zoe, Emma stepped forward.

'Hi, Clare.'

'Hello. How are you?'

'Good, thanks. I've been thinking . . . if it's not too late notice . . . I *would* like to have a stall at the fête.'

'Of course it's not!' Clare smiled. 'What would you like to sell?'

'I'll go with jam and chutney, like we discussed before.' Emma slid the straps of the tote bag off her shoulder and set it down on the table then carefully got out the three jars she'd brought with her. 'I have some samples here but I also have ideas for some others. I just need to get some more fruit.'

Clare picked up the jars in turn. 'Ooh! Look, Kyle, Emma's made strawberry jam, and raspberry and gin jam, also a tomato chutney.'

'Yum!' Kyle clapped his hands. 'Can we try them?'

'Of course.'

'Kyle, go and get some spoons, would you?' Clare asked.

'Won't be a moment.' Kyle hurried away in the direction of the kitchen.

'So, you've been busy?' Clare smiled at Emma.

'I finished cleaning up my mum's studio and tidied the garden and there's so much fruit and veg there that it seemed a waste not to do something with it.'

'How lovely. And your dad's looking really well.'

'I think so too.'

'I heard from my mum yesterday, actually, and she asked how your dad was. She's travelling around Europe in a campervan with the vicar. Well, the *former* vicar.'

'Iolo?'

'Yes! They got together last year and they're having a fabulous time cavorting on foreign beaches and camping all over the place.'

'That's wonderful. I'm envious.'

Clare nodded. 'Me too. But, having said that, I'm also really enjoying being home in Little Bramble. I've certainly been busy since my return last year.'

'With your job, the Christmas Show and the fête?'

'And Mum's dog, Goliath, *and* having Kyle around. He's a houseful, my son.'

'He seems lovely.'

'He is. I just wish he didn't fall in love so quickly because he's had his heart broken numerous times. But then, having said that, I guess I can't talk now.'

'About heartbreak?'

'About love.' Clare's cheeks coloured and she gestured across the room. Emma followed her gaze.

'That's Sam.'

'Your . . .?'

'Lover!' Clare giggled. 'I feel funny saying it but boyfriend seems too young and partner feels too . . .'

'Official.'

'Exactly that! Like he's my business partner or something.' Clare nodded. 'I'll call him my lover for now but only really as a joke.' Then Clare dashed around the table and took the arm of a woman pushing a double pram. 'Jenny, sweetheart, please sit down!'

The pretty woman who Clare led to her chair had greasy blonde hair pulled back in a ponytail, a very pale face and dark shadows under her eyes. But she smiled as she sat down and Clare parked the pram next to her.

'Emma, this is Jenny. You might know each other?'

Emma smiled at Jenny. 'Vaguely. I think I recognise you, but it really would have been years since we spoke.'

Jenny nodded. 'You're Greg's daughter.'

'That's right.'

'I was friendly with Ted at school, like Clare.'

'Of course! Good to see you again.'

'I doubt it. I look terrible and I am *exhausted*.' Jenny wiped a hand across her brow. 'These two are still feeding four times a night so it feels as if the moment I drop off, I'm being woken up again.'

'That sounds awful.' Emma frowned.

'I swear my nipples are down to my knees now and I'm constantly starving.'

'Do you want some jam?' Kyle was back with some spoons. 'Anything to avoid nipple talk again.'

Clare shot him a warning glance, then rolled her eyes at Emma.

'Sorry, Kyle, but you'll understand one day.' Jenny poked her tongue out at him.

'How will I?' Kyle's eyebrows rose. 'I don't plan on breastfeeding.'

Kyle and Jenny stared at each other before bursting into giggles.

'Don't make me laugh, Kyle, my bladder control is shot too.'

'TMI, Jenny, TMI.' He shuddered dramatically then pointed at the jars on the table. 'Have some jam and forget about your saggy nips and weak bladder.'

Emma looked from Kyle to Jenny to Clare and Clare winked at her. It seemed that these two had an easy enough relationship where these levels of banter were perfectly acceptable. Kyle was a very funny young man.

'Got any scones?' Jenny asked.

'Scones?' Kyle frowned. 'I can get some scones.'

Clare grabbed a purse from her bag that was hanging on the back of the chair. 'Get a loaf of bread too. Might as well make the most of this.'

Kyle nodded then sashayed out of the hall again.

'He's a good one.' Jenny nodded. 'Really looks out for his mum and her friends. He's so rude, sometimes, too, but it just makes me laugh.' She yawned loudly. 'Excuse me.'

'Why don't you have a cuppa and a scone then I'll come home with you and watch the twins while you have a nap?' Clare offered.

There was a squeak from Jenny then she burst into tears. Emma stood there awkwardly while Clare handed Jenny some tissues. 'It's OK, Jen. You're just tired.'

'I'm tired and hormonal and a geriatric mother. I swing from laughter to tears in mere seconds. Please excuse me, Emma. That's what I get for . . . for . . . loving my husband.'

Emma frowned, not sure what Jenny meant.

'We had sex – because even after all these years together I still can't keep my hands off him – and I got pregnant. Totally didn't expect it at forty-five but it seems it can happen. And twins too.' She shook her head but a soft smile played on her lips.

'Can I get you anything?' Emma asked, feeling the need to do something useful.

'You don't know where everything is in the kitchen, do you?' Clare asked.

'Well, you did lend me that mop and bucket so I've been in there and I can make an educated guess.'

Clare shook her head. 'It's fine. I'll be quicker. You sit with Jen a moment and I'll make us all a cuppa. We need to try your jam anyway and it'll be a good chance for everyone to get to know you better.'

'Sure. That would be nice.'

Emma pulled up a chair and sat next to Jenny while Clare went to make tea. Emma's dad was still chatting away to Zoe and Jenny was slumped over, blowing her nose.

'They're so cute,' Emma said as she peered into the pram.

Something swept over her, making her almost dizzy as she gazed at the tiny faces with perfect little noses and rosebud mouths. One baby was wearing a blue Babygro with a little blue hat and the other was wearing pink with a frilly crocheted bonnet. They were utterly beautiful and it hit her that she'd never have this herself. It wasn't something she'd struggled with and motherhood hadn't been something she'd longed for, but the sight of these two tiny beings stirred something inside her. The feeling faded almost as quickly as it had arrived, but even so, she felt quite moved by the babies' perfection.

'I don't try to stereotype them.' Jenny sniffed. 'It's my twins, you see. They dress them up like this so they can tell the difference.'

'Your twins?' Emma frowned.

'Yes, I have older twins too. Both girls. And they love dressing the babies up. I wish they loved getting up with them in the night too but then, even if they did, it wouldn't do any good because they don't have the milk to feed them.'

'Umm . . . I don't know much about babies and feeding them, but couldn't you express or use formula milk? Could your husband or daughters feed them for you so you could get some sleep?'

Jenny sighed. 'I could, but because of my age I feel like this is my last chance to do this and I'm afraid that if I don't keep feeding them, then my milk might dry up. It didn't come in immediately and took a few tries to get it flowing, but once the babies latched on properly, it was amazing. It's not easy at all but I feel so lucky to be a mum again. Even if it doesn't seem like it with all my moaning and groaning and emotional outbursts.'

'Don't be so hard on yourself.' Emma gazed at the babies again, beautiful little people, currently oblivious to the world. 'They're perfect.'

'Thank you. Their dad and I think so. Although we do miss sleep.'

'It'll come again.'

'It will. I know that from having my two older girls. Well . . . there was a phase when I got a bit more sleep but then as they got older and started driving and going out drinking – not at the same time, of course – I started worrying again and not sleeping as well and . . . I guess it's a bit of a cycle, really. Do you have any?'

'Children?'

Jenny nodded.

'Oh, no. Never the right time, really. Or the right person.'

Jenny's brows knitted together. 'Didn't you used to go out with Connor Jones?'

'I did.'

'That's right, because you dumped him on your eng—' Jenny's eyes widened and she covered her mouth. 'I am so sorry! The problem with exhaustion is it removes any filter. I didn't mean for it to come out like that.'

'It's fine.'

'No. It's not. I'm really sorry. None of that is my business at all.'

'It happened a long time ago, but I can't take it back, no matter how hard I might try.'

'Life is tough, Emma.' Jenny placed a hand on Emma's arm. 'We make decisions for reasons that make sense to us at the time. I can't deny that there have been days when I'd have happily kicked my husband to the kerb. But then I remember how he lets me warm my cold feet on him in bed, how much he loves our children and how attractive I still find him and I'm glad I didn't.' She laughed to show Emma she was joking. 'And who else would rush out at 3 a.m. to buy me incontinence pants because I wet myself every time I sneeze?'

Emma opened her mouth, trying to think of an appropriate reply.

'It's OK.' Jenny flashed a warm smile. 'It's not as bad as I make out and I guess I say some of these things just to relieve stress through laughter. Although even that makes me wet myself.'

Emma choked back a giggle. She had a feeling she was going to enjoy getting to know Jenny.

'Here we are.' Clare was back, carrying a tray of mugs and a teapot and behind her came Kyle with a brown paper bag. 'And Kyle has got us fresh scones, bread and croissants so we can try out this delicious-looking jam.'

They all sat down around the table for an impromptu tea party. Zoe poured the tea, Greg passed the mugs along and Clare spread the different jams onto flaky, buttery croissants, plump sultana scones and thick slices of bread. Emma relaxed with her new friends, talking about plans for the fête, tucking into the spread and sharing memories of what it had been like to live in Little Bramble over the years.

It was a wonderful way to spend the afternoon.

Chapter 20

'Are you sure about this, Emma?' her dad asked as they made their way to the village hall the next morning. The sun was shining and though the air was cool, the blue sky hinted at a hot day ahead.

'Absolutely, Dad. It'll be good for us both.'

Her father plucked at the jogging bottoms she'd told him to wear, then at the loose T-shirt. 'But I don't feel very smart.'

'Dad, you look fine. We're going to an exercise class. You're not meant to look smart.'

'But I like my normal clothes.'

Emma smiled as they walked. It was sweet that her dad liked to dress smartly, especially when going out in public. It was an old-fashioned thing that had been instilled in him as a boy; he felt that he had to put on his good clothes if he was going anywhere.

At the village hall, they waved greetings to some of the villagers they knew then went inside. The hallway was dark and cold, the heating off because it was summer and the sun hadn't warmed this side of the building yet. Aromas of toast and coffee teased Emma's nostrils and she pressed a hand to her belly. She'd only had a banana for breakfast, not wanting to exercise on a full stomach, although she had encouraged her dad to have a bowl of granola with chopped apple and a large glass of orange juice.

'If only your mum could see me now.' Her dad shook his head. 'Whatever would she say?'

'She'd say that she was proud of you and impressed by the effort you're making to stay fit and healthy.'

'I suppose so.'

They went through to the main room and Emma's stomach did a loop the loop because there were around twenty people in there already. They were all wearing appropriate clothing to allow free movement and some even wore sweatbands.

'Emma!' Clare waved at her from a mat at the front. 'I saved you both a space.' She pointed at the two yoga mats on the wooden floor and Emma tried to stop herself from grimacing. This was her first time at tai chi, so being at the front was her worst nightmare.

'Oh . . .' She led her dad over to Clare. 'Would we not be better off at the back? We'll probably get it all wrong this time and I'll end up embarrassing myself.'

Clare tightened her ponytail and shook her head. 'You'll be fine. There are other newbies here too and no one cares what anyone else looks like. When I started doing this back in the winter, it took me a while to get into it, but you'll soon get the hang of it. Just remember to breathe and stay relaxed. And be grateful – at least you don't have to do it with my mum standing next to you in her undies.'

'Her undies?'

'She always does tai chi outside in her underwear because she says it's good for the circulation.'

Emma wondered if Clare was joking. 'Bracing, I would imagine.'

'Exactly!' Clare leant closer. 'This will be so good for your dad.'

Emma nodded. That was the main reason she'd agreed to come to the Saturday morning tai chi class when Clare had raised it yesterday afternoon. Apparently, Clare's mum, Elaine, had taught Clare and Kyle and now Kyle ran classes in Little Bramble village hall.

She had to do this for her dad and for her new friend, Clare. She didn't want to let them down and yesterday they had told her all about the benefits of the exercises, especially for the elderly.

She helped her dad to remove his trainers, smiling because he'd worn his best socks, then kicked off her own trainers and set them aside. Standing still on her mat, she took some slow breaths and tried to let the tension in her shoulders slip away.

'Good morning, campers!' Kyle jogged onto the stage in front of them. He looked like he was about to teach an eighties aerobics class in silver metallic leggings, black shorts and a black vest top with thick grey leg warmers. He had a silver headband on and matching wristbands.

'Campers?' Emma whispered to Clare.

'It's his sense of humour . . . acting as if we're at a holiday camp in the eighties.'

'Ahhh. Of course.' Emma tried not to laugh because Kyle was certainly flamboyant.

'When we started tai chi, he didn't dress like that, but Kyle loves clothes and thought it would be fun to dress up. Not for me, though.' Clare gestured at her baggy joggers and T-shirt that looked about three sizes too big. 'This is Sam's. I borrowed it as I stayed at his last night.' Dots of pink appeared in her cheeks and a smile played on her lips. She had the glow of a woman in love and it gave Emma a sense of hope.

'Is Sam coming?' Emma asked.

'Not today because he has morning surgery, but he does come sometimes.'

'OK, then!' Kyle clapped his hands from the stage. 'I know that we have some beginners here today so can we give them some good old Little Bramble encouragement.'

Applause echoed through the hall. Emma's dad had a huge grin on his face and she was pleased she'd decided to bring him. This could be good for them both. After all, when was the last time she'd gone to an exercise class and been surrounded by other people? She'd been so worried that everyone would be judging her when she'd returned to the village but that hadn't been the case at all; in fact, apart from Connor's anger, and Zoe's initial coldness, Emma had found only friendship and acceptance. Oh, and there was Sadie and her glaring eyes, but Emma had only seen her twice so far and she wasn't about to let one woman's behaviour worry her.

Kyle stood with his legs ankle-width apart then took a deep breath.

'Do what I do, people. Follow my moves and keep up. I'll take it slow.' He laughed. 'For those of you who don't know, nothing about tai chi is rushed, so don't worry. If you make a mistake, let it go then carry on.'

Emma kept her eyes on Kyle, breathing as he did, moving as he did, and her concerns about getting things wrong slipped away. From the corner of her eye, she could see her dad doing the same and when she stole a proper glance at him, his face was a mask of concentration, his posture upright, his breathing deep.

Kyle's movements were mesmerising, full of grace and elegance. At times, he looked as though he held a ball of energy between his hands and was pushing and pulling at some invisible force. Emma followed him as closely as she could, sometimes going the wrong way and sometimes almost losing her balance, but no one else seemed to care.

When the thirty-minute session came to an end, Emma felt relaxed, clear-headed and content. But she also felt as if she was on the brink of something and when a tear slipped from her eye and ran down her cheek, she wasn't surprised. During the class, emotion had swelled inside her, taking her by surprise. It had ebbed and flowed with the movements, and she'd felt as if things were loosening, unwinding, things that had been tightly coiled inside for a very long time. Her body and mind had seemed to work together in the pursuit of well-being, and she was amazed at the uplifting effect of the exercises.

'Well done, everyone!' Kyle smiled at them. 'For our newcomers and for those of you who might have forgotten, there are many benefits to tai chi. It can reduce stress by relaxing your body and clearing your mind, helping you to realign. Regularly doing tai chi can lower blood pressure and alleviate arthritis pain. The focus on breathing throughout the exercises increases oxygen flow and this can help increase energy and alertness. As a result, it enhances your mental capacity, aiding concentration and keeping your mind sharp. And all this without putting excessive strain on your joints and ligaments.'

Emma looked at her dad, took in his easy smile, bright eyes and rosy cheeks and knew that he'd enjoyed it as much as she had. If they did this regularly, the benefits for him could be transformative, could help ease the early dementia symptoms he'd shown, perhaps even reverse them. He'd admitted that not eating properly, not sleeping well and not caring about himself had made him feel more confused and he'd been low and lonely, but this could be another good thing to aid his recovery. She couldn't change his age but she could help him cope better with ageing. It would, she knew, also be good for her. On the cusp of her fiftieth birthday, she should be taking better care of herself and tai chi was one way to do this.

'Did you enjoy that?' Clare asked.

'Very much. I'm fairly certain Dad did too.'

'Do you think you'll come again.'

'Definitely.' Emma smiled. 'When's the next class?'

Connor pulled up outside Greg's cottage and cut the engine. He wondered if it would always feel strange coming here, if, every time he did, he would be assaulted by memories of happy times – and the not-so-happy ones.

It had been a busy week and he'd managed to finish Sadie's kitchen and the latest order for a local customer. He was on top of things and all he needed to do for the next two weeks was ensure that everything was ready for the fête. He'd come to Greg's to bring some jars from his mum for Emma and he found himself strangely excited at the thought of seeing her and was glad his mum had asked him to come. Apparently, Emma was making jam for the fête and needed as many jars as possible and he was already wondering where he could get more jars if he needed an excuse to come back.

He got out of the van and went around to the back to get the cardboard box of jars then carried it to the front door. The cottage was beautiful in the summer with the roses climbing around the door, their sweet, heady aroma filling the air. It looked different since Emma had come home, more vibrant, as if she'd brought its lifeforce back with her. The clean windows were thrown open, music played somewhere inside – was that an acoustic guitar? – and just knowing that Emma was inside made him feel differently about going there. The cottage now held potential, for what he wasn't quite able to put his finger on, but he felt as if there was more to come.

He knocked on the door and waited, wondering why his mum had asked him to bring the jars over. She could have done it herself but he was glad she hadn't. He had his suspicions that she was meddling, but with the best intentions. She loved him and had loved Emma, had seen her as a member of her family for a long time. It was natural that she had missed Emma too and he knew they'd spoken recently. Maybe she was trying to push him and Emma back together somehow. He hoped as well that they could even be friends again at some point.

'Connor.' Greg waved a hand as he stepped back. 'Come on in.'

'You're looking well, Greg.' It wasn't a hollow compliment; Greg really did look good.

'We went to that tai chi class this morning at the village hall and I feel like a thirty-year-old again.' Greg patted Connor's shoulder as they walked through to the kitchen. 'Well, almost.'

'Tai chi, eh?' Connor set the box of jars on the table. 'I think I need some of that.'

'You haven't tried it?'

'I tend to spend a lot of Saturday mornings catching up with things at work, so no, I haven't tried it.'

'It has many benefits.' Greg filled the kettle and turned it on. 'Emma said we're going to go every week.'

'Brilliant.' Connor smiled, wishing his heart wasn't pounding quite so hard at the thought that Emma might be in Little Bramble every Saturday. 'I think I'll have to give it a try.'

'Come with us next weekend.' Greg frowned. 'There won't be a class the following week because of the fête but it'll continue after that. It would be great to have you there too.'

'I'll try to make it but I've got quite a bit to do before the fête, so maybe after that.'

'Don't put it off for too long, Connor. I know you're still young but it's never too early to start looking after yourself.'

'Thanks, Greg, I'll bear that in mind.'

'Oh, hello.' Emma came in through the back door. She was wearing what looked like gardening clothes with a smudge of mud across her forehead and she held a trowel in her right hand. 'I didn't hear the door.'

'That's because you've got The Carpenters blaring out in the studio.' Greg winked at Connor.

'Well, you were strumming away on your Fender Telecaster when I went out there.' Emma grinned at Greg.

'Some things don't change.' Connor smiled. 'This cottage was always filled with music, especially The Carpenters.'

'Not just The Carpenters.' She raised an eyebrow. 'I had to put up with your music too. What was it? U2, Bon Jovi, Guns N'Roses.'

'You said you liked them.'

Her eyes flashed and she lifted her chin, reminding him of the young woman he'd once loved. She was still beautiful and he found himself imagining what it would be like to hold her again, even just one more time.

'I didn't mind. Except when you played them really loudly in the car!' She laughed and he joined in. 'My eardrums have never recovered.'

Could things be easier between them now that he'd apologised? Now he understood how Emma had felt back then? He had shared so much with Emma that there would surely always be a bond between them. Their history could never be erased.

Greg cleared his throat and Connor shook himself. Heat crawled into his cheeks as he met Greg's laughing eyes. He'd been on a trip down memory lane with Emma and it had been enjoyable. They had, if he wasn't completely out of touch, almost been flirting. He returned his gaze to Emma, who had gone to the table and was looking at the box.

'What's in here?'

'Jars from Mum.'

'Wonderful! Tell her thanks.'

'Will do.'

She put the trowel down then frowned at the mud that crumbled off it onto the table. 'Oops! Better clean that off.' She grabbed some kitchen roll and scooped the mud onto her hand then dropped it in the bin. 'Dad, I've just had a good look in the garden and there definitely aren't enough strawberries for more jam so we'd better go and get some.'

'That sounds like a nice way to spend the afternoon,' Greg replied.

'Shall we go now? No time like the present.'

Connor shuffled his feet, feeling like an outsider.

'Connor . . .'

'Yes?'

'I don't suppose you'd like to come with us?'

'Strawberry picking?'

'If you haven't got any other plans. It's just that we could use another pair of hands and it might be fun.'

Connor cleared his throat. 'I don't have plans and I'd love to come. Remember that time when we were eighteen and went with your mum?' He couldn't help himself and he knew he'd have a twinkle in his eye.

Emma's lips parted and she stroked absently at her throat. 'I remember.'

'Right, you two, let's pack some sandwiches and we can have a picnic after we've been through the strawberry fields.'

'Good idea, Dad.'

'We can go in my van,' Connor said. 'More room.'

'Great.' Emma looked down at herself. 'I'll just pop and change, though, as these are covered in mud.'

She headed upstairs and Connor sat at the table, trying not to let the grin that was growing inside him spread across his face. He didn't want to seem too keen to spend the afternoon with Emma and Greg because deep inside he was terrified of scaring her away again. He knew he probably needed to be cool, but that just wasn't who he was and it never had been.

'Good to see you two youngsters getting along so well.' Greg's voice was muffled by the fridge because he was rooting around in there for something then he came to the table and set down a lump of cheese and a packet of ham. 'She always had that gift, didn't she?'

'What's that?'

'The ability to make us smile and feel grateful to be alive.'

Connor nodded, knowing that Greg had hit the nail on the head. Emma had always brought vitality and happiness with her, had been able to make her family and Connor smile, even when times had been tough. It was one of the things about her that he'd loved. And yet the downside of loving her had been devastating and there was no way he could survive that again.

In that moment he vowed to be sensible and practical, to enjoy Emma's company but to guard his heart. Maybe she would stay in the village as his mum had told him she planned to do, but equally she might disappear again, so Connor would prepare himself for the latter. Just in case. Not that he'd picked up any signals from her that she felt anything other than friendship towards him anyway.

But this afternoon stretched ahead of him, just asking to be enjoyed, and he intended on doing exactly that.

Chapter 21

Emma stood up straight and stretched. This strawberry picking was hard work. Her back and shoulders were already aching and she hadn't yet filled the basket she'd brought with her. Her dad had picked some strawberries from the first row of plants, but she'd seen him wince more than once, so asked him to go and get them some cold drinks from the farm shop and the picnic blanket from the car. Now he was sitting on the blanket under a tree. After the tai chi class that morning, she suspected he was probably feeling tired because she certainly was. Being out in the fresh air would be good for him.

On the next row along, working hard, was Connor. He was crouched down, gently but deftly removing strawberries from their plants, and Emma found her gaze repeatedly drawn to him. She'd been pleased, if a bit surprised, when he'd agreed to come with them, and it was almost like old times being with him and her dad like this. The only things missing were her mum and their youth.

'How's it going?' Connor had turned around and was heading towards her. He stepped over the plants and showed her his basket. 'This enough?'

'Wow! You've done well.'

'Better than you by the look of it, but then I was always good at strawberry picking. Some might say I was the best.'

There was mischief in his eyes and it took years off him. His brow shone with perspiration and his cheeks were flushed but he looked happy. Something inside Emma started to unfurl slowly, making her think of how the petals of a flower open to the sun in a slow-motion video. They had a common history and nothing would ever erase what they had shared.

'You were . . . and still are.'

He held her gaze and everything around them seemed to melt away. It was just Connor, the man she had loved, two baskets of fresh strawberries, the sun warming their skin and the breeze gently ruffling their clothes.

'I . . . We should get back to Dad.' Emma said the words but didn't move. Her feet felt glued to the grass.

Connor tilted his head slightly. 'We should.' The way he looked at her made her feel like the only other person on the planet. She remembered that feeling and knew that it was one of the things that had bound her to him.

'There's a bottle of wine and some lunch in the cooler in your van.' Her voice was husky.

'I'm actually ravenous.'

'Me too.'

He shifted the basket to one arm, then raised his free hand and gently brushed her cheek. Electricity shot through her, filling her whole body with a fierce yearning.

Connor leaned closer and his eyes moved to her mouth then he lowered his head towards her. She gasped, her pulse racing, her body responding instantly. His breath was warm against her skin.

Lost in the moment she wanted this. Wanted him. More than ever before.

But it was wrong.

She stepped back and broke eye contact.

'Sorry,' he said. 'You had a strawberry leaf on your cheek. I got it off for you.'

She couldn't speak.

'I'll get the things from the van.'

Emma nodded as he walked away, then shook herself. What was that? Was he going to kiss her? Did he think it would be OK to kiss her? For a moment she'd wanted him but then she'd remembered everything, remembered Sadie. He was with her and Emma would never disrespect another woman in that way. She felt sure that Connor wasn't the sort of man who'd cheat either. Was it just their old connection overpowering them both?

She carried her basket over to where her dad was sitting and he smiled up at her.

'Were you successful?' he asked as she sat down.

'Successful?' Emma thought of Connor touching her cheek, the green of his eyes and the gold flecks at the centre, the sheen on his skin from the heat and the effort and her heart squeezed. 'Yes. I think so.' It was as though she'd been sleepwalking for years and she was waking up slowly, discovering who she had once been again. It had only ever been Connor for her; she'd never fallen in love like that again. But none of it mattered because there was Sadie.

'Good, good!' Her dad leant forwards and looked into her basket. 'We can wash some of those and have them with lunch.'

'And some champagne. I packed the reusable plastic champagne flutes.'

Connor brought the cooler and his basket of strawberries over to them and set them down on the blanket. Her dad got the champagne flutes and bottle of bubbly out then handed it to Connor. 'Would you mind? My grip isn't what it was. Physically or mentally.'

Emma started and looked at him, but a teasing smile played on his lips. 'Cut it out, Dad!'

'Sorry.' He chuckled.

Connor peeled away the foil covering the cork then placed his hand over it and wiggled it until there was a pop. Emma held up the flutes and Connor filled them then set the bottle down against the tree trunk. 'What are we celebrating?'

Emma looked at her dad then back at Connor.

'The beautiful weather, a successful harvest and our health.'

'Cheers.' Connor gently tapped Emma's flute with his then did the same to her dad's.

'Right, Emma, what sandwiches did we pack?' Her dad opened the large Tupperware container and spread out the sandwiches and several foil-wrapped parcels.

'There's a quiche in there too, Dad.'

They sat in the shade of the tree and ate cheese and onion quiche, cheese and ham sandwiches and freshly picked strawberries, discussing Connor's business, Emma's work and memories of her mum and Connor's dad. There was something incredibly comforting about being with someone who knew her family so well, whose family she knew. It was a bond that could never be broken.

Conversation flowed like the champagne, although Connor only had the one small glass because he was driving, and Emma realised how very easy being with him was – as long as they kept some physical space between them and didn't allow their old passion to overflow again.

As the champagne warmed her blood, relaxing her limbs and mind, it was, she thought, such a shame that he was already taken.

Connor had dropped Emma and Greg off at their cottage and helped them carry everything inside. Emma had offered him a cup of tea, but he'd felt in need of a shower and a nap after the afternoon's labours. She'd walked him to the door and waved goodbye, and he'd driven away with a sense of lightness in his chest, as if a weight had been lifted after a very long time.

It had been a lovely afternoon. There was something very special about eating the fruit when it had just been picked, sweet, juicy and fragrant, the taste of high summer. It had taken him back to that day when he had gone strawberry picking with Emma and her mum.

After picking a load of strawberries, they'd gone back to the village and Emma's mum had gone off to her studio. Connor and Emma had gone for a walk, taking a tub of the strawberries and some perry – basically a cider made from pears – they'd bought at the farm. They'd made their way along the woodland walk then climbed over a fence into a field and settled under a tree. The strawberries had made Emma's lips red and the cider had brought colour to her cheeks. She'd been irresistible and they had kissed for ages, holding each other tightly as they whispered about enduring love and the future they dreamt of sharing. They had been so young and filled with hope, naïve certainly, but optimistic in that way that the young can be before reality creeps in.

But seeing Emma again and being around her had recaptured some of that sense of optimism. He felt that if he could spend more time with Emma, then there would be the chance to rediscover who he had once been and who they had been together. He had liked himself when he'd been with Emma and it dawned on him now that he hadn't liked himself very much at all since then. He'd got on with things, had made a success of his business, but the same couldn't be said for his romantic life. It was why he'd ended up spending so many years with Sadie: he'd come to believe that he didn't deserve more, that he should be able to make the mother of his child happy. Not being able to do so had made him feel so low and his self-hatred had grown, so it had been a vicious cycle. He wanted to be the man he'd been before, to believe that he could be happy with himself, that he could love again.

Thank goodness Grace hadn't been damaged by her parents' relationship, had been able to grow into a confident woman with drive and ambition. Pride in her filled his chest; he had got one thing right at least.

Instead of heading straight home, he went to The Lumber Shed. The need to create was burning inside him and he'd had an idea about something he wanted to make. He needed to get started right away so it would be ready in time. It would be a gift for Emma – and a way of letting her know that even if nothing ever happened between them again, she would still always have a special place in his heart.

The next morning Connor awoke to his phone ringing. It was a FaceTime call from Grace, so he accepted it then sat upright in bed.

'Hello, Dad!' She smiled at him, her cheeks flushed and her eyes bright. Her blonde hair was pinned up loosely and a few tendrils had fallen down around her face.

'Good morning. What time is it?'

'Just gone ten, so nine there.'

'I slept in!' he exclaimed.

'Working late?'

'I was at The Lumber Shed, finishing a job.'

'On a Saturday? I thought you agreed to try to focus on finding a date?'

'No I didn't. I agreed to *think* about it at some point in the future. Besides which, you've only been gone just over a week, so give a man a chance.'

Grace rolled her eyes. 'OK, I'll let you off this time.'

'What's it like out there? Give me all the details.'

He lay back on his pillows and listened to Grace's voice and her easy laughter as she filled him in on her accommodation, the people she'd met and the sights she'd seen.

'So you love it?' he asked.

'It's amazing, Dad. You'll have to come and visit me.'

He smiled. 'Perhaps I will.'

'What are your plans today?'

'I'll get up in a bit then have some tea and toast, probably pop into work for a bit.'

'Are you having lunch with Nanna?'

'I'm not sure yet. Her house is so full of bunting now that I'm not sure there's room for cooking.'

Grace laughed. 'Oh, I miss you all.'

'Don't miss us too much. You're out there to enjoy yourself.'

'I know.' She blinked. 'I'm going for brunch with friends this morning. The coffee out here is delicious and the pastries are to die for.'

'Good for you.'

'What about you, Dad? Have you done anything other than work since I left?'

He was about to fib but Grace gasped. 'You have, haven't you? I can see it in your face.'

'What?'

'You look different.'

He ran a hand over his morning stubble. 'It's probably because I haven't shaved yet.'

'No, it's not that. It's something else.'

'If you must know, I went strawberry picking yesterday.'

'How lovely. Who with?'

He cleared his throat. 'Emma and Greg.'

'Really?' Her eyebrows shot up her forehead. 'How did *that* go?'

'Well, since I apologised to Emma, things have felt a bit better. You helped me to understand how she must have felt all those years ago and it's eased the tension for me.'

'What about her?'

Connor thought about the lovely afternoon they'd had, about how much he'd enjoyed being with Emma and Greg and about the look in Emma's eyes when he'd brushed the leaf from her cheek. Then he thought about how he'd leaned in to kiss her and how she'd stepped out of reach.

'Dad? You're blushing.'

'Am I?'

'What happened?'

'I'm not sure.'

'Do you still have feelings for Emma?'

'I don't know.'

'Did you kiss?'

'Grace!' He shook his head. 'I can't discuss things like that with you.'

'Why not?'

'You're my daughter.'

'And I'm here for you, even if not physically right now.'

'Thanks.'

'Dad, look, if you have feelings for Emma you should be honest.'

'I'm not sure that she'd want that. I did go to kiss her. Not deliberately but something inside me made me want to, and she pulled away. Which is quite understandable if you think about it because we've only seen each other a few times since she came back and why would she want to kiss me?'

'Because you're just adorable.'

'Ha ha. Anyway, I'm sure it's just nostalgia or something making me feel this was.'

'It could be that you actually did want to kiss her and that you still really like her. Kind of like unfinished business between the two of you.'

'Oh, Grace, I don't know. I've only ever had two proper relationships and I messed both of them up. I'm no expert at all this. And speaking to you about it feels kind of strange, so let's stop now.'

Grace giggled. 'You have to talk to someone – and if it's a case of me or Nanna, then I'm probably the better choice.'

'Right. Thanks for that.'

'I'm going to go and get ready now, but remember that there's no harm in telling someone how you feel. Sometimes it's the best thing to do because that way there can be no misunderstandings or regrets.'

He nodded, thinking of what he'd been working on at The Lumber Shed the night before. What would Grace say if she knew about *that*?

'Speak soon, Grace.'

'Bye, Dad, love you.'

'Love you too.'

Grace disappeared from the screen and he put his mobile back on the bedside table. Maybe she was right; maybe she was wrong. It was all far too complicated and confusing to deal with. He pulled the duvet up over his head and closed his eyes, hoping to grab another hour of sleep and forget about it all for a while longer.

Chapter 22

Emma unlocked the door to the studio and went inside. She'd got up early to check her emails and reply to the urgent ones as well as to send some sample edits on a few projects. She'd worked at the kitchen table while outside the sky changed from navy to lavender to rose gold.

One of the stories she'd done a sample edit on had a rescue dog in it and it had made her think again about Zoe's suggestion. Some canine company would be nice. It would give her a reason to get out and walk and it would also be lovely to have another creature around the cottage and to snuggle with on the sofa.

She had a busy day ahead because she wanted to get on with jam making to use up all the strawberries, then she was hoping to make some chutneys too, ready for the fête. She'd found some interesting recipes, one for a tomato chutney with chili and ginger and one for a gooseberry and red onion chutney. She'd also ordered some more spices online and they were due to arrive today so she could get on with experimenting with flavours. She was fascinated by how the measurements of spices could create such different results and was keen to try out some ideas of her own.

When she opened one of the cupboards to get the sugar out, she groaned. She had almost run out so a trip to the shop was in order before she could get started.

'Connor, I'm just not happy with how you left my kitchen.' Sadie glared at him in her hallway.

'I've looked at it again, Sadie, and I can't see what the problem is. I've a lot on at work and need to get going.'

He'd dropped by her cottage on his way to The Lumber Shed because she'd phoned him first thing, insisting that one of the cupboards was about to fall off the wall. It wasn't, not at all, but he'd checked and double-checked just to put her mind at ease. He was worried that since Grace had gone, Sadie was more stressed than usual.

'Please take another look.'

'It won't fall off the wall, Sadie, I promise.'

'Stay for breakfast.'

'I've already had breakfast and I need to get to work.'

He opened the front door and stepped outside but she was hot on his heels and grabbed his arm.

'Look at me, Connor.'

He did. At her wild eyes, her blonde hair that had fallen out of its ponytail, at the silky robe she was wearing. She was a beautiful woman who needed to move on with her life.

'Why don't you go and eat,' he said, 'then spend the day with your parents? Or with a friend? It's going to be a scorcher and a day outdoors would be good for you.'

'Why don't you come back inside?'

'No, Sadie. This has to stop.'

Suddenly she flung herself at him, wrapped her arms around his neck and pressed her mouth to his. He froze, shock seizing him for a moment, then he gently untangled her arms from his neck and took a few steps back.

'What was that, Sadie?'

'I love you!'

'You really don't. Please, Sadie, let this go.'

'Never!'

She flew at him again, wrapping her arms around his waist, and he staggered as he tried not to step on her bare feet.

'That's enough!' He raised his voice now and walked along the path and out onto the street. 'Sadie, you need to get some help. I don't want to hurt you but we're not together and never will be again. For your sake – and for Grace's sake – please speak to someone.'

He got into his van and started the engine, his heart racing as he tried to keep his eyes on the road ahead. He'd tried for over ten years to be kind, but it hadn't helped Sadie or him. She'd clung on to the idea of their relationship, in spite of it being over for so long, in spite of Connor's pleas for her to let him go. He hoped that she would get some help, that her parents would support her and that she'd be OK. She was lonely, believed she needed a man to make her feel better about herself when in fact, the only person who could do that was Sadie herself.

He'd phone her parents when he got to work to ask them to check on her, although he knew they did regularly anyway. They adored Sadie, had put her on a pedestal, and it had led her to need that kind of adoration from everyone around her so she'd struggled when people didn't feel that way about her. Perhaps going to see Grace in Paris would be good for Sadie, show her that there was a life to be lived away from Little Bramble . . .

Emma had been walking to the shop when she'd heard voices and had slowed her pace, peering ahead. When she'd realised that it was Sadie and Connor in the front garden of their cottage, she'd felt like turning back but she was aware of Sadie looking at her from her garden.

As she passed, Sadie flung herself into Connor's arms and they kissed. Emma had dragged her gaze away from them and marched onwards, not wanting to witness their passion.

Her stomach churned and her mouth was dry as she hurried away, but she'd seen what she'd seen – and if she had any doubts left that Connor and Sadie were very much a couple, they'd been put to bed at last.

'Are you sure you don't want a coffee or tea?' Connor asked as Sadie sat down in his office the next day. He took the seat behind the desk, placing a barrier between them.

After yesterday's scene in her garden, he'd thought he wouldn't see her again for a while, but here she was.

He'd opened the window but the afternoon was hot and sticky and he was keen to get back down to the workshop, where it was cooler.

'No, thanks, I'm fine.'

Sadie flicked her hair over her shoulders and crossed her legs. She was wearing what looked like an emerald kaftan with a grey feather print and silver gladiator sandals that tied around her ankles. Her blue eyes were surrounded by thick black fake lashes.

'Is everything all right with Grace?' he asked, pulling out his mobile and checking for missed texts or calls, suddenly worried.

'Yes, she's fine. I spoke to her last night and she's having a wonderful time. She said it's incredible out there. In fact, that's why I'm here.'

'OK . . .' Connor folded his hands in his lap.

'I'm going abroad sooner than expected.'

He watched her carefully, trying to keep his expression neutral but dismay was already pooling inside him.

'How soon?'

'Tomorrow.' She waved a hand. 'It's OK, don't worry. I'm not going to cramp Grace's style if that's what you're thinking. I'm going to fly out to Paris and stay in a hotel for three nights then I'm heading on to Milan and then to Greece. I haven't been away in ages and this will enable me to have a break but also see Grace.'

'You're going travelling?'

'Yes. I'm going for a month so I can have a decent break.'

'Well, that's very positive. Have a good time.'

'I will. I have a friend in Milan and she's coming to Greece with me so we can have a proper girls' holiday.'

He nodded. 'What time's your flight tomorrow?'

'Three.'

'Do you want me to take you to the airport?'

She shook her head. 'I'm going to get an Uber.'

'Really? I don't mind.'

'I think it's probably better that you don't. I need to make this the start of a new chapter in my life and I don't want my feelings muddied by your presence.'

'Muddied?'

She rolled her eyes. 'Connor, don't be an idiot. I hate you for what you've done to me but yesterday made me realise that I have to get away from this village – and from you.'

He pressed his lips together, not wanting to say the wrong thing.

'It was the wake-up call I needed. You have never looked at me in the way you looked at Emma and it – it breaks my heart to say but it's true. The irony of it is that I spent years being afraid that she'd come back and take you away from me, but now that she's here, I'm finally free from my own stupid dreams.'

'Sadie! Emma and me, it's not–'

'No! Don't you dare feel sorry for me. You've done too much of that. I don't want your pity. I do regret wasting so long pining after you, but I've been doing some serious thinking and I also think that I used you as an excuse. I was afraid to leave Little Bramble and knew that if I fell in love with someone who wasn't from the village, then they might well want to live elsewhere. I wanted to stay here where I felt safe, close to my parents and to the life I knew.'

'There's nothing wrong with that, Sadie.' Connor had wanted to do the same, hadn't wanted to leave with Emma because he'd believed he had everything he needed right there in the village. Until Emma left, that was.

'You know what?' Sadie asked as she stood up and smoothed her dress down. 'I think that you and Emma could have something together now. She's been away, has spread her wings and you've built your business into a success. None of us are getting any younger and we only get the one life.'

Connor wasn't sure if this was a trap and if Sadie was about to explode again, so he just shrugged.

Sadie went to the door and Connor stood up. He wanted to believe her, to accept that she was being genuine about moving on, but it would take time. Sadie had clung to what they'd had for so long that he couldn't have faith in the idea that she could walk away until it actually happened. She'd always been unpredictable and he worried that it might be a trick.

'I know I've said it before, but I really am sorry for any hurt I caused you, Sadie.'

'Stay safe and well, Connor.'

'You too – and give Grace my love.'

'Always.'

Sadie padded down the steps to the workshop floor and Connor went back into the office and closed the door behind him. He hoped she was feeling as positive as she'd made out, but only time would tell.

Chapter 23

The day before the fête arrived, bringing with it grey skies and torrential rain. Emma was meeting Clare at the village hall and she put on bright yellow wellies, a raincoat and took an umbrella with her. The walk to the hall was a strange one because the day wasn't cold, but warm and humid, and she hoped with all her heart that the weather the next day would be a lot better.

She climbed the steps to the village hall then shook off her umbrella before stepping into the hallway and gingerly removing her coat. She left it with her umbrella in the hallway.

'There you are!' Clare was sitting at a table with Kyle and Sam.

'Sorry I'm a bit late. I went out to the studio to do a final count of stock then Dad wanted help with something and before I knew it, it was gone ten.'

'That's fine.' Clare shook her head. 'I only got here twenty minutes ago because I had an early shift at the stables. We're just sorting out final numbers for the stalls because two from outside the village have cancelled in light of the weather and . . .' She covered her face with her hands and groaned. 'It's like the Christmas show all over again! The snowstorm almost ruined that and now the fête could be ruined by the rain.'

'Don't worry.' Sam wrapped an arm around Clare's shoulders and hugged her tightly. 'The forecast for tomorrow is better.'

'Yeah, Mum, it'll be fine.' Kyle nodded.

'We could always move things in here,' Emma suggested, watching her new friend's face carefully.

'It's an idea, Clare.' Sam nodded. 'Worth considering if things do take a turn for the worse. Kyle, shall we go and check who's here this morning then we can think about what time we're going to start setting up?'

Kyle shuddered. 'I don't fancy trying to set anything up in that.' He stared out of the window at the darkening sky.

'Well, it might be a case of a very early start tomorrow.' Sam cleared his throat. 'But either way, we'll do it.'

The two men walked away, and Clare groaned again then rubbed her cheeks as if trying to get the blood flowing.

'Sam's right, I know he is.' Clare sat up straight and pushed her shoulders back. 'It will all be fine. OK, for my peace of mind, Emma, will you take that copy of my list and when I call out the stalls, will you tick them off?'

'Of course.'

Emma was very impressed with the range of stalls. There would be a wide variety of stalls, including a craft stall for children, food and drink stalls, one for The Lumber Shed, a greyhound rescue stall to raise money for the local charity, an equine stall selling horse-riding gear and promoting Old Oak Stables, one for the local farm shop and then Emma's jams and chutneys. There would also be a bouncy castle for the children and face painting. It sounded like the perfect way to spend a Saturday – and if the weather improved, it could be wonderful.

'In theory, that all sounds good, right?' Clare smiled at Emma, but her eyes revealed her anxiety.

'It sounds amazing, Clare. You should be proud of what you've done here.'

Clare shook her head. 'I can't take all the credit. I just got stuck in to help because my mum's gone away and one of the women who usually organises everything is ill, then another one said she was keen to hand over the reins to someone else. I guess it's kind of the way that these things go in a small village, right? One generation hands over to the next and so on.'

'That sounds about right.'

'I'm happy to do it, though. And Sam and Kyle have been amazing, as have you, of course.'

'Me?' Emma frowned. 'I've hardly done a thing.'

'You've brought back the jam stall, which your mum used to do such a good job of, according to lots of people I've spoken to. If I was asked once, I was asked a thousand times if there would be jam and chutney for sale.' Clare smiled. 'People like jam and something to go with their sandwiches.'

'They're useful additions to have in the cupboard.' Emma's face twitched.

'Good for toast, sandwiches, cakes, turkey and chips . . .'

Clare snorted then and Emma started to laugh.

'I'm sorry, Emma, it must be the tension. The most ridiculous things suddenly seem funny.'

'I completely understand.' Emma waved a hand dismissively. 'And it *is* funny. I mean, who knew jam and chutney could be so integral to village life?'

From outside came a sudden flash and Clare jumped. 'Please no, not lightning!'

'Oh dear.' Emma got up and went to the window. The rain was hammering down now, running in rivulets down the glass and pounding the pavements and roads outside. She could barely make out the green because of the sheet of water blurring the way and knew that it didn't bode well for the state of the grass.

Behind her, a chair scraped across the wooden floor and then Clare came to join her.

'It's typical, isn't it?' Clare said. 'British weather's so unpredictable.'

'Sadly, that's true, but do you know what?' Emma turned to Clare. 'I have a feeling that tomorrow will be better.'

'I hope so.'

'Come on, let's get a coffee then go and do a sunshine dance to dry up that rain.'

'Thanks, Emma.'

'My pleasure.' Emma slid her arm through Clare's then they went to the kitchen to make coffee while Emma wracked her brain to try to think of a way to raise Clare's spirits.

Storm or not, the fête would go on!

Connor leant forwards to inspect his work and a loud wolf whistle almost sent him headfirst into the tin of varnish. He turned to find Sam Wilson in the workshop, a big smile on his face.

'I didn't hear you come in.'

'That's probably got something to do with the storm and the radio – not to mention how carefully you're concentrating on applying that varnish.' Sam reached Connor's side and stood with his hands in his jean pockets. 'That is *really* something. New or upcycled?'

'New. I carved it myself. From upcycled wood, though. I upcycle a lot but I wanted to check that I could still make something from scratch.'

'It's nice. Is it for sale?'

Connor shook his head. 'It's a gift for someone.'

'Something like that is a pretty special gift so I'm guessing it's for a pretty special person.'

Connor gave a self-conscious laugh. 'You're not wrong.'

'Clare said that Zoe had mentioned something about a certain lady who's returned to the village. I've met her myself and she seems really nice.'

'I'm sure I don't know who you mean.' Connor stared at his shoes.

'You don't want to say anything and that's fine. I understand completely.' Sam rubbed a hand over his dark springy curls. 'Anyway, I just came to check that you're all set for tomorrow. I did try to ring but your phone was off and I had to run a few errands so thought I'd stop by.'

Connor pulled his phone from his pocket and saw that he'd accidentally turned the volume down. 'It should have vibrated at least but then these jeans are so baggy I wouldn't have felt it. But yes, all set for tomorrow, although . . .' He nodded at the section of sky visible through the window. It overlooked fields and trees and usually was like a landscape painting that showed off the changing seasons, but today it was dark and gloomy, the sheets of rain occasionally pierced by a fork of lightning.

'I know. Clare's terribly worried.' Sam grimaced. 'We're really hoping tomorrow will be better.'

'We all are.' Connor nodded. 'A lot of people have worked very hard for this, especially Clare.'

'Yeah . . . and . . . I was hoping to make the day extra special.' Sam coughed then pulled a small box from his pocket. 'She makes me so happy and although I never thought I'd feel like this, I want to spend the rest of my life with her and it feels like the right time to ask, when she's worked so hard to make this fête a success.' He opened the box.

'Wow!' Connor peered at the ring. 'That's what you call a diamond.'

'I've even spoken to Kyle. I wanted to check he'd be OK with me springing this as a surprise.'

'It's a lovely idea and I'm sure Clare will be delighted.'

'I hope so. There's always that element of anxiety around it though, isn't there? Will she want this? Will she be shocked? I mean, she only got divorced last year so it could be that it's too soon for her.'

'Have you discussed it?'

Sam shrugged. 'Kind of. You know, like when someone proposes on TV I've tried to test the waters. But she could say no, which would be devastating, or say yes – but only because she's been put on the spot.'

Connor swallowed hard; Sam was closer to his own truth than perhaps he knew.

'Well, why don't you see how the day goes and then you can get a sense of how she might react? Although I've seen you two together and you look very much in love.'

Sam nodded and a big grin spread across his face. 'I'm a lucky man. If she hadn't come back to the village last year . . .'

'It was meant to be.' Connor used the phrase that his mum did when trying to offer comfort and reassurance.

'I think so.' Sam put the ring back in his pocket. 'Hopefully, by the end of tomorrow, I'll be engaged to the woman I love. Or I could be hiding away and crying into my pillow.'

'I hope it'll all work out for you.' Connor patted Sam's shoulder. 'It would be a great way to end the fête.'

'Thank you. See you tomorrow then.'

'Sure will.'

'Oh . . . and Connor?'

'Yep?'

'Good luck with your gift.'

'Thanks.'

Connor lowered his gaze to the workbench in front of him. It wasn't a diamond ring, but it was something he'd carved with his own hands, that he'd created with Emma in mind, so he really hoped that it would make her smile.

He felt nervous for Sam, knowing what a big step proposing was, but he had a feeling it would work out for the kindly vet and lovely Clare.

When you know, you know, he thought.

Emma gazed around the studio and smiled. She was filled with an enormous sense of achievement looking at the results of her recent hard work. She'd filled four boxes with jars of jam and chutney and spent the afternoon adding labels that she'd printed off at the village hall to the jars. She'd designed the labels a few days earlier, then emailed the design to herself. Clare had told her she could print them on the colour printer at the hall because she hadn't got a printer at her dad's yet. Along with the fabric lid toppers that she'd created by cutting up some old shirts that her dad had given her, the jars looked quite professional. She was looking forward to arranging them on her stall tomorrow.

She paused at the door and listened. The rain was still falling heavily. The afternoon had been gloomy, but inside the studio with the light on and the Aga burning, she'd felt cosy and safe. Her dad had been inside with Dilys, showing her how well he was getting on with his guitar playing, and that had left Emma free to work out here. Emma loved editing because it was a creative process in which she helped authors to make their work shine, but cleaning up the studio, caring for her dad, sorting the house and garden and making the jams and chutneys had been different. It had been a physical process, one that involved rolling up her sleeves and getting stuff done and she'd enjoyed it. She had changed, her perspective had altered, and she knew that she had grown as a result. Making the decision to stay had brought her a peace of mind that she hadn't had in a long time.

As she stood there, she closed her eyes and breathed in deeply, then something washed over her. It was more than a sense of peace and contentment, more than a sense of achievement, more even than happiness. A scent permeated the air, of fruit and sugar, roses and honeysuckle, baking and woodsmoke, and it enveloped her like a warm hug.

'Mum,' she whispered. Goosebumps rose on her arms and something brushed against her cheek as soft and light as a feather.

She opened her eyes slowly, but there was nothing there. Just the clean and tidy workshop, the boxes and the warmth emanating from the Aga. There was the sound of the rain on the roof, her breathing, and a wood pigeon cooing as it sheltered from the rain in a nearby tree.

Whether it was being in this place where she'd spent so much time with her mum, her imagination or something not so easily explained, she felt a deep connection to the woman who had raised her and she wanted to hold on to that feeling. Coming home had been the right thing to do and at the right time for her and for her dad. Perhaps for her mum also. She knew that if she'd come home a year or even two years ago, she'd have resented the impact it would have had on her life in London.

Finally, however, the time was right.

She turned off the lights, let herself out of the studio and locked the door behind her, keen to give her dad a big hug and tell him how much she loved him. The hug would be from herself, but also from her mum, because she knew, in her heart, that that was what she would have wanted.

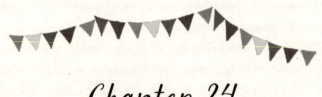

Chapter 24

The weather on the morning of the fête was better than Emma could ever have imagined. The rain from the previous day was a distant memory and the sun was shining brightly. She got to the village green just after eight to set up her stall and ensure that everything looked just right.

'Where do you want me?' her dad asked.

'Let's go and take a look at the stall and we can see how much space we have. Then we can get you settled.'

'I'm quite excited,' he said.

Emma's heart squeezed. Excitement was a positive emotion, so another good sign.

'Are you sure you're warm enough?' Emma glanced at his flat cap, fleece jacket and navy gilet. She'd been worried about him feeling the cold in the fresh morning air and had suggested that he wear layers that he could remove as the day warmed up, including two pairs of socks, a T-shirt and a long-sleeved shirt underneath his outer garments.

'Plenty, Emma, don't worry. I'm really looking forward to the day. It'll be lovely to be outdoors and to catch up with everyone. Look, there's Zoe.' Her dad pointed over at the village green, where Zoe was standing talking to Marcellus David who was, for once, not wearing his postal uniform. It was strange seeing him without it but he did look very smart in navy chinos, a white shirt and a gold waistcoat.

As Emma and her dad approached, Marcellus grinned, his warm welcome as ready as ever.

'Well, hello there, Emma and Greg. So good to see you both looking so well. The country air is doing you good, Emma, and having your daughter home is doing *you* good, Greg.'

'Doesn't she look wonderful?' Emma's dad turned to her and Marcellus and Zoe nodded. Emma felt a bit like a pony on display at a show, but also kind of flattered to have their approval. She would turn fifty in just a few days, so having compliments on her appearance was quite pleasant. In her early twenties, she'd thought anyone over forty was old, but almost thirty years on, she knew the reality was very different and that reaching fifty was actually something to be celebrated. Seeing Connor again had confirmed that for her, because *he* wasn't old, not at all; he was still handsome and strong, full of energy and vitality. Fifty was going to be something she would embrace, especially now she felt a weight had been lifted.

'You do look good, Emma.' Zoe smiled at her.

'Thank you.'

'She's been incredibly busy making jam and chutney.' Her dad gestured at the cart Emma had pulled behind her from the cottage. The jars were all safely tucked in, surrounded by bubble wrap to prevent the glass rattling as they walked. 'Her mum would've been very proud.'

He blinked hard and Emma put a hand on his arm.

'I'm OK, angel, just happy.'

That got Emma in the throat and she rubbed at her neck to try to ease the tension.

'I think it's going to be a day of high emotions,' Zoe said. 'For all of us.'

'It will be a very good day indeed.' Marcellus clapped his hands. 'And we will hopefully raise plenty of money for the greyhounds.'

'That's the plan,' Zoe said. 'Let me show you to your stall, Emma, and when you're set up, there's someone I'd like you both to meet.'

Zoe led them around the green to a row of stalls, each one consisting of a long foldable table with a white canopy and two chairs behind it.

'This is yours.' Zoe pointed at the one at the end of the green closest to the Red Squirrel pub.

'Convenient for a nice pint or two,' Emma's dad said, making her and Zoe laugh.

'You're not drinking beer today, Dad. It's going to be hot and you need to stay hydrated.'

'I was just thinking that a nice pint of cider would go down well with lunch.'

'That's OK then.' She hugged him with one arm around his shoulders.

'The greyhound charity stall is in the middle of the green,' Zoe said, 'and The Lumber Shed stall is just there.'

Emma followed Zoe's pointing finger to a large stall on the opposite side of the green that was divided by a walkway and some grass. She wondered if the placing of her stall so close to Connor's had been deliberate or if Clare had placed her stall here because she was the last one to sign up. Either way, she didn't mind, and the thought of being so close to Connor sent an unexpected thrill of excitement through her. She squashed it though, aware that she had no right to look forward to seeing him.

'I'll leave you to get settled, then when you're ready, pop over and see me.' Zoe walked away, looking very smart and professional today in her green T-shirt with the greyhound logo and khaki walking trousers.

'You know the charity is always looking for volunteers?' her dad said as they spread a checked tablecloth over the fold-up table then clipped the sides down. 'For all sort of jobs.'

'Like what?' Emma asked. 'I can hardly imagine myself doing home checks or cleaning out kennels. Not because I wouldn't want to, more because I've never done anything like that.'

'I was thinking more like admin jobs. You have editorial skills and they could do with a good editor to help with the newsletter. The bloke who's been doing it is a terrible typist and makes lots of errors.'

'Dad!' Emma shook her head. 'If he's volunteering it's hardly fair to criticise him.'

'It's embarrassing, though. I receive the newsletter every quarter. In one edition, there was an article about a winter ramble and the recommendation was "Don't forget your hat, scarf and *willies*".'

'*Willies*?'

He nodded. 'Obviously, it should have said wellies, but he must have accepted the autocorrect on his computer then failed to check before it went to print. And there's more.'

'What else?'

'"We'd like to send a big thank you to *dead* Mrs Jones who kindly volunteered for the Christmas day *shit* at the kennels".'

'No!'

'Yes.' He nodded, his expression perfectly serious. 'It gave the shift a whole new meaning, and as for poor Mrs Jones . . .'

Emma was giggling now.

'And . . .' Her dad had started to place jars on the table so Emma began setting them up in pyramids of different flavours. 'When the chairman retired last year, they thanked him for his "hard work, energy and *self-defecating* humour".'

Emma snorted at that. 'That's too much.'

'Gives old Billy Chapman a whole other side to his personality, doesn't it?'

Emma had to stop what she was doing and hold her stomach as she laughed. She'd almost forgotten how

322

funny her dad could be, always making she and her mum smile with his jokes and puns, with his quirky outlook on life. Had he lost those things recently, or had she overlooked them, seeing him as his age rather than the person he still was?

'Dad, you do make me smile.'

He gave a small bow then doffed his cap at her. 'That's music to my ears. You *should* smile, Emma, all the time. You've always been very hard on yourself and without good reason.'

She gave him a hug and kissed his cheek, grateful for this time with him and even more so for how much better he seemed. He had lights in his eyes, a spring in his step and, it seemed, his old sense of humour was returning.

When everything was organised, Emma stepped back and peered at the stall.

'Does it seem OK?'

'It looks wonderful.'

The stall had country chic with its checked cloth and colourful bunting that had been wound around the posts supporting the canopy. The bunting stretched out from each stall to the next so they all appeared to be linked together. For Emma, it represented how the people of this little village were working together to raise money for the charity and to create a lovely day for everyone. The link between the villagers was one that couldn't be broken, just as the links she had to the village had endured over the years. Then there was the link between her and Connor.

It was still there, fragile, damaged in some ways, but unbroken and she suspected that having survived almost thirty years since they'd parted, it would always survive. It was a comforting thought. Even if they could only be friends now, that was far better than not having him in her life at all. She hoped he felt the same way.

On the stall, jars filled with different colours of jam and chutney were divided into sections on the table with a pyramid at the rear to showcase the flavour and the offer of a discount if someone bought three or more. The labels named the contents as well as the ingredients and she was glad that she'd experimented with herbs, spices and alcohol because strawberry and prosecco sounded perfect for summer and redcurrant and cassis jelly would go well with cheese and cold meats. There was something to appeal to all tastes and she felt proud of what she'd achieved. She was a good editor but she was so much more than just her job, a fact she'd forgotten in recent years.

'These look good.' The voice in her ear sent shivers of delight down her spine and she turned to find Connor next to her.

'Thanks.'

'Can I place an order now and collect them later? I don't want to miss out.'

'Of course.'

She packed the six jars he wanted into a small box and set it back on the trolley, then Connor paid her dad the money.

'First sale of the day!' her dad said as he dropped the money into his zipped apron then patted the outside.

'Plenty more to come, I'm sure. Oh, and Mum said she has something she wants you to see.' Connor raised his eyebrows.

'She did. We're all set up so I can pop over there now. Will you be all right for five minutes, Dad?'

'Absolutely. Perhaps you can find me a cuppa while you're away.'

'I'll do my best.'

Emma and Connor crossed the green and passed the Norwegian spruce that stood tall and broad at the centre. It had been there for as long as Emma could remember, and she'd spent many Christmases singing carols and sipping hot chocolate or mulled wine as she gazed at the festive lights around it. The tree was a part of the village and she was too. She knew that now and wished she hadn't been afraid for so long.

'The tree's grown.'

'It's huge, isn't it? Although on a day-to-day basis, I don't really notice.'

'I think because I've been away, it's probably more obvious to me.'

'Absence makes the heart grow fonder?' His voice was softer as he said the words and she glanced at him as they walked. Was there more to his words than a reference to the tree?

'Actually, Connor, I'm beginning to believe there's some truth in that. I mean . . . Little Bramble looks better than ever.'

'It's a good place to live. Anyway, here you are.' Connor raised a hand in greeting. 'Hi, Mum.'

'Hello, you two.'

Zoe was standing with two other women who were wearing the same green outfit as her and they smiled warmly at Emma and Connor. 'This pair are volunteers with the charity – Mary and Lulu.'

'Hello.' Emma nodded at them, then at another woman who was approaching the stall.

'And this is Jess. She's bringing the dogs from the kennels for us today and I'm going to pop home and collect Digby and Toby in a bit. I didn't want to bring them too early in case they got cold, but it's warming up now and they'll be able to have their beds in the shade.'

Jess was leading two greyhounds towards them, both wearing yellow jackets, and as they got closer, she read the writing on them: *I'm looking for a home.*

'Thanks, Jess.' Zoe took one dog's lead from the other woman and stroked its head gently. The greyhound was small compared to Digby and Toby and black and white with large brown eyes. 'Emma, this is who I wanted you to meet.'

Emma looked at the dog and it peered up at her, blinking its big eyes and waving its long tail. 'She's only fifteen months old, so still quite a young dog. She wasn't raced because she wasn't fast enough, but she was very timid when she came to us. I don't think she'd been very well treated and she was initially nervous around men, but she's spent time with some of our volunteers and with Connor and she's coming round. Sam's been wonderful with our dogs, doing as much of the work pro bono as he can, and he's given her a full bill of health. She's been neutered and fully assessed and is ready to find a home.'

Emma stepped closer to the dog then crouched down and held out a hand. The dog sniffed it then gave her palm a lick.

'Oh . . .' Emma ran her hand over the soft narrow head and the silky ears. 'She's beautiful. What's her name?'

'Harmony.'

'It suits her.'

'I think so.'

'What do you think?' Connor asked as Emma stood up.

'Me?'

'She's looking for a home.'

'I think she's beautiful and someone will love her.'

'Someone like you?'

'Oh! You mean me? And Dad?' Emma's heart skipped a beat. 'Of course! That's what you meant. Sorry, my brain isn't working as quickly as it should be this morning.'

So Connor's in on this too.

'Take her to meet your dad, see how they find each other. And don't panic, Emma. Rehoming isn't an overnight process. We have to ensure that the dog and potential owners are well-suited, so even if you do like the idea of adopting, we'll make sure everything's right first.' Zoe handed Emma the lead.

'See you in a bit.' Connor smiled then whispered, 'There's no pressure at all. Mum thinks you and Greg would be a lovely family for Harmony and that she could be good for

Greg, but it has to be right. Just spend some time with her and see how you feel.'

'OK. Thanks.'

Emma took a deep breath and walked away, holding the lead tight, feeling that she'd been given something very precious to look after indeed.

'Who's this then?' Emma's dad asked when she reached the jam stall.

'This beautiful lady is Harmony.'

'Isn't she graceful?' Her dad held out a hand and Harmony sniffed it.

'She can be a bit nervous with men at first, apparently, but soon comes around if she senses that you're kind.'

'Bloody awful how some of these dogs are treated on the racing circuit.'

'I know.'

'Doesn't she have fantastic markings? Kind of like a cow.'

'Dad!'

'Well, she does. She could've been called Moo Moo or Molly Moo.'

Emma laughed. 'I think Harmony suits her better.'

'I agree. She's like a beautiful harmony. I wonder if she likes guitars?' Her dad tilted his head at the dog. 'Is she staying with us for a while then?'

'If that's all right. She can help us with the stall.'

'That's not quite what I meant.'

'Oh?'

'Is she coming to stay with us at home?'

The dog dipped into a low bow and Emma's heart squeezed.

'I think that's a yes from her.' Emma's dad smiled.

'Well . . . I'm not sure because the homing process is very complicated and we would need to have a home check and ensure that we can offer Harmony the proper support that she needs and—'

'Emma, slow down.' Her dad held up a hand. 'We're good people. We have a lovely home with a large safe garden and she wouldn't be the first dog we've had.'

Emma scrunched up her face as a memory flickered deep in her mind.

'Don't you remember Cassie?'

'I think I do but that was a long time ago.'

'Cassie was the dog we adopted before we had you. She was a Doberman Spaniel cross with beautiful black and brown colouring and soft floppy ears. She was around seven when we adopted her from an elderly woman who was going into a nursing home. Your mum loved that dog and we had her until you were about eighteen months old. She passed in her sleep one night, aged twelve. I don't think your mum ever got over losing her, which was why we never had another dog. She said it was just too painful.'

'I always wanted a dog, growing up.'

'I know and I did try to work on your mum but it was one thing she was resolute about.'

'And how do you feel now about having a dog? There are many benefits to becoming a dog owner and—'

'I know, don't you worry. I've read all about how to keep my body and mind healthy for as long as possible. Oh!' He looked down and Emma followed his gaze. Harmony had stepped closer to him and was now leaning her slim frame against his leg. He smoothed a gnarled hand over her coat and she gazed up at him.

'I think she likes you,' Emma said, moved.

He nodded, his top teeth pressed into his bottom lip.

'Are you OK?'

'I'm . . . Yes.' He nodded but his voice wavered. 'Just . . . this is nice. I also read that when dogs do this, it's their way of giving you a hug.'

'Why don't you have a sit-down and I'll go and get that tea I promised you?'

'That would be lovely.'

Emma gazed at her dad and Harmony again before walking away, her heart brimming with joy as her dad sat down and Harmony moved closer to the chair as if glued to his side, looking as if she'd been a part of their family for years, not minutes.

And she knew that they *would* adopt Harmony because, as with some things in this life, it had already been decided for them.

The morning passed in a blur of sales and bookings for future jobs and Connor barely had time to grab a drink, let alone go and see how Emma and Greg were getting on with Harmony. She was a beautiful, gentle dog and he hoped that Emma and Greg would want to rehome her. His mum had a good instinct for matching dogs with their families and when she'd suggested that Harmony might be the perfect fit for Greg and Emma, he'd agreed that it was worth finding out.

He accepted a cup of coffee now from his mum and sipped it, relieved to have some caffeine.

'Thank you. I needed this.'

'Even though it's so warm?' His mum pushed her hair back from her brow. 'Who'd have thought that the weather would turn out to be so fine for the fête with all that rain yesterday.'

'It's *fate*.' He grinned. 'As in f-a-t-e.'

'Ha ha, Connor. But I agree, it's as if Mother Nature is smiling on us today.'

Connor looked around at the green. People stood in groups talking, others browsed the stalls, children ran through the adults and skipped around the Norwegian Spruce and the air was filled with music from the loudspeakers set up around the green, with chatter and laughter, the smells of hotdogs, burgers and cut grass. It was everything anyone could hope for a village fête to be. A big country village party.

'We've had some interest in homing some of the other dogs today too, so that's a brilliant sign. I'll be busy with home checks and adoption forms over the coming weeks.'

'Good news, Mum.'

'Definitely, because the more dogs we can successfully rehome, the more room there is at the rescue centre for us to take others.'

'Of course.' Connor nodded. 'Hi, Emma.'

Emma had come over to the stall and was waiting just behind his mum.

'Hi. Sorry, I could see you were talking and didn't want to disturb you.'

'No problem. What's up?'

'Nothing . . . well, actually, I've given Harmony some water but I think she could do with a lie-down. She's been sitting next to Dad but I wondered if I should pop home and grab a blanket or something for her to lie on.'

'No need.' Connor's mum shook her head. 'We've got some at the stall, so I'll grab one and take it over to Greg.'

'Thanks.'

'How's she getting on?' Connor's mum tilted her head as she gazed at Emma.

'Really well. Dad has taken to her and she seems to like him too. He said he's always wanted another dog but Mum was against it because she was heartbroken after she lost Cassie years ago.'

'Cassie?' Connor frowned.

'Yes, the dog they adopted before I was born. Mum found losing her too painful.'

'It is dreadful when they pass but the love and happiness they bring with them and the lives we can offer them make it all worth it.' Connor's mum smiled. 'At least, I think so. Imagine what we'd miss out on if we didn't have them.'

'That's what I think too.' Emma nodded.

'I'll go and get that blanket and have a chat with your dad.' Connor's mum left him and Emma alone at his stall.

'Have you been busy?' she asked.

'Very. This is my first drink.'

'That's not good. I could have brought you something sooner if I'd known.'

'It's fine. I'll make up for it now with plenty of water, but I did need a caffeine hit first.'

'So what are you selling?' She peered behind him.

'Come and have a look.'

He took her arm and led her to the long stall that had been erected for The Lumber Shed. 'We have mini chairs and desks for children, tables and chairs, sideboards, chests, rocking horses, decorative bowls, love spoons, cheeseboards . . .'

'It all looks wonderful.'

'And most are made from reclaimed wood or at least part-made. We do a lot of upcycling.'

'You always were conscious of environmental issues.'

'Kind of a tree hugger?' He wiggled his eyebrows.

'Definitely.' Her smile lit up her face and he wanted to touch her cheek.

'These are lovely.' She picked up a cheeseboard in the shape of a heart.

'Perfect for cheese and crackers or a nice soda bread.'

'Mmm. I haven't had soda bread for ages.'

'I'm fairly certain there's a stall here selling it. The farm shop one, actually.'

'I'll have to get some.'

'The farm shop stall stocks all types of cheese and bread, as well as heather honey, chutney and pickle, I think.'

'Competition!' She laughed.

'Not really. There are so many people here that you'll probably both clean up by the end of the day.'

'I hope so. Although Dad would be happy to take plenty of jam home with us. I told him he needs to watch his sugar intake but he's all about enjoying himself now.'

'Walks with Harmony will help keep him fit.'

'That would be so lovely.' Her face fell.

'What is it?'

'I'm thinking about adopting her but what if we don't pass the home check?'

'I'm sure you will, Emma. Mum knows you well, don't forget, and you have a lovely safe home for a dog to live in.'

'Harmony seems to like us.'

'She'll be good for your dad too.'

'I hope so.' She held up the cheeseboard. 'How much for this?'

'For you, it's free.'

'Oh no. I insist on paying.'

'It's a gift.'

'Connor, you can't go giving your stock away, especially as a percentage of the money is going to the charity too. Now, how much?' She pulled a purse from her pocket.

'All right then but . . . uh . . . I do have something I'd like to give you later and that *will* be a gift.'

She met his gaze and he could have sunk into the depths of her eyes. But the memory of her stepping away as he'd gone to kiss her came back like a bucket of icy water. She didn't seem to feel the same way he did.

'Deal. I can't wait to see it.'

He rubbed at the back of his neck. 'I'm nervous now in case you don't like it.' *Or don't like me,* he thought.

She wanted Little Bramble now, but would she want him as well?

Emma put a hand on his arm and her touch sent tingles rippling over his skin. 'I'm sure I will.'

As the day wore on, Emma took a break to have a wander around the fête. Dilys had arrived an hour earlier and she said she would man the stall with Greg and Harmony while Emma had a look at the other stalls.

The next stall across from hers was selling beautiful silver jewellery, from rings with semi-precious stones to pendants on fine silver chains and bracelets with charms. It was all very pretty and skilfully made. Emma smiled at the stall-holder, who was helping a teenage girl to try on a bracelet.

Further on was an equine stall selling jodhpurs, riding hats and boots, as well as saddles and bridles. Emma paused to look at the jodhpurs, thinking they would be quite comfortable.

'We have more stock at the stables, but you're welcome to try any of these on.' A woman with a mop of bright ginger curls and freckles across her nose and cheeks picked up a pair of navy jodhpurs and held them out. 'These look like they'd fit you.'

'Thanks.' Emma nodded, feeling a flush creep into her cheeks.

'Do you own horses?' the woman asked.

'No. I don't, actually, I–'

'Do you ride?'

'No. I've . . . uh . . . never learnt.'

'Well, it's never too late to try.' The woman hung the jodhpurs back on the rail then held out a hand. 'Verity Baker. I'm the owner of Old Oak Stables.'

'Oh, I know the stables.' Emma shook her hand.

'Are you local, then?'

'Was. I mean . . . I am now, I suppose. Again.'

Verity frowned. 'Hold on, I think Clare might have mentioned you. Are you Emma Patrick?'

'That's right.'

'Thought so. Greg's girl. Nice to meet you.'

Emma hid a smile at Verity calling her a girl; she was clearly older than Verity, who looked to be in her late thirties at most.

'You too.'

'Why don't you take a card and then when you decide to try out horse riding, you can give me a call? We can book you in for lessons. It's excellent exercise and the horses are lovely.'

'Thank you.' Emma accepted the card and pocketed it.

'Hello there!' Verity had already moved on to another customer, so Emma walked away, feeling both warmed by Verity's open manner and a bit windswept by her brusqueness. Verity was clearly someone who didn't spare the horses when it came to business. Emma smiled at the pun.

'There's a lovely smile.' Clare greeted her with a kiss to each cheek. 'How's it going?'

'Great, thanks.'

'I see you met Verity.' Clare smiled. 'She's lovely but can be quite blunt. Did she try to sell you lessons?'

'Yes.'

'Worth a try if you like horses. I love it at the stables, but then I was horse mad as a kid. Not everyone feels the same.'

'I might give it a go if you can teach me.'

'We'd have great fun. Do give it a go!'

'I will – I'll book some lessons next week. Which stall are you on?'

'I'm moving between helping Verity and Zoe, as well as checking on the children's craft stall that Jenny's twins, Tilda and Lizzy, are running.'

'Oh, that's right, she has grown-up twins too. They like to dress the babies up, don't they?'

'All the time.'

'Jenny really has her hands full.'

'The girls help her out when they can and her husband's a gem.' Clare brushed her hair back from her face. 'Gosh, it's very warm, isn't it?'

'A perfect day.'

'Come on, let's have a stroll and see what else is here.'

Clare took Emma's hand and tucked it into the crook of her arm. They paused at different stalls, including the farm stall, a gin stall with some delicious-sounding craft gins, one selling candles and another selling cookies of all shapes and sizes.

Emma's mouth watered at the aromas of food, from crepes and coffee to hot dogs and onions. There was something special about food cooked in the open air, something so satisfying about the smells of frying onions and freshly ground coffee beans. Her new friend was beaming at her side, her dad was safe and well with their potential new dog and the day had gone well. It had been so long since Emma had been surrounded by so many people and even longer since she'd paused for enough time to appreciate the simple things in life. The only thing that was bothering her was Connor. Being around him again was proving to be more challenging than she'd envisaged. She couldn't deny that she still found him very attractive, and he seemed so warm towards her now, even flirty. The way he looked at her made her blush . . . and yet, he was with Sadie, so Emma had to accept that and stop her heart wanting more.

'Shall we get some food?' Clare asked.

'That's a great idea. I should take something back for Dad as well. His appetite has certainly grown recently.'

'Bless him, that's good news. Crepes?'

'Yum!'

They stood in line, watching as the couple at the stall used a scoop to pour batter onto hot plates. When the crepes started to lift at the edges, they flipped them over with spatulas then waited for the other side to cook.

Emma ordered a chocolate spread one for herself while Clare ordered a spiced apple and sultana one. When the crepes were ready, they strolled over to a quiet spot and sat on the grass to eat. Emma kicked off her shoes and felt the grass tickling between her toes. The crepe was light and buttery, the chocolate spread thick and nutty and she polished it off quickly. Simple pleasures were the best.

'Good afternoon.' A voice echoed across the green and static crackled followed by a shrill ringing. Emma winced and Clare grimaced. 'Ahhh . . . sorry about that. Should be better now.' Marcellus David was standing on a small raised platform in front of the Norwegian Spruce, a microphone in his hand. 'Thank you all so much for supporting the Little Bramble Summer Fête. As you can see, we have a wonderful array of stalls and many visitors from out of the village. We are delighted to host this special event on such a lovely day. I'm about to have someone pick the winners of the raffle, so make sure you have your tickets ready. The prizes are fabulous! Huge thanks, by the way, to those of you who worked tirelessly over recent weeks to sell raffle tickets and to those of you who bought them. The money from the raffle will go to our local greyhound rescue charity to help the hounds in need. Also, I need to thank the locals who have donated wonderful prizes. OK . . .' He peered out into the crowd. 'If I could have a volunteer to select the tickets from the bucket held here by my lovely assistant?' He gestured to his left, where a tall woman with short grey hair and broad shoulders stood holding a grey bucket. 'For those of you who are unaware, Miranda Fitzalan is one of our local vets and owns the practice along with Samuel Wilson. They have also donated a prize of a full cat or dog health check for one lucky winner.'

'That's very generous,' Emma said, thinking of Harmony.

'They do a lot for the community.' Clare smiled, her eyes shining. 'Sam's very generous with his time.'

'He seems lovely. Right, I'm going to grab something for Dad to eat and take it back to him. Thanks for the crepe.'

'You're very welcome. See you later.'

Emma nodded then headed back to the crepe stall.

'And the first ticket is . . .' Marcellus's warm Caribbean lilt carried over the crowd and there were excited murmurs as numbers were announced and people went to claim their prizes. Emma's dad had bought five strips of tickets and she hoped he'd win something. It would make his day.

She ordered a cheese-and-ham crepe and a spiced apple one, then made her way back to the jam stall, weaving through the crowds and taking care not to drop the food. It had turned out to be such a wonderful day and she was thoroughly enjoying being part of the community again. She'd been filled with pride when Marcellus had commented

340

on the generosity of locals because she was one of those locals again.

She was almost back with her dad and Harmony when she heard a blood-curdling scream that sent a chill through her veins.

Chapter 25

All around Emma, people gasped and crowded around. She squeezed past them, no longer caring that the crepes were getting squashed. All she did care about was getting to her dad. She was sure the scream had come from his direction.

'Where's the first-aider?' someone shouted, increasing Emma's anxiety, so that when she burst through the onlookers and saw her dad on the ground next to the stall, she fell to her knees at his side.

He was crouched down, leaning forwards, his shoulders hunched, Harmony staring down at him.

'Dilys, what happened?' she asked, noting the concern on Dilys's features.

'I'm not sure. One minute he was chatting away, the next, there was a terrible scream.'

'Dad?' Emma laid a hand gently on his back. 'Are you OK? Do you need a doctor?'

'Not from your dad, Emma.' Dilys shook her head. 'From the dog.'

'What?'

Emma leant forwards and realised that the dog was not, in fact, checking on her dad; it was the other way around.

'I'm all right, Emma, just worried about this lovely girl. One minute she was fine and the next she let out the worst scream I've ever heard.'

'Poor Harmony.' Emma stroked the dog's head and she blinked up at her.

'I'm here. I'm the first-aider.' It was Zoe. 'What's wrong? Greg, what happened to you?'

Zoe joined them on the ground, placing a hand on Greg's arm.

'It's not Dad, it's Harmony.'

Zoe frowned. 'Harmony? What is it? What's wrong?'

'She let out the worst scream and started hopping around and now she's holding up her paw,' Emma's dad said and Emma saw that he was gently supporting the dog's leg.

'Let me take a look.' Zoe checked the dog's paw and leg over carefully. 'Poor girl. Looks like it could be a wasp sting.'

'Where?' Emma peered at the dog's thin leg.

'Right there.'

Zoe pointed at a small swelling.

'She's been stung, has she?' Sam had just arrived on the scene, his tall frame casting a shadow over them all.

'Looks like it.'

'OK. Zoe, can you grab some ice and a wet towel?'

'Of course.'

Zoe hurried away and Sam knelt down and checked Harmony over. Emma's shoulders ached with tension as she waited for the verdict. She'd never expected to care so much about a dog so quickly, but she wanted more than anything for Harmony to be OK.

'She seems fine.' Sam smoothed Harmony's head and nodded. 'But we'll need to get some ice and a cold cloth on the sting to help with the swelling and any pain.'

Zoe returned with the ice and cloth and Sam held them over Harmony's leg. Emma was aware of people surrounding them but when she looked up, all she found in their eyes was care and concern. This little dog was a part of the community as much as any of the people and everyone wanted to ensure that she was OK.

'Emma, if you can hold that in place, I'll go and tell Marcellus to carry on. He stopped when we heard the scream. I think we all froze.' Sam stood up. 'I won't be far if you need me again.'

Emma nodded. She couldn't speak because her throat had closed up and when she looked at her dad again, she could see that he was struggling too. She held the cold cloth on Harmony with one hand and rubbed her dad's shoulder with the other.

When people had wandered away to continue with the raffle and Emma felt able to speak, she turned to Zoe.

'Will she be OK? You don't think we were neglectful, do you?'

'What? Of course not, Emma. Wasps sting dogs and people alike, but you've learnt a very valuable lesson today about greyhounds.'

'They don't like being stung?'

Zoe laughed. 'That's true, but also, they do tend to scream if something startles them. It's one of the worst sounds you can hear and sends terror into many hearts, but it will often be something like a claw catching on a blanket or someone brushing past them when they're dozing. It's rarely something awful, but it will sound as if it is.'

'Poor Harmony.'

Emma wrapped her free arm around the dog's long neck and kissed her head.

'I don't think she's poor Harmony at all today,' Zoe said. 'In fact, I think she's happy Harmony because she's found her family.'

'The home check?' Emma was puzzled.

'We need to do that and to ensure that this is definitely what you and Greg want, but from what I've seen of the three of you today, the decision has already been made. Keep that ice on her leg for a bit then settle her on the blanket and she'll probably have a snooze.'

Zoe got up and left Emma, Greg and Dilys at the jam stall, but Harmony didn't have a snooze. Instead, she happily shared Emma's dad's crepes then leant against him as he sat on the chair, gazing at him as though he was the most wonderful human in the whole world.

Emma's stall emptied as late afternoon settled over Little Bramble and soon all that was left was the checked table-cloth and the bunting that waved gently in the breeze. The heat had faded as the sun got lower in the sky and now the horizon was a beautiful vibrant pink with orange and purple hues. The air was delicious, laced with scents of crepes, coffee and barbecues and Emma felt that summer had well and truly arrived.

'That was a successful day.' Her dad patted the bulging money apron.

'It was a *perfect* day.' Emma stretched her arms above her head.

The green was calmer now, although some people still milled around snapping up last-minute bargains from stalls and sipping on cider and beer from the refresh-ments stand, while others had wandered over to The Red and sat outside on the pavement at tables or in the pretty beer garden.

'What happens about this little beauty?' her dad asked as he rubbed Harmony's ears.

'I'm not sure. I suppose she'll have to go back to the kennels overnight or to her foster family, at least until Zoe has done a home check.'

Her dad's face fell. 'I hate to think of her going back there.'

'It's a good place, Dad, and they really love the dogs.'

'I know that! Of course I do, but won't she be lonely?'

'I wouldn't have thought so. I'm sure she'll be OK.'

He gave a small laugh. 'Perhaps I meant that *I'll* be lonely! She's a beauty and I've enjoyed having her company today. She's soft and warm and her breath is . . . not the sweetest I've ever smelt, but she's lovely and I don't want to say goodbye to her.'

'Do you want to apply to adopt her?'

'Can we?'

Emma looked at his pleading eyes, at how the dog seemed so attached to him already and she knew that there was no way they wouldn't apply to adopt Harmony. It was, she realised, as if the dog had chosen them.

'We most certainly can. I'll speak to Zoe about it right away.'

'Did I hear my name?' Zoe said as she went to Harmony and rubbed her ears. 'How's her leg?'

'It seems OK,' Emma's dad said as he checked it for the thousandth time that afternoon.

Zoe knelt down next to Harmony. 'There's a small bump there but it'll go down.'

'Sam came back and checked her three times and said she's fine.' Emma's dad held out Harmony's lead. 'I suppose she needs to come back with you now.'

Zoe chewed at her bottom lip. 'Or . . . If you'd like, I could pop over later and do the home check for you? Bring some food, her bed and the adoption pack? You could see how she settles overnight.'

'Really?' Emma raised her eyebrows. 'That quickly? I thought there would be more to it.'

'Between you and me, Emma, there usually would be if I didn't know you, but I've been to the cottage lots of times so I know the garden's secure, and I know you both well. As long as you can tell me that you're serious about this, then I'm happy to let her come to you tonight.'

Emma looked at her dad and his eyes widened.

'We're serious,' she said.

'We are *incredibly* serious.' Her dad cleared his throat. 'Thank you, Zoe. Did you hear that, Harmony? You're coming home.'

Zoe placed a hand on her chest and sniffed. 'I love it when these dogs get a happy ending. They go through so much that seeing them find their forever home gets me every time.'

'We have our donation for the charity,' Emma said, and her dad held out the money apron.

'What about your percentage? For costs?'

Emma shook her head. 'It's fine. Take it for the dogs.'

'Thank you both. That's just wonderful. I'll put it with the rest of the takings and Marcellus will lock it away tonight, then we can count it and bank it on Monday.' Zoe gave Emma a quick hug then she walked away.

'Right, Dad, I guess we should make our way home.'

'Emma!' She turned to find Connor jogging towards them.

'Hi.'

'I . . .' He panted. 'Sorry . . . I have something for you, remember?'

'Oh, yes! Sorry, I'd forgotten.'

'Come with me for a few minutes?' He held out his hand. Emma glanced at her dad and he nodded.

'We'll head on home and see you there.'

'Are you sure?'

'I think I can find my way.' Her dad cocked an eyebrow.

'I didn't mean it like that!'

'I know, Emma, and I was teasing you. See you later.'

'OK.'

She glanced around, wondering where Sadie was.

'It's OK,' Connor said. 'I don't bite.'

She nodded then took Connor's hand and let him lead her to his stall.

There was a large object with a dust sheet covering it.

'This is what I wanted you to have.' Connor released her hand then swept the sheet away.

Emma gazed at it then at him.

'That's for *me*?'

He nodded. 'I made it especially for you. So you can work properly. I thought it could go in the studio and be your office as well.'

Emma ran a hand over the smooth surface of the beautiful desk, admired the leaves carved around the edges and the legs, the sheen of the wood.

'It's walnut. All upcycled but the desk itself I made.'

'Connor, it's incredible.'

'Like you.'

'Me?' She laughed.

'You are.'

'Connor . . . I don't know what to say.'

Had Sadie seen this?

'I'll bring it to the cottage for you in my van and carry it out to the studio. It's quite heavy.'

'Thank you so much. I'm sure this is more than I deserve.'

'You deserve the world, Emma.'

She met his gaze, his eyes dark in the twilight, his skin glowing from the sun and the heat and she couldn't help herself. This moment had happened so many times in her dreams and it was finally here.

She stepped forwards and flung her arms around his waist, pressed her face against his shirt and breathed him in. He smelt of sunshine, sandalwood, grapefruit shower gel and something else, his own masculine scent that made her heart race. It was a scent she recognised from long ago, that everything inside her recognised, and she wanted to lose herself in it. When his arms slid around her and held her closer, she had to swallow the moan of longing that surged in her throat.

They stood that way for what felt like hours but was mere seconds, only breaking apart when someone shouted goodbye.

They stood there then, slightly awkward in the way that two people who've once been as close as people can be often are. This man had seen her naked, kissed her everywhere, and she had slept in his arms, soothed by the beat of his heart, by his warmth and love. The feelings she'd had for him had been suppressed but not erased and now they rushed to the surface like bubbles in a bottle of fizzy drink that's been shaken.

The strength of the feelings made her tremble all over as she fought the urge to throw caution to the wind. If only she could not care who they were, where they were or who could see. She would take his hand, run her thumb over the calluses on his palm and his fingertips, raise it to her lips and kiss it then stand on her tiptoes and cup his face. She would press her lips against his, feel his breath sigh against her, his body relax. When he kissed her back, she would melt into him and everything else – the sounds of stalls being packed away, the grumbling of tired children and the whistles and rattles of the starlings overhead as they swooped and soared – would fade away.

But it couldn't be.

'I'm sorry,' she whispered. 'I shouldn't have hugged you like that.'

'Why not?' His voice was husky, his pupils dilated with desire. She knew exactly how he felt. She hadn't been held like that for what felt like a lifetime.

'I had no right. You're spoken for.'

'What?'

'Sadie.'

'Emma . . . I–'

'Could I have your attention, please, Clare Greene?' A voice crackled over the loud speaker and everyone remaining at the fête fell silent.

Emma frowned at Connor and he shrugged then nodded. 'I know what this is,' he whispered.

'What?' she asked.

'Wait and see.'

He pointed at the Norwegian Spruce, where Sam Wilson was standing on the small platform with a grinning Marcellus David at his side.

'Clare Greene! Where are you?'

A ripple went through the remaining crowd and Kyle hurried towards Sam. 'She's coming. She just popped to The Red to use the loo.'

Sam laughed and shook his head. 'Timing is everything, right?'

Clare appeared then and Kyle ran to her. 'Come on, Mum, Sam's waiting.'

'What for?'

'Just get a move on.' Kyle hurried Clare over to Sam then stood back and folded his arms.

'OK,' Sam said as he held the microphone up in one hand and took one of Clare's hands in the other. 'Clare . . . Thank you for today. It has been amazing. Thank you, also, for how wonderful my life has been since you returned to Little Bramble.'

'Sam . . .' Clare looked around them. 'What's going on?'

'I wanted to thank you properly for being such an incredible woman. You are my best friend, my partner, my lover.'

'Sam!' Clare tapped his arm playfully and he laughed.

'It's OK, I'm sure Kyle knows.'

Kyle nodded. 'It's true.'

'You are a wonderful mum to Kyle and daughter to Elaine, you are the best dog mum to Goliath and an amazing friend to Jenny, Zoe, Emma and many more. You are the most remarkable woman I've ever met and I love you, Clare. I love you so much that I have a very important question to ask you.'

Clare looked around, her eyes restless as they landed on familiar faces. When she glanced at Emma, Emma gave her a thumbs up and a big smile.

'Clare Greene,' Sam dropped to one knee and held out a small box, 'would you do me the huge honour of agreeing to spend the rest of your life with me?'

Clare gasped and her hands flew to her mouth.

Time seemed to stand still, then slowly, she started to move. She held out her left hand and Sam fumbled to get the ring from the box then slid it onto her ring finger.

'Yes! A thousand times, yes, Sam. Oh my goodness! I can't believe this is happening!'

'You're saying yes?' Sam stood up and held Clare's shoulders. 'You'll marry me? Be my wife?'

'Yes!' Clare nodded and tears rolled down her cheeks. 'Of course I will.'

Sam scooped her up and they kissed and kissed and kissed.

'Get a room, Mum!' Kyle rolled his eyes, making everyone laugh.

Emma sighed, delight for her new friends filling her chest.

'The perfect way to end a perfect day.' Connor reached out and brushed her cheek. 'But I hadn't finished what I was saying.'

Emma looked around as applause began, cutting Connor off, then spreading out around the green and across the village as everyone heard the news. She joined in, clapping hard as she tried to push her disappointment and sadness away. Some things were meant to be, some weren't.

Something tightened in her chest even as she moved her hands, as Connor cheered beside her and as Marcellus congratulated Clare and Sam over the microphone.

The tightening intensified as Emma saw the happiness in every face around her, recognised the sharing of joy, was reminded of how it had been back then.

The tightening seemed to squeeze the air from her lungs and then it popped, and she staggered backwards. Connor stopped clapping, concern contorting his features, and he held out a hand, but she looked at it, shook her head, turned and stumbled away.

She pushed past people, ignoring their questions and concern, not seeing who they were or even caring, because all she knew was that she had to get away.

Away from Connor. Away from the villagers. Away from her past.

As quickly as she could.

Chapter 26

Emma got home to find that Zoe was there with her dad and Harmony, so she rushed to the bathroom to try to compose herself. She couldn't let them see her in such a state and knew that Zoe would be very concerned, for her, but also for Connor.

When she'd splashed some cold water over her face and brushed her hair, she looked a bit more presentable, although her eyes held something wild within them.

And poor Connor! He'd given her such a beautiful gift then she'd run away from him. In fact, she had done the exact same thing she'd done all those years ago, only this time it wasn't her engagement party she was running from.

What was wrong with her? Why couldn't she ever get things right?

She needed to pull herself together, go downstairs and speak to Zoe about adopting Harmony and put her dad first. Her feelings for Connor were complicated and the hug they'd shared had only confirmed that. The power of their connection had hit her hard, reached inside her and dragged a whole load of complicated emotions to the surface. But she couldn't act on those feelings. Connor was in a relationship with another woman – the mother of his child – and had been for years.

She didn't know what she was going to do, or where she'd even begin trying to deal with what had happened, but there would be no more running away. This was her life and she was going to live it.

With or without the man she loved.

Connor stood in front of the desk he'd made for Emma, unbelieving. They'd had a good day, had held each other, and he'd believed that they were knocking down some of the barriers between them. The way Emma had held on to him so tightly he'd known that she still loved him, that she had never stopped.

And then in an instant everything had changed.

Sam had proposed.

Everyone had clapped and cheered.

Emma had let go of his hand and run away.

Again!

He hurt, but over the years he'd learnt not to react to things immediately. With age came wisdom and he knew that this was not as simple as it might seem. Something had scared Emma and she'd fled, just as she had done all those years ago. She'd had good reasons then – she must do now as well. Maybe it was all too soon for her.

His first instinct was to go after her and take the desk to Greg's cottage but he suspected that Emma probably needed some space and he would give her that space. So many years had passed since they had been together that he knew one more day wouldn't make any difference in the grander scheme of things.

When she got downstairs, Emma took a deep breath then went into the kitchen. Zoe and Greg were sitting at the kitchen table with mugs of tea and Harmony was lying on a folded duvet on the floor at his feet.

'Hello, Emma.' Her dad smiled. 'We thought you'd be a while yet.'

'No . . . I, uh . . . thought I'd better get back to see Zoe and talk this adoption through.'

'I brought the duvet down off the spare bed. Zoe said that a folded duvet is as good as most beds for greyhounds because they can stretch out on them.'

'Although, I have to be honest with you,' Zoe raised her eyebrows, 'she'll probably end up on the sofa with you – and if you let her upstairs, possibly on your bed.'

Emma's dad laughed. 'I have no problem with that. It's been a while since I've slept next to a beautiful female.'

'Dad!' Emma shook her head.

'Sorry. Couldn't help myself.'

'Toby and Digby have beds in my room because I found that they didn't settle well downstairs. They're quite clingy and though we've worked on the separation anxiety, it's something that greyhounds can suffer from. They're so overcome at being cared for by kind humans that they become afraid of losing that love and affection.'

Emma sank into a chair. 'That's terribly sad.'

Zoe nodded. 'But when they find their family, it's wonderful.'

'How's she been since you brought her home?' Emma asked.

'She went for a wee in the garden and Zoe said that's a good sign and she's had a sniff around downstairs. She's spent time with Zoe and others from the charity so she has been inside a home before.'

'One thing to watch out for is worktop surfing.' Zoe pointed at the worktops. 'Greyhounds can reach where smaller dogs can't, so don't leave any food you don't want them to have within reach. Especially not anything that could harm them, like chocolate or grapes.'

'Right.' Emma's dad nodded.

'I have a booklet here for you with some dos and don'ts and plenty of advice, but if you join the Facebook group too, you'll get most questions answered there. Greyhounds are popular pets and the community is a very warm and welcoming one.'

'I'll join for us, Dad.'

'Can you set me up a Facebook account too?' he asked.

'Of course.' Goosebumps rose on Emma's arms. Her dad was keen to learn and interact with other people because of Harmony and that was a very positive sign. He'd always refused to sign up to Facebook in the past, not liking the idea of it.

'If you read the forms through and sign them, we can go ahead with the adoption. No pressure this evening, though. I'll leave them here and pop back tomorrow. I've already brought her food over, Emma, and explained to your dad how much to give her. You'll need to consider getting a stand for her food and water bowls and things like coats for when she goes out and possibly pyjamas if it gets cold here at night.'

'A stand?' Emma asked.

'Yes. To raise the bowls off the floor, otherwise she'll struggle to reach her food.'

'Because she's tall and has a long neck?'

'That's right. But I'm sure Connor can sort that out for you anyway. He made me two for my boys.'

Emma's mouth had gone dry and she struggled to swallow.

'And what about pyjamas?' Emma's dad asked. 'Where do you get those?'

'Well, actually, Grace is a dab hand at making them and she might have left some spares at Connor's so I'll check, but you can order most of these things online these days.'

'Right.' Emma nodded. There was a lot to remember but it would be a welcome distraction.

'I'll leave you to it, but any problems or concerns just give me a ring. Anytime, day or night.'

Emma walked Zoe to the door.

'Your dad looks happy,' Zoe said as she stepped out into the balmy evening.

'He really does.'

'Are you OK, though? You're quite pale.'

Emma choked up at Zoe's concern. How would Zoe feel if she knew that Emma had just deserted Connor again?

'Look . . . if it's something that's happened between you and Connor, then don't worry. You don't have to tell me and he might not either, but I told you before and I'll tell you again . . . I care about you, Emma, and I'm always here for you. I love Connor, he's my flesh and blood, but you're family too. You two might rekindle things but you might not and that's fine.'

'How could we possibly rekindle things?'

Zoe frowned. 'I don't understand. I mean, if you don't have feelings for each other anymore then that's one thing, but I've seen you together and I don't think that's the case. I feel it would be a great shame if you didn't see how things could go.'

'But he's with Sadie.' Emma's voice squeaked as she spoke.

'What?' Zoe's eyes widened. 'What makes you think that?'

'I've seen them together and I've seen the Facebook photos and they have Grace and–'

'I don't know what you've seen on Facebook, Emma, but they must be old photos. I know that sometimes Sadie might like to propagate the idea that she and Connor are a couple, but they haven't been together in ten years.'

'Really? But I saw them hug!'

'Did you? Or did you see Sadie hug Connor?'

Emma frowned. 'I-I guess it could have been her hugging him.'

'Connor never loved Sadie the way he loved you, Emma. It was all a mistake but once he knew Grace was on the way, he couldn't turn his back on them. He gave it a go but it was never right and, to be honest with, he never got over you.'

'Oh . . .'

'Exactly. Something to think about, right? Now take care – and remember, if you want to talk about anything, I'm here for you. No judgements, just love and support.'

'Thank you, Zoe.'

Zoe hugged Emma tightly then left and Emma slumped against the door frame.

She *did* care about Connor, might possibly still love him, and yet she'd been compelled to run away. She'd thought it was because he was with Sadie and she was battling her feelings for him but now she knew he was single, did that alter things enough for her?

She needed to take some time to think and hopefully everything would become clear.

By ten o'clock, Emma's dad was dropping off in his chair, his head nodding, his soft snores dragging him back to consciousness. Emma told him to head up to bed, but he tried to protest, worrying about Harmony. The dog was settled on the folded quilt on the hearth and Emma had placed a fleece blanket over her as the temperature had dropped.

She wondered how these dogs managed when they came straight from the racetrack, often injured and malnourished, jumping at their own shadows. Harmony had jumped up a few times as the sounds of the old cottage settling after the heat of the day disturbed her, but she'd soon settled again when Emma and her dad had spoken soothingly to her. Harmony wanted to put her faith in the people around her and Emma admired her for it. If she could let go of her past, could love again, then surely Emma could do the same.

She pulled her legs up to her chest and wrapped her arms around them. A deep sadness penetrated her entire body, making her shiver and ache as if she had the flu. She'd had reasons for running away from Connor, as she had done in her twenties, had felt that staying wasn't an alternative she could live with. If she had spoken to Connor about it calmly, rationally, back then, would he have understood? Could they have worked something out? Those were things she would never know the answers to. She would never be able to change what had happened.

She folded in on herself, head on her arms. The tears came then and she let them, grateful, at last, for the release. Emma wasn't good at letting go, had swallowed her emotions so many times over the years, but she'd reached the point where she had to let it out or she would never properly heal.

Suddenly, she wasn't alone anymore. A cold nose nudged her arms, her hands, sniffing at her and tickling, then a tongue brushed her forehead. She looked up and found big brown eyes gazing intently at her. It was as if the entire world was captured in Harmony's gaze and Emma cried harder. She cried for Harmony and for dogs like her, for her dad and his loneliness, for his fears about losing his memory, she cried for her mum and for the things that had passed and for everything that had happened since she ran out on Connor that first time.

When Harmony jumped up next to her on the sofa, she sat back and the dog shuffled closer, resting her pointy head on Emma's lap. She released a long low grunt as Emma stroked her head then nudged Emma repeatedly every time she slowed her stroking.

'I'm sorry, Harmony. This isn't a very nice first night with us for you, is it?'

The dog blinked her big brown eyes.

'Things will be better, I promise. I'm just a bit sad.'

When her tears finally slowed, Emma pulled a tissue from her pocket, wiped her eyes and blew her nose. Crying like that had been liberating and now she felt empty, as if everything that had built up inside her for years had been freed into the air and finally she could begin again.

She lifted Harmony's head then slid down so that she was lying next to the dog and pulled the throw off the back of the sofa over them both, appreciating the warmth of Harmony next to her, the strong beat of her heart. It clearly took a large chest for a heart so big and compassionate, so ready to trust again in spite of what she had been through. Harmony grunted again and Emma realised that it was a sign of contentment, so she let out a low imitation grunt then kissed the soft head.

'To new beginnings, Harmony. For both of us.'

Chapter 27

'Happy Birthday!' Greg sang as Emma walked into the kitchen rubbing her eyes.

'Oh! Morning, Dad.'

'Hello, sleepyhead.' Lucie smiled at her from over a steaming mug of coffee and next to her, Phoebe waved.

Her friend had brought her partner to the village to look at a property and they were staying at Greg's for a few days, including Emma's fiftieth birthday.

'Where's Harmony?' her dad asked.

'Still in my bed.' Emma laughed. 'It's a good job it's a double or I'd never get any sleep.'

'That dog!' Her dad shook his head. 'Spoilt already.'

Emma watched his face, how it glowed now with health, and she sent out a silent thank you to the universe for bringing her home again. Returning to Little Bramble hadn't been a completely smooth journey but it had been a good one and though initially reluctant to face the ghosts of her past, she was glad she had.

'Sit down.' Lucie patted a chair. 'There's bacon, eggs, mushrooms, smoked salmon and champagne. We're all starving because we've been waiting for you to get up.'

'It's only just gone ten!' Emma protested. 'And I *am* fifty now, so I need my beauty sleep.'

'You're a spring chicken.' Her dad kissed her head.

Emma rolled her eyes at Lucie, but she loved how sprightly her dad was, how he teased her gently in the way he used to and how easy it was to live with him. She hadn't thought it would be as an adult, but he'd surprised her with his acceptance of anything and everything and how well they got on as two grown-ups living together again after so many years apart. They were very much alike, two peas in a pod, Lucie had said, and it made for a tranquil existence.

It had only been five days since the fête but in that time, Emma had sorted herself out. She'd contacted an estate agent to put her London flat up for sale, as well as her neighbour so he knew what was going on, and she'd let all the publishers she worked with know that she intended on moving out of the capital with immediate effect. She could commute when necessary for meetings and publication events, to network with authors and agents, but her life was back in Little Bramble again and knowing that had given her a wonderful sense of peace.

There was only one thing still troubling her and that was Connor. They hadn't spoken in the days following the fête, and she hoped he'd decided to take some space to think about what had happened, just as she had. Then, last night, he had sent her a Facebook friend request out of the blue. The gesture had made her smile because she'd spent years wondering how she'd respond if he ever did and now he finally had. She accepted immediately, and Connor must have been waiting for her reaction, because he waved at her and they had a conversation on Facebook messenger. Connor asked if he could come by today to wish her happy birthday and to drop off the desk and her stomach fluttered at the thought of seeing him again.

She thought she knew what she wanted now, but she wasn't sure she'd be certain until she saw him, spoke to him, gazed into his eyes and asked him what he felt.

Lucie placed a plate piled high with salmon, eggs, bacon, mushrooms and toast in front of her, along with a flute of Buck's Fizz.

'I thought we'd start with Buck's Fizz with breakfast then move on to straight champagne in the garden.' Lucie grinned at her.

'Ugh! That stinks.' Phoebe pushed her chair back and covered her nose. 'Sorry. It's just the hormones.'

She rushed out of the room and Emma heard her feet on the stairs.

'Morning sickness.' Lucie grimaced. 'I'd better go and check she's OK.'

Emma raised her glass to her dad.

'Cheers.'

He clinked his glass against hers.

'Happy birthday, my beautiful girl.'

'I can't believe I'm fifty, Dad.'

'I can't believe you're fifty either, Emma, but don't be sad about getting older. I really enjoyed my fifties, and my sixties. My seventies too, actually.'

'I'm not sad. I'm quite looking forward to the next decade. I've learnt a lot over the years but more than ever this past year. Things started to change months ago, way before Christmas, actually, and coming back here for Christmas then leaving again really got me thinking about things. My life had become so much about online interaction and not much else. Don't get me wrong, the internet and social media platforms can be wonderful and they make the world a much smaller place, but it's not enough when it's all you have. I'd become like a hermit – if it hadn't been for Lucie, I'd have barely seen another soul.'

'That's not a good way to live.'

'I know. And that's why finding myself doing the shopping in my pyjamas in the early hours of the morning was a wake-up call. Add to that the phone call about you and it hit me how much was passing me by. I . . .' Her throat constricted and she sucked in a shaky breath. 'If . . . If I hadn't come back, I can't bear to think of what might have happened to you, to me and to Harmony.'

Her dad shook his head. 'It's OK, Emma. Everything happened as it should. You came back when it was right. I needed a wake-up call too, you know. I wasn't taking care of myself and neither were you. All that matters now is that we have time together with Harmony and that you are happy.'

'And you, Dad.'

'I'm very happy, Emma. Can't you tell?' He sipped his drink and smiled at her. 'I'm giving another Zoom lesson later and I'm really looking forward to it.'

Emma smiled. Her dad had started to teach his grand-children guitar via Zoom. It was chaotic at times with the three of them competing to play the chords, and Ted had groaned at the noise, but it was also lovely to see her dad having a chance to bond with her brother's children even though they were so far away.

Her dad's eyes widened as the sounds of four paws coming down the stairs echoed through the hallway.

'Good morning, Miss Harmony.' He stood up and opened the back door. 'Would you like to use the conveniences before breakfast?'

The dog licked her lips then trotted outside, her tail wagging as she went.

'She's made herself so at home, hasn't she?'

'It's like she's been with us for years, not days.'

'I couldn't bear to be without her now,' Emma said as she munched on a piece of toast.

'Nor me. She's part of the family.'

When Harmony came back inside, Emma's dad stroked her head then went about making her breakfast.

'Don't forget to give her some salmon,' Emma said.

'Of course not. She's having the works this morning. It's not every day Emma turns fifty is it, girl?'

Harmony slid into a play bow, her tail wagging in happy wide arcs.

'Zoe said we've been lucky with her. Some of the dogs take a long time to settle in because of previous trauma and because being inside is completely different for them, but Harmony's time with foster families as well as Zoe acclimatised her.'

'She's finding her feet and becoming who she was meant to be.' Her dad winked at her and she nodded. He was talking about more than just Harmony.

When the doorbell rang, Emma's heart skipped a beat. She stood up, aware that she was still wearing her pyjamas and hadn't even washed her face.

'I'll go,' she said, quickly running a hand through her hair, thanking her hairdresser for encouraging her to have it cut short so she didn't have to worry too much what it looked like first thing in the morning.

Harmony jogged ahead of her, then waited while she opened the door. It was Connor and he smiled as he crouched down to greet the dog. Harmony got to welcome guests first these days and that was just fine by Emma. When he finally stood up, she waited for him to speak.

'Happy birthday.'

'Thank you.'

'I've got the desk in the car, as well as a stand for Harmony's bowls.'

'Brilliant, thank you.'

'I'll go and get them.'

He carried the feeding stand through to the kitchen, greeting Emma's dad as he went, then he fetched the desk.

'You want this in the studio?'

'If you don't mind.' Emma led the way, grabbing the key from the hook in the kitchen.

She unlocked the door and Connor carried the desk inside, setting it in front of the window.

'It looks perfect there.' She ran a hand over the warm wood, appreciating how much time and effort Connor had put into making it.

'I can just imagine you doing your edits in here.' Connor looked around. 'The light will be perfect and you can always get a lamp for when you're working through the evening.'

She shook her head. 'I'm going to cut down on the jobs I accept.'

'Really?'

'I was trying to do too much because I was terrified the work would dry up. But there will always be work for an experienced editor and I have a lot of contacts who will still send jobs my way. I just want to slow down a bit, enjoy being here with Dad and Harmony. I'm selling my London flat and it's tripled in price since I bought it, so I'll have savings and that will take the pressure off financially.'

'I don't blame you wanting to slow down a bit.' Connor nodded.

'I'll commute when I need to, but it won't be that often.' She licked her lips. 'Connor . . .'

'Yes?'

'I'm really sorry about how I reacted at the fête.'

He shook his head. 'It's fine, Emma. I understand. That hug . . . then the proposal. It brought back a lot of memories.'

'Everything just swirled around me and I panicked and gave in to my urge to run. Also, I thought you were with Sadie.'

'Mum told me.' He nodded. 'But I haven't been for a long time.'

She winced. 'I'm so sorry. I feel awful. I should have asked but I'd seen you together and had seen her hug and kiss you so I just assumed you were a couple.'

'I was a bit hurt and confused at the time but I thought you just didn't like me in that way or were confused and giving me mixed signals. There was a lot of pressure.'

'Pressure?'

'Of not being enough and yet being everything.'

'Yes.'

'I've struggled at times with what happened, but I've made mistakes too and I understand now that life isn't perfect, people aren't perfect. Grace helped me to understand it more than anything. We're all just doing what we can to survive.'

'I want more than to just survive.'

'Me too.'

He held her gaze and she walked slowly towards him.

'After you proposed, the pressure was incredible. It built and built in me, as did the fear of not being enough and, if I'm honest, so did the fear that *you* wouldn't be enough and that our life here wouldn't be enough for me. I don't want to hurt you by saying that, but I worried that if I stayed and didn't go to London as I'd always wanted, then I'd resent you and you'd be hurt . . . more than you were by me leaving as I did. If we'd got married, had children, my leaving could have been so much worse.'

'I always worried that I wouldn't be enough for you.'

'The thing is – you were. You were wonderful. But I was young, and I needed to know that I'd made the right decision. I didn't want to get married and have children and just be a wife and mum. That might sound terrible, but I wanted so much more. I'd seen other women settle down like my mum and make their husbands and children their world, which is great, but I always wondered what happened when the children were grown and left. Did the wife end up being home alone, feeling like her worth was only tied up in those things? That thought terrified me. I needed more, *still* need more, to be the best version of myself. I have to be me in order to have enough to give. Does that make sense?'

'Absolutely.'

'I know that some women and men are happy not working, not having careers, but having one was the right thing for me.'

'I know . . . and I always loved that about you.'

He took her hands in his and she felt the calluses against her skin, the evidence of years of hard work and manual labour.

'You did?'

'I did and so I should have been more supportive. I should have encouraged you to spread your wings and do whatever you needed to do, promised I'd be here for you when you wanted me.'

'No, you needed more than that, Connor. You deserved more than that.'

'So we're agreed that we're both valuable people?'

'We are.'

'And that we've come a long way since you left?'

'We have. I think that the final straw that made me run was seeing how happy everyone was for us. My parents and yours, other people in the village – they just all seemed so delighted that it put an enormous amount of pressure on me. I was terrified that I'd hurt not just you but them if things continued as they were. It was suffocating.'

'I know what you mean. But at the time I didn't think about how that would have impacted upon you.'

'Add to that my yearning to see what else was out there in the world and it was all too much.'

'I'm so sorry that I didn't see that, Emma.'

'Don't be sorry. It happened and I wish I'd dealt with things better than I did, but I was so young and scared and yet, madly in love with you. When I ran, I left behind my best friend.'

'I lost mine too.'

'Where do we go from here?'

He touched her cheek with his thumb, holding her gaze and she saw the tears in his eyes.

'I'm scared,' he whispered.

'Me too.' A tear trickled down her cheek. 'I never thought I'd be scared at fifty. I thought I'd have it all figured out by now.'

'So did I.'

They started to laugh, the people they had been and the ones they were now merging.

'I think it's OK to be scared, though,' Emma said. 'Just like it's OK to be happy.'

'I agree.'

'How do you feel about . . .' She took a deep breath to steady herself. 'Trying to be scared and happy together?'

'I'd like that very much.'

'That's settled, then.'

'There's something in the drawer of the desk.'

'For me?'

'Of course.'

She went to the desk and gently opened the drawer. There was an envelope inside. She lifted it out.

'Open it.'

She slid her thumb under the seal and inside was a card with 50 printed on it in silver and gold letters. As she opened the card, something inside it moved and she caught it before it fell to the floor.

'It's an email printout.'

'Read it.'

She scanned the email and gasped. 'I've always wanted to go to Paris.'

'I was hoping you'd never been because, if you fancy it, I thought we could go together.'

'You've booked something?'

He nodded. 'For the first weekend in September. Only two nights but I thought we could have a short break, possibly briefly see Grace because I know she'd love to spend some time with you and I'd like the two women I care about most in the world to get to know each other. I've paid for Eurostar tickets and a hotel. I only booked one room but if you like, I can book another.'

Emma read the email again and her heart lifted then sank.

'I can't go.'

Connor's face fell.

'You don't like the idea.'

'It's not that. I love the idea but what about Dad and Harmony? I can't leave them.'

'I took the liberty of speaking to Mum about this and she said that if you wanted to go, she'd help out with Harmony. I also spoke to Dilys and she said she'd be here for Greg too. I was nervous asking them because I'd hate for you to think that I was being presumptuous or anything. I just wanted to do something nice for your fiftieth.'

'It's lovely, Connor. The desk is incredible, and this is really special too.'

'I thought we could create some new memories together.'

'Let's do it!' She smiled. 'But don't book a separate hotel room. There'll be no need for that.'

'Really?'

'Really.'

His eyes darkened and he pulled her towards him, lowered his head and kissed her. She sighed against him, her body awakening in his embrace, her heart opening to him, the man she had always loved.

When they paused to catch their breath, he nodded towards the cottage.

'Did I see smoked salmon and eggs on the table?'

'And Buck's Fizz.'

'Shall we have a double celebration?'

'That sounds like a very good idea.'

They left the studio, hand in hand, and walked towards the cottage. They had faced challenges in their past, but from this point on, they would face everything together.

There would be no more running away because Emma was exactly where she wanted to be. At last.

Acknowledgements

My thanks go to:

My husband and children, for your love and support. You – and the dogs, of course – are my everything.

My wonderful agent, Amanda Preston, and the LBA team.

The amazing team at Bonnier Books UK – with special thanks to my fabulous editor, Claire Johnson-Creek, for seeing the potential in my stories and making them shine, and to the very lovely Jenna Petts, for all your hard work and enthusiasm.

Thelma for your love, support and wise words over the years. I hope that if I ever get to ninety, I'm as energetic and inspirational as you.

My very supportive author and blogger friends, especially (and in no particular order): Ann, Wendy, Jules, Sarah, Bella, Phillipa, Kate, Holly, Laura B, Annie, Laura K, Andi and Ian.

Sarah, Dawn, Deb, Sam, Clare, Yvonne, Emma, Kelly and Caryn for always being there.

All the readers who take the time to read, write reviews and share the book love.

The wonderful charities Greyhound Rescue Wales and Hope Rescue for the incredible work you do every single day, and to Alan Thomas and John McConnachie for suggesting the name Harmony for Emma and Greg's greyhound.

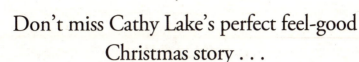

Don't miss Cathy Lake's perfect feel-good
Christmas story . . .

Recently divorced, the family home sold and her son all
grown-up, Clare is at a crossroads. She's dedicated her
whole adult life to her family, and now it's time she
did something for herself.

In the lead up to Christmas, Clare decides that a bit of time
in the countryside might be just what she needs, so she moves
back to Little Bramble, the village she grew up in. But living
with her mum for the first time in years – and not to mention
Goliath the Great Dane – can be challenging.

When Clare finds herself running the village Christmas show,
it feels like she has purpose in her life again. Bringing together
people from all sides of the community, and all walks of life,
will Clare manage to pull off a festive feat like no other?
And will she find the new start in life – and possibly
love – that she's been looking for?

Available now. Read on for an extract.

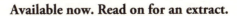

Chapter 1

'Look at me, Mum!'

Clare Greene's heart fluttered. She turned, expecting to see her son, but instead her gaze fell on the empty space in the back garden where the swing used to be. The house and garden were full of ghosts and, as she made her way round one final time, she was being assaulted by memories and voices from the past.

Closing her eyes, Clare could picture her son, Kyle, swinging high, remember her anxiety that he'd fall off and hurt himself. But his laughter as he'd soared through the air and the joy on his face as he'd called to her, keen to garner her approval, had made the fear worth it. Her ex-husband, Jason, had taken the swing down years ago, but it had stood there for a decade, from the time Kyle was seven, and he'd had so much fun on it. Kyle was twenty-one now and at university in Bath studying performing arts – a grown man and no longer her little boy.

A cold wind whipped around the garden, tugging at her coat, and she shivered. Time had passed so quickly: she was forty-five and often felt that her life had passed her by, that she had practically sleepwalked through the days. If only it were possible to have some of that time back to savour the good times . . .

Her heart lurched and she pressed a hand to her chest. Looking down, her eyes found her wedding ring. As difficult as it would be, she really needed to take it off. Jason had removed his when the divorce was finalised, sighing at the white mark that remained on his finger. Just like the emotional scars left by the end of their marriage, it would take some time for physical marks like that to go.

She trudged back up the garden to the semi-detached house, went in through the French doors and closed them behind her, lifting the handle slightly until it clicked, then turned the key. There was a knack to locking these doors. They should have had them fixed years ago, but it was one of a list of jobs that had never been done and now it would be someone else's problem. But the new owners would also have so much to enjoy here. Clare had loved her home and was sad to leave it, but she knew it was time, even though her throat tightened as she realised she would never walk on the lush green lawn again, never sit on the patio as she savoured her morning coffee, never listen to the jazz drifting from next door on sunny afternoons. Her fragrant roses would be tended to by someone else, the shed would house the tools and bikes of others, and the birds that flocked to the feeders would become accustomed to different humans.

Slipping out of her garden shoes and into her plimsolls, she made her way through the open-plan kitchen diner with its large fireplace and driftwood mantelpiece, her soft rubber soles seemed strangely noisy on the wooden boards, the sound echoing around the empty house, making it feel as though she had company. The furniture had been moved into storage and the clothes and belongings she couldn't bear to part with, such as Kyle's baby photo albums, from a time when people had actually printed photographs, were packed in her treasured Mini Countryman, the remaining finance on it cleared with some of her half of the house sale. The car had seemed to groan under the extra weight but she felt compelled to take them with her.

She passed the lounge where she had given birth to Kyle three weeks before his due date, taken by surprise as she'd thought the pains were practice contractions. He'd slid out onto the rug, red and furious at his early arrival. Kyle's entry into the world had been dramatic and he hadn't changed a bit; he still enjoyed being the centre of attention. Clare had been just twenty-four then, so young and innocent, convinced that life had plenty to offer and that she was destined for something special, even though she hadn't had a clue what that something would be.

How things changed.

In the hallway, where the October sun streamed through the window above the door, she took slow deep breaths, treasuring the sights, sounds and scents of home, storing them safely in her heart. Who knew when she would have a home of her own again? When her vision blurred, she knew it was time to get moving.

Her mobile buzzed in her pocket, making her jump, and she pulled it out to check the screen, expecting a message from the removal company. When she saw Kyle's name, her heart lifted.

Hey Mum,

Hope you're OK. I know today will be difficult, but you can do it! When one house door closes another one opens and all that. Let me know when you're safely at Nanna's.

Love you millions! X

Clare hugged her mobile to her chest for a moment, thanking the universe for the gift of her precious boy. Whatever happened, she had a wonderful son and she would always be grateful for that. After firing off a quick reply, she slid her phone back in her pocket then opened the door and stepped outside, put the key in an envelope and posted it through the letter box, preparing to start the next chapter of her life.

Clare was ten minutes away from the village where she had grown up, but it would probably take her twenty to get there because she was stuck behind a tractor. Her Mini ambled along through the narrow country lanes and her feet ached from braking and pressing the clutch as she had to stop/start the car. Behind her, a row of cars was building and she knew it wouldn't be long before some of the drivers started beeping at her, pressurising her to overtake. But Clare knew better; these lanes could be deadly and visibility was poor. There was always the risk of crashing into some idiot taking the bends at sixty miles per hour.

The whole journey from Reading to Little Bramble in Surrey only took about forty minutes, but she had to admit that she hadn't made it very often, particularly over recent years. There had always been an excuse, whether it was a dinner with Jason's colleagues from the prestigious law firm in Reading where he had been a partner, or an author event at the library where she had worked for twelve years as a library assistant (a job she had adored until they'd had to make some staff redundant six months ago due to cutbacks), or generally just feeling too tired to make the effort. A lump formed in her throat from the guilt. Her mum was seventy-five, fit and healthy, a busy member of her local community, but she wouldn't be around forever and in some ways she'd taken her for granted. They hadn't ever been that close but, even so, she was aware that she could have made more of an effort to visit.

She turned the radio on and listened to the DJ chatting to a celebrity author called Cora Quincy about her latest self-help book. Cora was all of twenty-five but spoke as if she'd lived a long and difficult life. Admittedly, Clare had read about Cora (a fashion model turned actress turned author who'd married someone from a boyband Clare could never remember the name of) online, and knew that she had endured a challenging childhood, but even so, her tone was slightly patronising. Clare had been married for almost as long as the woman had been alive – surely she had more life experience to draw on, more wisdom in the bank? And yet here she was: homeless, jobless, clueless about what came next.

The traffic came to a standstill as the tractor stopped to make way for an approaching car. Clare pulled up the handbrake and turned, gazing at the hedgerow to her left, almost bare of leaves now in October's colder days. Dark twigs poked out of the hedge, threatening to scratch any vehicles that got too close, and others stretched up to the sky like gnarled brown fingers. Beyond the hedges were fields where farmers grew corn and vegetables, where livestock roamed and nurtured their young.

As a child, Clare had thought she'd grow up to be a vet or own her own stables. She'd loved the wildlife around the village, had been a keen horse rider who had spent Saturday mornings at the stables then worked on Sundays at the local farm shop just outside Little Bramble, where she got to feed the chickens and ducks in her breaks, care for the motherless lambs in spring and play with the fluffy collie pups. Yes, she'd had a good childhood, even if she hadn't been as close to her mum as she'd have liked. At university, she'd studied English Literature (after deciding at sixteen that taking A-levels in the sciences was not for her), met Jason, and her ambitions had slipped away like smoke on the breeze. She'd been so infatuated with him, so taken by his apparent maturity and intelligence that she'd have followed him to the end of the earth if he'd asked her, so when he proposed, she'd accepted without hesitation.

The tractor started moving again and Clare released the handbrake and set off again at a snail's pace.

'Oh, absolutely!' Cora's decisive tone burst from the car speakers and broke into Clare's thoughts. 'I'd spent far too long worrying about what everyone expected of me, trying to be that perfect creature that pleased the world, and then one day . . . BOOM! I had an epiphany! I was like, alleluia! Eureka! And all that jazz.' She giggled, clearly very pleased with herself.

'And so . . . do you have a message for our listeners?' Darryl Donovan, the long-time Radio 2 DJ asked.

'I do, Darryl, I really do. Whoever you are and whatever you've been through, put yourself first. Decide what *YOU* really want and go for it! I realised, and your listeners can too, that I had to live my life for *me* before I could be with anyone. If you don't love yourself, how can you possibly love anyone else?'

Clare rolled her eyes. It was all very well saying that at twenty-five. It was a message Clare had heard many times in the past, but not one she'd ever managed to take on board. She'd been a daughter, a wife, a mum, a library assistant (although that had been something for her because she'd enjoyed it so much) so her roles had been centred around others and she'd been content with that. The idea of shaking off those responsibilities and doing things solely for herself seemed unimaginable.

Now, for the first time in her life, Clare realised that she felt very much alone.

Clare had always been a daddy's girl and tried to make her father proud whenever she could. When he'd died ten years ago, he'd left a gaping hole which she'd struggled to fill. She didn't have a close relationship with her mum. Elaine Hughes had always been busy with her own life – for many years with her job as a drama teacher, then later on with her work as a chief examiner and as chairwoman of the village amateur dramatics society. With Jason bringing his and Clare's marriage to an end, she was no longer committed to making him happy, but this in itself was another difficult loss to deal with. And then there was Kyle: her darling son, her reason for everything, her joy. But Kyle was grown up and had gone off to university, leaving Clare feeling redundant in that aspect of her life as well, especially after losing her job. Her whole life had changed when she'd least expected it. She'd been prepared for Kyle leaving home, but losing her job and her marriage at the same time was too much.

Would it be possible for Clare to start again and live her life for herself? Could she turn things around and discover what it was that she really wanted?

The left indicator on the tractor started flickering and it pulled into a layby, so Clare put her foot down on the accelerator and drove past it, singing along to the uplifting track from the eighties that the celebrity had chosen as her theme tune.

Perhaps the young woman wasn't so naïve after all.

Return to Little Bramble this Christmas in . . .

The Country Village Christmas Wedding

Clare Greene and Samuel Wilson are getting married and everyone is excited for the event of the year. But Clare and Sam are busy people and have left organising their wedding to the last minute.

Luckily, wedding planner Hazel Campbell has recently moved to the village. She had the perfect life in Edinburgh with a successful business and what she thought was a loving fiancé. But when she caught him with her maid of honour on the evening before their wedding she fled, leaving her whole life behind.

The idyllic village of Little Bramble seems like the perfect place for Hazel to start over. As Hazel throws herself into planning the perfect country village Christmas wedding, she starts to find herself again and realises that a second chance at love might be on the cards for her as well.

Coming 2021. Pre-order now.